Killswitch

Victoria Buck

Killswitch

Contact Information: titleadmin@pelicanbookgroup.com

All scripture quotations, unless otherwise indicated, are taken from the Holy Bible, New International Version(R), NIV(R), Copyright 1973, 1978, 1984, 2011 by Biblica, Inc.™ Used by permission of Zondervan. All rights reserved worldwide. www.zondervan.com

Cover Art by *Nicola Martinez*

Harbourlight Books, a division of Pelican Ventures, LLC
www.pelicanbookgroup.com PO Box 1738 *Aztec, NM * 87410

Harbourlight Books sail and mast logo is a trademark of Pelican Ventures, LLC

Publishing History
First Harbourlight Edition, 2016
Paperback Edition ISBN 978-1-61116-739-9
Electronic Edition ISBN 978-1-61116-738-2
Published in the United States of America

Dedication

To the future. May we meet it with grace.

Other Victoria Buck Titles

Wake the Dead

1

Life underground mystified the man who used to own the world. Chase leaned against a white partition in the bunker constructed under an abandoned museum. Getting here had consumed his thoughts. Even his dreams.

He scanned the sixty-foot-wide room that used to be nothing more than a cavernous hole. Computers and holographic displays filled the space now, along with a group of people all intent on giving *God* credit for this techno-cave. Odd.

Maybe there *was* a higher power behind it. Something had pressed Chase, caused him to give up everything. Urged him to seek refuge in this strange world.

Or maybe it was just his coding, since he'd gotten blown apart and reassembled—turned into a transhuman.

Whether Providence or programming, he'd made it. Now he'd do what he came to do: connect these people with others like them around the world. Protect them. Keep them a step ahead of government forces bearing down on them. But somebody had better tell him what all this was about. Why the believers held to their faith. His other reason for coming—to find the truth.

But *here*? Was every branch of the Underground Church literally underground?

The middle of the busy command center housed ten computer stations, three to four feet apart. Old-fashioned bulbs hung from the white drop ceiling. In the thirty-eight hours since his arrival, he'd become acquainted with the massive network of information and communication programs. The exoself—the computer built into his very being—now seemed at one with the systems Mel had constructed. No wonder, she'd designed him too. At least in part.

She lifted her deep brown eyes and gave him a reassuring smile, then she motioned toward the door to his right. He returned the smile and nodded. Almost time for the meeting.

Melody Reese—the third reason he didn't stop looking until he found this place. He watched her move across the room. Maybe seeing her again had been at the forefront of his reasoning.

She'd been the one to organize his days at the Synvue complex, making the coffee and handling the calls. Friendship might have become something more if their lives hadn't taken such an unbelievable turn. The whole world knew what had happened to Chase, but Mel had harbored secrets. She'd trained in Artificial Intelligence and Chase never knew it. Not until she was gone. After his transformation, they told him that he didn't need an assistant anymore. Mel was reassigned. Then she disappeared.

They'd had little time to talk now that they were back together. She wasn't the same girl he'd known in Chicago. Black curls, longer than when he'd last seen her, framed her pretty face. The sparkle hadn't abandoned her eyes. In fact, they had a fire in them now. An urgency.

Of course, Chase wasn't the same either.

He took the hallway leading to the rest of the compound. He hadn't interacted much with these people. They didn't know what he could do for them. He possessed unlimited intel and processing capabilities—the stuff Mel hid in the exoself. Now he'd upload the programs into this massive computer.

When he wasn't merging the exoself with the systems, he rested. It'd been a while since he had a bed of his own. And he spent some time with the only other resident he knew, his mother. Kim Redding: stellar mom, upstanding citizen. Active member of the underground? Of all people. Mom had accepted the Lord. That's what she told him. No more surprises could exist in the universe. Was it because of him? Did she need something to cling to when they made her son a transhuman?

Transhuman. The term hadn't caught on, though the movement had started decades ago. Chase was the computer man, a cyborg. A bionic disappointment, as far as he could tell, to the millions who once adored him.

He hated the labels. He was just a man.

He continued through the complex until he reached the largest of six meeting rooms, where he took his place on a make-shift platform. No amount of paint and silicon could diminish the dank odor of a cave. He forced a breath out his nose and waited for his audience to arrive. Mel said it was time for him to speak to the people. Ninety-seven lived and worked in this branch of the underground. What did they think of him?

They shifted in a few at a time and sat in white resin chairs. Not unlike most of the believers Chase had encountered over the last several weeks, they were practiced in unobtrusive charity, offering whatever Chase needed then moving on with little to say. Nobody had time to explain this reckless existence.

But it seemed they were anxious to hear *his* story. Three men dawdled at the back of the room. All the chairs were taken. Chase stepped across the platform.

A few people were missing—some mothers and their small children. And his own mother. She stayed in the command center to monitor the computers, which was fine with Chase. He'd already told her everything. Well, almost.

Also missing was the cocky guy the group called Switchblade. He'd gone up top in the little town of Herouxville, but the exoself didn't have access to Switchblade's agenda. Probably out spying on local officials, making sure they hadn't noticed the Underground Church had set up operations below the streets of the Quebecian village. The guy had a hero complex.

These people didn't know Chase could wipe out the communication programs of the local police with one carefully directed thought. That would take care of the would-be spy's high opinion of himself.

Chase brought his focus back to the gathering. In the past he'd stood before thousands, while millions watched on GrapheVisions across the continents. Something in his gut grieved the loss of stardom. Maybe Switchblade wasn't the only one short on humility. He shook off the yearning for his old life and addressed his waiting audience.

"Good morning. Most of you know me as Chase Sterling. My real name is Charles Redding. My mother was the one who nicknamed me Chase. It was Synvue that changed my last name. I'm changing it back." He smiled. "But what Mom says, goes—I'm still Chase. Never argue with my mother. You may have noticed she's the only one who refers to the supercomputer you've built here at Blue Sky Field as the 'desktop.'"

Laughter rose from the crowd. Chase let the moment pass before continuing.

"I was the beloved host of *Change Your Life*. I remade pathetic souls—plucked them from a life of hardship and dropped them into a dream existence where they had everything they'd need for the rest of their lives. Riches, beauty, position, restored health. I considered it the ultimate salvation to take people with failing bodies, or unattractive ones, and make them thrive, make them stunning. The envy of everyone who witnessed the miracles. Then I made them wealthy beyond their wildest dreams, gave them the career—the government assignment—they'd always wanted. Or if they didn't want to work, I made sure they had enough funds to squander until they died."

Chase spotted Mel at the end of the first row of chairs. She gave him a nod and he continued, "As you know, I became a project, a scientific endeavor of the Western Republic."

A few derogatory comments and groans preceded one voice, feminine and aged. "We must pray for our leaders. God appoints them for a time and purpose."

More remarks followed, some too unkind to be directed at an old lady.

Chase raised his hands. "Let's not get caught up in knocking the WR." The crowd settled and Chase continued, "I worked within the entertainment network, Synvue, which is controlled by the WR. Or maybe it's the other way around." He stepped to the edge of the platform. "Those of you who've been underground for some time may not know what happened to me. I'm sure you've all heard something of my injuries. Of my death."

Whispers carried confusion through the room.

"I was reborn. The first of an evolutionary leap. So said my creator."

The murmuring continued. Chase's superior hearing picked up every word.

"He thinks he's reborn?" someone whispered.

"He doesn't *know* his Creator," another added.

These people were ready to toss him out.

He glanced at Mel. She pulled out her VPad and Chase read the text in his mind as she typed:

They have a different understanding of what it means to be reborn. They don't really go for the whole evolution thing. And God is the only creator.

"OK," he said. "I guess I know as little about you as you do about me. Let me explain. I didn't die, I suppose. I was mortally wounded and then rebuilt with bio-genetic lab-grown organs that will never wear out. My vision, hearing, and strength were enhanced. And I have computer-generated intelligence and a connection to multiple cyber systems around the world."

A roomful of eyes stared. Jaws dropped.

"And I think I can be useful to you. I want...to help you."

He waited. If their expressions were an indication, they weren't convinced.

Mel rose from her seat and joined him on the platform. "I told many of you about this already, so don't look so surprised," she said. "I know it's a lot to take in. I designed and installed programs and added them to his processors to give us—the Underground

Church—a way to connect all the branches around the world. To help us with supplies and transportation. With protection. Chase is willing to let us utilize these programs, even though I didn't have his permission for any of this. Everything that was done to him, whether by me or by the scientists who rebuilt him, happened without his knowledge. He lost the life he once had and got transformed into the something he didn't want to be.

"He could have stayed up top and lived like a king. There's no one else like him. But he chose to escape, to become a hunted man, to seek us out, and to help us. Please, give him a chance."

"If he's a hunted man," a voice called out. "How do we know they won't hunt him down and us with him? We heard what happened to the group in Atlanta."

"Exactly," Switchblade said from the back of the room. His black eyes seemed to laugh, but his thick arms crossed to deny any humor in the situation. "In fact, I think they've already tracked him. We got federal deputies in town and I don't think they're here for the local cuisine. Didn't see nobody with a plate of *poutine*."

People rushed from the room. Frantic voices faded into the hallway. Mel wrapped her hands around Chase's arm. The laughter in Switchblade's eyes found his lips, which formed into a judgmental smirk before he dashed away.

"They tracked me. I thought I could hide." Chase pulled free from Mel's grip. "I should never have come here."

2

Chase and Mel followed the crowd to the command center. Already pulling data from computers in the town's police station, the exoself found nothing to indicate a problem. Of course, WR Feds would use their own systems. Chase searched for a connection.

His mother worked in front of a large transparent monitor. Her fingers glided across the screen, moving data from one position to another, much as Dr. Fiender had done when he first showed Chase the exoself. No need for such a display now—Chase could read the data flowing inside him without the visual aids. He located four VirtuPads registered to the WR. Communication passed between them and Chase processed the voice transcripts:

No reason to believe he's still in this hole of a town. The old woman said she gave him clean clothes and sent him on his way—said he was looking for a farm or something.

Chase didn't need to hear anything else. They'd questioned Molly, the sweet elderly lady who'd helped him when he first arrived in town. No telling what they did to her. His strength sensor activated and he threw back his shoulders.

"I have to go." He headed for the door that opened to stairs leading upward.

Mel reached for him but he pulled away. She hurried after him. "What do you mean you have to go? You can't go up top."

He faced her. "They've been to see Molly."

"How do you know that?"

"I just know." He swiped his hand through his hair. "Look, Mel, I can read their communication. I know what they're doing."

"So, what are they doing?"

"Looking for *me*, of course. I've got to see if Molly is all right."

"I'll go."

"Don't be ridiculous," a man said from behind them. Amos, a short, balding man in his fifties—the leader of this group.

As Bear had been the head of the underground in Atlanta, Amos was the overseer of Blue Sky Field. But *this* was the location that managed all the branches in the world. The man in charge had an awesome responsibility. Chase had only seen him once before the meeting today. He seemed to spend a lot of time in his private quarters. They hadn't even been introduced. Now it appeared they'd skip the handshake and get right to work.

Amos sat at a computer station. "They know who you are, Melody. If they catch you, they've got Chase. They know he'll come after you."

"Of course I would come after her, and I'm going to check on Molly," Chase said. "They could have killed her."

"That's entirely possible." Amos's words held little emotion.

Chase spun around and rushed for the door.

Switchblade blocked the exit, his feet spread apart, his arms crossed. "Can't let you go up there. I'll go to Molly's. She likes me. Brings me those muffins of hers every time she comes to a meeting."

Chase stiffened. "I feel responsible."

"You *are* responsible." Switchblade lunged forward and pointed a finger close to Chase's face. "But I'm going. Check your brain, Charlie. See if those deputies up there know anything about me." He pulled the hood of his jacket over his close-shaved head and put on a pair of mirrored glasses. "They don't know me from Adam. As far as they can tell, I'm just an out of place punk who never did nothin' for the WR, 'cause the WR never did nothin' for me. I'm good to go."

Chase folded his arms and lifted his chin. "What's your real name?"

Switchblade stepped close, lowered the glasses, and glared down into Chase's eyes. "Don't care to divulge that information, Charlie. You got anything in that exoself to read my iris? Not much of a computer man if you don't."

"Yeah, I've got it. Stop calling me Charlie." He did a quick sweep of WR job assignments, schools, housing, prisons—this guy had to have a record. But no, as far as the government knew, he was just another lost cause out of the system. No name—just a vague record of him being born in Cleveland, and his age—thirty-two.

Wait, there *was* a former job assignment. He spent two years as a bodyguard for Synvue.

"You worked for Synvue? When?" Chase asked. "And why don't you have a name?"

The man shoulder's tightened and his upper lip twitched. "I'm going up now."

He faced the door and flipped open the locks.

"I got all the way here from the Southwest Territory without getting caught," Chase said. "I'm going with you."

"No," Amos said. "Switchblade will contact us as soon as he knows anything. You're here to help us. What would it profit for you to get caught?"

The man was right. Chase watched the hooded wannabe hero take the stairs three at time.

"Come on, boss. Let's go check the data. Maybe we can find something." Mel took his hand and led him back into the command center.

His mom had the same consoling smile she'd given him twenty-five years ago when he struck out in a Little League game. He started toward to her, but then focused instead on the monitors near the other side of the room. It wouldn't do anything for these people's confidence to see him running to his mommy.

He'd gathered extensive data from the four WR VPads. A group assembled as he sat at a keypad to categorize the information. His mother joined them. Had she caught the way he'd avoided her? Her wink and half-smile said that she had and she wasn't offended.

"They can't track me using traditional methods because of the exoself." Chase leaned back and dropped his hands from the keys. "But I may have made a mistake."

"What mistake?" Amos asked.

"I met up with my show's producer in NYC. She found me there and I told her what I was doing—that I wanted to help the Underground Church. Not the smartest thing to say."

"You saw Kerstin?" Mel's tone darkened. "Why would you tell her that? Why would you tell her anything?"

"She was sick and I..." He hadn't told these

people, not even his mother, everything he could do. Of course, Mel knew. She was there when the scientists installed the device enabling him to detect illness simply by touching a person.

"She needed a kidney, and I told her to go to Robert. Then I asked her to let me go. And she did."

Mel drew back from the crowd as she lowered her gaze to the floor. Was she angry with him for trying to save a life?

"You told this woman you were coming here?" Amos didn't overreact. The leader seemed like he could handle anything.

"No. Just that I was going to try to find your group. She must have notified the Feds to look for anybody transporting believers. Your communication about moving goods and people is lacking security measures. But I can take care that." Chase searched beyond the twenty or so people standing around him. Mel sat alone at a station, typing on a keypad. "If it's not too late."

"How did they find Molly?" Mom asked.

"A few questions in town led the deputies to a lady living in the outskirts who takes in strangers and frequents unregulated meetings. That made her a suspect to harboring believers."

Amos circled the group and poked a screen at another station. "She was one of only five believers in town who hadn't joined us here. The ones up top are essential. The WR may have gotten all five. What a loss." The man blinked his droopy blue eyes. "But...to die is gain."

"What's that supposed to mean?" Chase looked at Mel. "The incoming data doesn't indicate anyone's been killed."

But something was there in the communication between the agents and superiors. It wasn't good. Chase kept his eyes on Mel until she looked at him.

"What is it?" she asked.

"They're on their way to a detention camp. All five of them. Somebody get in touch with Switchblade. You can do that, can't you?"

Amos pulled a VPad from the pocket of his brown vest.

"Tell him not to go near Molly's," Chase said. "It's a trap."

The leader prompted the call. "Might be too late."

3

The hiders in Blue Sky Field had VPads. The church in Underground Atlanta had avoided them like snakes. Thanks to Mel, a techno-revolution was taking place in the underground. Authorities seeking to shut down the activities of the church could no longer track their use of electronics.

Chase could process both sides of the conversation on any nearby VPad, and he listened in on the private call.

Amos spoke first. "The upside believers are gone. Don't go near Molly's—they're waiting for somebody to show up there."

"How do you know that?" Switchblade asked.

"Chase says so. Get back here. That's an order."

"That robot don't know everything. I'll just take a look. Nobody will know."

Chase grimaced. *Robot*? Let the thug get caught.

Mel grabbed the VPad from Amos. She eyed Chase as if she knew what he was thinking. Maybe she did. Maybe she hadn't told him she could read his mind.

"Switch, he picked up on communication from above. If he says they're gone, they're gone. Get out of there."

Switch? How long had Mel been using a pet name for this guy? Chase crossed his arms and took three steps back. But the conversation continued. He could've stopped the transmission if he'd wanted to, but he didn't.

"OK, Melody. I'm coming." Switchblade ended the call.

This guy didn't follow the orders of his leader, but Mel could turn him?

Mel handed the VPad back to Amos. "Where are they?" she asked Chase. "Can we get them back?"

"I'm working on it. There are three detention centers within seventy miles of here. One is for dissenters. One is for common criminals. The other one is a mix." Chase dropped into a chair. The people, once again, gathered around him. His mother put her hands on his shoulders. "I've got it, or at least I know what's on the report. I don't know why they would try to trip us up—they don't even know I can access their systems."

"What if Kerstin told them?" Mel's voice carried a chill.

"She doesn't know everything." Chase crooked his head toward Mel but didn't make eye contact.

"Maybe Fiender filled her in when she showed up for a transplant."

"He wouldn't do that. Anyway, I don't know that she even went to him. She could get a kidney elsewhere."

"Not like yours. That's what you wanted for her. Right?" She moved closer, her arms folded tight.

His eyes met hers. "There's really no need for—"

"For organic replacement. I know that." Mel sat next to him and touched a large-screen VPad. "Show me where they are." She pushed her curls behind her ears.

Chase instructed the exoself to display a real-time

view of the surrounding area. "Here." He pointed to an intersection fourteen miles north.

Mel touched the screen to zoom close to ground level. "I don't see anything."

"WR satellite block. Trust me, it's there." Chase prompted a code—one of the codes Mel had hidden in the exoself. The image of the wooded area changed and a structure at the end of a dirt road filled the screen.

"How did you do that?" Mel asked.

"I used your code. You know, the four S's."

"Sympathizers, supplies, secret houses, safe travel," she said. "But Chase, the code connects the underground, and the underground is not connected to the WR, or to whatever satellite you just hacked. So how did you do it?"

"The fourth S—code thirty-one, eight. To know if a location is safe, the exoself looks at it without a WR block. The code removes the block." Chase's gaze met Mel's. "You know that. You wrote the code."

Mel touched a letter on the keypad and then rose to check one of the screen-free displays. The image of the detention center appeared. With one finger, she pulled it upward. A 3D image of the building hovered before her.

Chase joined her at the display. Wire fence surrounded the complex. A transport vehicle headed out, and the large metal gate slid shut. After that, nothing moved. No sign of anyone on the ground.

Mel seemed to study Chase. "I didn't program you to remove a WR block. Thirty-one, eight should help us find safe passage. It will tell us who's on the move, so to speak, within our own organization."

Chase shrugged. "You know more about this stuff

than I do. After Robert put me in control of the exoself and shut down everything in me that allowed WR monitoring, he said I wouldn't have access to government systems. But I do. I don't know how or why. All I know is I used that code and the block lifted."

She focused on the display.

A smaller building stood to the right and rear of the main structure. "What do you know about the first code, Mel? Thirty-two, seven. What was your intent when you programmed me?"

"To hide you. It's the reason you can't be tracked."

"Yeah, and so far it's worked. I hope." He lowered his voice. "But did you know it's a weapon? It not only hides me, it protects me. To the death of anyone who threatens me. I don't even have to the pull the processor. The exoself does it without any instruction from me."

"Chase, that crazy." Mel's eyes narrowed. "The exoself is a computer. You're the one who tells it what to do."

"Maybe that's the way it started." Chase touched the display and rotated the main building. "But I think, in order to protect itself, it will do whatever it has to do to make sure I'm safe." He glanced at his mom. Worry lines marked her gentle face. The people here called her Birdie, because she liked to sing. She wasn't singing now.

He looked at the screen. "I couldn't do all this before I got to Atlanta. It started when I unlocked your code, Mel. And it's getting better, faster."

Mel put her hands on either side of her head. "OK, we'll talk about this later. Right now we need to figure out if there is any way we can get our people out of this place."

"I can dissolve the walls on this image. Do you want to know what's going on inside?"

Mel's eyes widened. "You can see through walls?"

"Not exactly. I can see through a satellite image of a wall because that's what the satellite can do."

"And you can do this with *my* code?"

"Same one—safe travel." Chase pulled the code again and the image changed, slower this time, to reveal the rooms inside the main building.

The five detainees lined up before a man wearing WR police garb. No sound. By the way the man pointed and waved his right hand in his captives' faces, he must be yelling.

Molly stood in the middle, a tall man and young woman on her right, two teen boys on her left. None of them moved. Their mouths remained shut. Their hands were behind their backs.

"Chase, what do you think will happen to them?" his mother asked.

"If anything gets entered into the database at the compound, I can intercept it. For now we can only watch."

Mel touched the little building in the back and pulled it forward. "What's in here? Why can't we see into it?"

Something inside him told Chase not to look. But he pulled the code and the walls faded.

Groans sounded behind him.

"That's enough, Chase." Amos touched the top right corner of the display and it went black.

"I had a bad feeling," Chase said, "but I wasn't expecting this."

4

Monitors sparked to life as people got to work on different tasks. Some calculated the average time a detainee was held in a center when there were no formal charges. Others mapped various routes to the location holding the five believers. Chase continued to read the communication passing between the WR henchmen who'd intruded on the little town above his head. Nobody said a word about the device in the outer building.

Mel had left the room. Chase tracked her location to a computer in her private quarters. Mom was gone too. A few people moved about on the far side of the complex. Only Amos and Chase were left in the center.

"I don't think they'll be released." Amos shook his head." At least not any time soon."

"I know. A week ago they might have been. But now—"

"Now they're taking these things more seriously."

Chase put his elbows on the desk and rubbed his forehead. "Now they're looking for me."

"I didn't say that." The leader of the underground sat next to Chase. "I didn't even think it. If the authorities thought they'd make contact with you, they'd let them go."

Chase leaned back in the chair. "It started a few days ago—Christians being detained like this. Even when I was in Atlanta, the cops let a girl go the same day they took her in. But the data shows that hasn't been the norm recently."

"How many arrests have you tracked since you left Atlanta?"

"Over 200. Just three of those have been released."

"Heaven help us," Amos said. "What was so special about the three who were released?"

"I only know what gets put in the reports—names and locations. At least I can tell you where they got arrested. By now, could be they've gone underground."

Amos flashed a quizzical look. "Yes, hopefully the three are in hiding." He rose and slipped his hands into his jeans' rear pockets. "But maybe not. Tell me their names."

Chase pulled the information from the exoself. "All men, all arrested and then released in NYC. Nathan Gaines, Jack Oakley, and Gunner Ramos. Ring any bells?"

"The first two, no. The last one is a supplier."

Chase pulled the code and found the name. And some history. "He used to be a preacher. Arrested seven times for fraud and money laundering. Lost his tax exemption long before every other church did. Now he's supplying the underground. Making up for past sins?"

"Why would the Feds let him go when they're holding 200 other believers in detention centers?"

"I wish I could tell you. I don't know what I'm supposed to do about it—about any of this. I'm just an endless supply of information."

"Are you having second thoughts about joining our cause?"

Chase was supposed to be here—he was

programmed to help and protect these people. But how could he get five people out a detention center? What about the other 200 being held by the WR? How many more were there around the world? He didn't even want to know.

He pushed away from the gleaming white desktop.

"What's wrong?" Amos asked. "Chase, you can't give up."

"Don't you people pray or something when the odds are against you?"

"I'm praying right now."

Chase looked Amos in the eyes, and something coursed through the exoself. The men who were released all had the same series of numbers after theirs names. 0043250. Chase ran WR detention center manuals. In seconds, he had the answer. "They're not believers."

"What are you talking about?" Amos asked.

"The three men who got released. Their activity in the underground is a ruse. They work for the government. They got picked up by mistake—they were with a group that got arrested. When the WR checked them out, they let them go."

"Chase, can you—"

"I'm attaching the release code to the five who were taken in this morning."

"You think those officials are going to believe that all five are informants? Three of them are just kids."

"Do you have a better idea?" Chase took his seat at the desktop and pulled the code. The monitor showed the detention center. "There are four officials at the facility. They're all low-level guards. They see a release code come up in their orders, they let the five go. At least, that's what I hope will happen."

"Give it a try," Amos said.

Chase pulled a code and the exoself opened the system. Footsteps made him glance sideways. Switchblade. Back from town. Safe and sound.

"Melody says we got five trapped in some stinkin' center. You gonna get them out with your super powers?" Switchblade pulled off his sunglasses.

"I'm working on it. Go get Mel. I need her help."

"I'll get her," Switchblade said. "But what are you doing for the five?"

"Attaching a code to their names that will tell the officials they're WR snitches, not believers."

"That's the most asinine plan I've heard in long time." The man's broad shoulders lifted as he wheezed out a laugh. "When…If they get out, the Feds are gonna tap them for information. They'll be forced to work against us."

"Have a little faith, Switch." Chase smiled.

"Faith—what do you know about *that*? And don't call me Switch, Charlie." He bulldozed his way between the tightly positioned computer stations.

Mel returned within a minute, Switchblade right behind her, and sat at the station. "Why is it that you can get in on WR transmissions and send out information to the underground, but you can't just send a message to my VPad?"

"The exoself doesn't allow me to communicate directly with individuals. I think it has trust issues. I was permitted to send one message to Robert, but that's all."

"That's just crazy, boss. Trust issues? The exoself is not a person." She shook her head. "What do you need me to do?"

"I'm attaching a code to the names of the detainees. I know Molly, but not the rest of them. Tell me their names and I'll pull their histories. Then go to the first S—sympathizers. We'll feed in some phony backstories."

"Haven't the Feds already seen their profiles?" Mel asked. "Why doctor the information now?"

"They're just getting started. Orientation stuff. The Feds haven't reviewed them individually. But we have to hurry."

"Got it," Mel said. "We'll start with Molly. Last name Bedél."

"Native of the area. Raised by Christians." Chase studied the same profile the officials would soon read. Then he added something. "She got kicked out of the local church before it shut down. Supported government sanctions forbidding distribution of literature. After that, she became an agent of the WR."

"Oh my," Amos said. "We're going to lie our way through this?"

"You're not lying, I am," Chase answered. "And I'm allowed to lie. Right? I'm a sinner."

"Son, we're all sinners. We just don't feel good about it."

"I feel good about getting these people free, so I'm going feed to lies to the bad guys," Chase said. "I'll deal with the consequences later."

"Second name, Finley Moreau," Mel said. "She's eighteen. Also a native. Her parents are not believers. Molly's influence brought her in."

"Perfect," Chase said. "Molly recruited her to work for the WR." Chase instructed the exoself to add the false information.

Mel continued the list. "Kirel Previtt. Twenty-nine.

Native of the Northeast Territory—Maine. Moved to Herouxville after getting into some trouble with smugglers. Snuck Bibles into illegal shipments to the EU. Fled to avoid prison, but he still lives up top like the rest of the five."

"OK, there were drugs in the Bibles. He fled to keep his business going. The Feds caught up and offered him a deal—report on the church or go to prison for the drug dealing."

"You're feeding in the information so fast, Chase," Amos said. "I'm afraid you're going to make a mistake."

Others had gathered around, whispering behind Chase. Breathing. Couldn't they back up a little? Despite the pressure, the beat of his lab-grown heart never altered. His blood pressure remained perfect. He could do this.

"Next name," he said to Mel.

"Do these together. They're brothers. Twins, in fact. Simon and Silas Devereux. Orphans. Their parents were killed when their church fought against its closing. The building was burned to the ground. Twenty-four people died. That was twelve years ago. The boys were four. Now they're sixteen. They live with unchurched grandparents but sneak off to meet with believers."

"They blame the church for their parents' deaths," Chase said. "They want revenge."

"That's not true," a girl cried from the group at Chase's back.

He peered into the crowd and spotted the girl "Of course, it's not true. I'm making this up as I go along." She couldn't have been more than sixteen. Poor kid— this was a tough way to live. "I'm trying to get them out. Remember?"

"I'm sorry, you just sounded so sure of yourself." She almost smiled. "You sure know how to tell a...You're good at making up stuff."

"I've been pretending for years. I guess it was good for something."

"What now, boss?" Mel asked.

"Now we watch and wait."

5

Chase, Amos, Mel, and Switchblade moved to the 3D display. Others followed, eager to see what would happen when the Feds in charge of the round-up noted the orders to release the detainees. The orders Chase had wriggled into the system.

The near compliment of a teenager was the only appreciation shown by the good people of the underground. They'd step off their moral high ground and thank him when the five were free.

"Thanks, exoself, old buddy." Chase would offer some gratitude if no one else felt inclined.

"You don't even know if you did the job," Switchblade said. "Don't see nobody opening the front door."

"Wait." Mel motioned to the display. "Look at this."

One of the men in the compound moved away from the five and studied his VPad. He spoke quickly, shook his head, and typed on the small screen.

Chase intercepted. "The code is in place. They've all been identified as informants. Orders are to release them." He slumped into the nearest chair and huffed. "After they've been debriefed on local activities."

"I hope they can lie as good as you, Charlie," Switchblade said. "They talk to them one-on-one, those Feds'll catch on."

Chase broke into communication between the

deputies and the VPad relaying messages to the detention center.

The people surrounding him waited and stared at the holographic image.

One Fed slung his weapon to his back. Another crossed his arms. And then another walked to the door, waved his hand in front of the security device, and swung the door open.

Molly and the rest of the group, their confusion not well hidden, hurried outside to a waiting transport. They climbed in. The gate gave way and the vehicle headed out.

Chase spun on his heels to face to the believers and spread his arms. "And so we've sent another lucky soul—that is—five souls—to begin anew." He smiled. "You're welcome."

"What exactly did you just do?" Mel asked. "And don't tell me that you used my programs."

"I sent word to the man in charge that the absence of the detainees would arouse suspicion if all five missed the meeting occurring in one hour. The upside believers would get spooked and scatter, ruining the operation. The five should be released and returned to town. ASAP."

Whooping began in the back of crowd. Mom cut through the crowd of worried expressions and kissed Chase on the cheek. The young girl who'd given the back-handed compliment joined in the cheering. Mel hugged him. He pulled her close and smiled.

"You got lucky." Switchblade's deep voice lifted above the others. "Now tell me this—who's arranging that meeting? All the up-top believers from Herouxville are in a government transport. And they don't lie as fast as you do, Charlie."

"Despite the misleading information, God has gotten our people out of a mess," Amos clapped his hands together. "And God will get them back safely."

What? God hadn't hacked the system and lied his way out of this situation.

"Switchblade has a point," Chase said.

"I'm glad you see that." Switchblade puffed out his chest. "They gotta come underground. And never go back up."

6

Chase monitored the communication trails as the transport took the narrow road back to town. Did these people realize what he'd done? Most of them were off to one side now, praying or something. Thanking God.

But that's why Chase was here—the dreams, the words from his dad. This *was* God's idea. Wasn't it? What did he expect? A pat on the back?

He hated siding with Switchblade, but the guy was right. Molly and others weren't safe staying in town. They had to disappear.

Amos held out his hand. "We're grateful to you, Chase. What you did today was tremendous."

Chase took the man's hand. A spark rushed through him. "Uh, thank you, Amos. Are you feeling all right?"

"Little tired, but that's nothing new. Right now I'm more relieved than anything. Why do you ask?"

"It's nothing. I'm relieved too."

Mel interrupted. "The transport just dropped off our group a block from here. The Feds are watching, so we're sending a messenger. They'll be directed to go to Kirel's apartment for a meeting." She sat at the work station next to Chase. "Can you get the Feds to leave once we've got the group inside?"

"I'll send instructions to pursue a group belonging to the Dissenters of the Republic headed south to bomb a WR base."

"More stories," Mel said. "Did somebody at Helgen program all this creativity?"

"It's not a story. The dissenters are going to bomb a base near the border—what used to be the border—at the north end of New Hampshire."

"You know what's going on with that group?"

"I was looking for a bone to dangle and up popped this chatter. I'm intercepting data from all over." Chase swiped his fingers through his hair. "It's a little overwhelming."

"OK, boss, take it easy. I don't know why, or how, this is working. We'll figure it out later. Right now, just go with it."

"Who's your messenger? Who's going up?"

"Switchblade. When there's a need to send someone up, he jumps at it." She lifted her brow and grinned. "Being in a cave makes him...unruly."

Cameras in town made easy work of verifying the five were on their way to the meeting place. Switchblade dropped the word and disappeared before the Feds even noticed. Chase instructed the exoself to send the call for federal back-up to move south. The five were inside the old brick building just a few minutes before the deputies got back in their transports and headed out of town.

"It's done. With any luck, the leak in communication won't stop that bomb," Chase said.

"It'll be a blessing if the bombing is thwarted. Lives will be saved," Amos responded.

"I don't get it." Chase turned his chair to face Amos. "First, you say to die is gain. Whatever that means. And then you want to rescue the bad guys?"

"They're misguided. They can find the better way. God willing."

These people really were odd. Chase needed to talk to Mel in private. Besides asking a few questions about the confusing methods and messages of the Underground Church, he had to tell her about Amos. No doubt after that handshake; the man was sick.

But that didn't explain his blasted contradictions. "Amos, can I ask you something?"

"Of course."

"The people in the Underground and the ones up top—you talk about them like you're fine with letting them get killed. Like they're expendable." Chase leaned forward and put his elbows on his knees. "But other people, like the Dissenters of the Republic, you want to keep from harm. To save them. I don't get it."

"Seems like foolishness, right?"

"Yeah, it does. But I know you're not a fool."

"I'm not *fine* with our people being killed, Chase, but we're fighting for something greater than ourselves. And they've freely given their lives—both physically and spiritually—to Christ. Don't misunderstand; we all grieve the loss, but we know we're moving on to be with the Lord when we die. But the lost ones are in danger of…"

"Of what?"

Chase's mom spoke from behind him as she rested her hands on his shoulders. "Sorry to interrupt. Molly and the others are here."

Chase leapt from the chair and headed for the stairs. He reached Molly within seconds and put his arms around her. The old woman shook and Chase patted her on the back. "A little too much adventure for you?" he asked.

"Much too much," Molly whispered.

He pulled back. "I'm so glad you're all right."

"I hear I have you to thank. Switchblade says you worked that exoself and got us out."

Chase glanced at Switchblade, who wasted no time in looking away.

"It's wonderful to see those sweet blue eyes of yours again," Molly said. "I didn't know for sure that you'd made it to the underground." She rubbed Chase's chin. "A couple of days thickened that beard. Looks good."

"I'm sorry you're stuck here. You can't go home, you know."

"Bound to happen sooner or later. But now we have no one up top to help with supplies."

Amos approached and offered Molly a hug. "The Lord will provide. He always does."

"Yes," she said. "Always."

Amos greeted the other new residents of the underground. The younger ones—the twins and the girl—would be missed by frantic families up top.

"Molly, did anyone say anything to those deputies about the underground?" Chase asked. "Do you think they have any clue there is a base of operations here in Herouxville?"

"I don't believe so." She surveyed the others gathered around her, and they all expressed the same. "We were very careful about what we said, and only answered direct questions. Even then…" She tilted her head and blushed a little. "I mean, we didn't exactly tell them the truth."

Chase smiled. He wasn't the only one who knew how to lie, after all. "But you all told the same story, right? No contradictions?"

"We were never split up, so no discrepancies."

Amos put his arm around Molly, guided her

toward the hallway, and motioned the other four to follow. "I think a debriefing is called for. We'll find out just what the WR knows about us after today's close call. Chase, you can join us if you want. Or I can fill you in later."

"I'll stay here and monitor activity up top. And I need to go over some things with Mel. We'll talk later."

Amos continued down the hall.

Chase spotted Mel in the far corner of the command center. Her hands covered her cheeks.

And Switchblade's hands circled her waist.

7

Chase retreated to his private quarters. An hour would be enough time for Mel to finish her business, or whatever it was, with Switchblade. He hadn't listened to their conversation. He'd give the people in this close environment their privacy by keeping the hearing enhancer off.

He should've listened. What was going on between the two of them? Mel had only been here a few weeks.

"I thought there was something between us," he said to no one. "Fool." He finished running the audio files from the deputies who'd come and gone. Seemed the crisis was over. He left for the command center.

Mel appeared in the hall, headed in his direction. Her hands were at her side, her eyes on him. "Where'd you go, boss? I wanted to talk to you."

Did she think he didn't know what was going on? It didn't take a transhuman to figure *that* out.

She threw her arms around his neck.

Chase held her close. Her hair smelled like lilacs. "What's wrong?"

"Nothing," she said. "I'm just so relieved."

"Can we just go somewhere and talk for a while? About something besides computer code and Bible riddles and where the next shipment of dried beans is coming from? Please, Melody."

She laughed, and the sweet sound lifted Chase's

spirit. "Did you find us some beans?" she asked. "We're running out of vegetables."

"They're ready for pick up but we've lost our contacts up top." Chase took her hand and pulled her toward his room. "I'm sure we can work it out. Right now, I want to talk to you. I've been here for two days and we haven't had a chance to be alone."

"Everything in the underground is so important," she said as he opened the door to his small room, which contained nothing but a single bed, a small table with a lamp, and one chair. "I feel like I'm always running, when all I'm doing is sitting at a computer station."

Chase entered behind her and shut the narrow door.

"Leave the door cracked. Protocol."

"Come on—we're not teenagers."

"But there are teenagers here. A few more of them than we had this morning. We set a good example by not doing anything that might appear inappropriate."

Somehow that was a relief. Switchblade would have to live by the same silly rule. Chase pulled the door open. Mel sat on the edge of the unmade bed. Chase dropped to the floor in front of her.

He sank into her deep brown eyes. His one true friend. All the years at Synvue, during his relationship with Kerstin, spending time with Mel had always been his favorite part of day. Only days before he'd gotten a hole blown through him did he realize there might be something more than friendship.

He never got the chance to find out. Until now.

"What's going on between you and that thug you call Switch?"

"What?" She shot off the bed

Chase got up from the floor and took her hands in his.

"I'm sorry. You seemed so glad to see me the other night and I thought..." He let her go and put his hands on his hips. "It's none of my business. I'm sorry."

"You're right." Her lips made a firm line and her right brow lifted.

"You can start up a relationship with whomever you choose. I have no business questioning you about it."

"No. You're right about me being glad to see you. I prayed for months but I didn't know if you'd ever show up. I don't have feelings for Switchblade."

Chase reached for her. But the voices from somewhere down the hall stopped him. He turned his back to her and pulled on the door knob.

"What is it?" Mel asked.

"I turned on the hearing enhancer so we wouldn't be surprised by passers-by. Amos is on a VPad with someone and he's not too happy. Something to do with that device we saw at the detention center."

"We'd better go see what's up."

He faced her and eased his arms around her. "We need to talk, Melody. About a lot of things."

"We will." She pulled him close and kissed him softly on the lips. "That, by the way, is an infraction. No overt displays of affection among singles in the underground."

"What's the punishment?" He returned the kiss, making this one last a bit longer.

"No punishment. Just encouragement from the other residents."

"That's odd. What sort of encouragement?"

She smiled wide and her eyes sparkled. "Oh, you

don't want to find out. Better not tell anybody about this."

Chase smiled and touched the dimple in her cheek. "Meet me back here later tonight?"

"To talk?"

"Yes. To talk."

He pulled her into the hallway and then let her go before anyone saw them. But he couldn't get the smile to leave his face. A few minutes with Amos might take care of that.

"It's time for lunch," Mel said. "And time for you to stop ordering room service and join us."

8

Chase and Mel sat at a table with several others in the compound's dining hall. Amos watched from a corner of the square room. A few people filled plates and set them out on a counter that separated the area with twenty rectangular tables from the kitchen.

Several children sat together on a blanket spread on the floor in a corner of the room. Their own little picnic. A woman bent near the little party and split open a couple of oranges, laying them on the blanket for the kids to share. When she rose, she rested her hands on her round stomach. There'd soon be another child in the underground. When the time came, who'd deliver the baby?

Molly sat beside Chase. Mom sat across from them.

"Birdie, your boy is here at last. Your faith was rewarded," Molly said.

"Yes. May our faith carry us through these perilous times." Her soft gray hair framed her face. She looked older—it'd been too long since Chase last visited his mother. But her blue eyes still glowed with vibrant energy.

"Mom, I overheard some things. Do you know what's going on?"

"You know more than I do, son." She accepted a plate handed to her by a young man. Lunch consisted of a dried hunk of some type of meat, an orange, and slice of white bread. Chase took his plate and picked up the meat.

"We pray first," Mom said.

"Sorry." He dropped the cold, hard meat as others got their plates. Ten minutes passed before everyone had been served. Then the servers served each other. What a waste of time. Amos was served. Then he got up and served the one who'd served him. At last, everybody had a plate.

"Bow your heads," Amos instructed. "Lord in Heaven, be with us here under the earth. Bless the ones above. Multiply our number while the time allows. Bless this food. We receive it as a gift from Your sovereign hands. You are our sustenance. In the name of Christ. Amen."

Chase waited for the others to dig in.

"Eat," Amos told him. "Then we need to talk."

Chase bit into the dried meat, which wasn't too bad, though it smelled like last month's leftovers. He folded the stale bread and dropped the meat into it. Maybe the exoself could locate a few jars of mayonnaise. Some cheese would be nice too. Someone broke open an orange. Chase breathed in the aroma and stuck his thumbnail into the top of his own fruit. He gazed at Mel. The best restaurant in the Synvue complex couldn't compare with what Chase had right here.

"Chase, what's with the grin," his mother asked.

Heat rushed to his cheeks like he was a kid with a crush. "It's nothing, Mom."

She took a bite of her sandwich.

Switchblade sat beside Amos and kept ogling Mel.

Amos rose from the table before the rest of the group had finished eating. He'd only picked at his lunch. Did he have any idea that he was so ill? Chase had to speak to him about it. But he wouldn't go alone. He'd talk to Mel first, and then the two of them would go together.

"Friends, I've spoken at length with an informant. Chase, I believe you know her. Windsong—she's a pilot."

"She hid me in her plane and got me to New York."

"Since then she's been delivering equipment for the WR." Amos regarded his people. "Some of you were in the command center this morning when Chase removed the walls, so to speak, at the detention center. But most of you didn't see what was hidden there. The device has not yet been utilized. According to Windsong, it's being set up in detention centers all around the Western Republic. The EU developed the machines and recently began shipping them around the world."

Chase instantly followed the trail of information as Amos spoke. He'd known what the device was for as soon as he'd seen it. Judging from the reaction of those in the command center, he'd assumed they all knew what they were looking at. But maybe not.

Amos motioned to the pregnant woman, and she and a couple of other moms gathered the children lunching on the blanket and led them out of the room.

Then Amos continued. "Some of you have seen drawings of the device. Production has begun. Several have been delivered to our continent."

"Two hundred of them," Chase said.

"You've found the information?" Amos asked. "And you know what they will be used for?"

"I knew when I saw it this morning, but I didn't

know how it worked. I wish I didn't know now. But I've got a complete manual."

"Then you know more than I do." Amos eased into his chair. "Please, will you explain it to us?"

These people didn't need to hear this. "If you all stay hidden, which is what I'm here to help you do, then you will never see one of the things up close." He looked at Amos. "Do I need to explain it?"

"Just tell us, son. We aren't afraid to die. But we don't want to be surprised."

A couple of teenage girls began crying. Chase hadn't even said anything yet. "Look, Amos, you're upsetting the younger ones. Can't we talk about this in private?"

"Tell us what you got, robot," Switchblade said. "The kids need to be tough. We don't hold nothing back."

At least the youngest children had been allowed to leave. Chase stared at Amos, who nodded and waited. "It's a laser device designed to...It's a guillotine. A modern, technologically outfitted guillotine."

The crying girls both left the room, along with a few others. Everyone else waited. Chase reached under the table and clutched Mel's hand.

"The report doesn't indicate that any of the devices have been put into operation, but they've been added to detention centers."

"Go ahead," Amos said. "Tell us how it works."

Chase pulled his hand from under the table. "I assume you've all seen a laser knife. You turn it on and the laser emits from the base and slices through...whatever. It's the same technology, but bigger. A person is put into position on a platform with his head facing the floor. A metal bar is fastened on each side of the platform, and the laser blade emits from one bar to the other over the person's neck. And then it... Well, you all know what it does."

"What is the name of the device, Chase?" Amos demanded.

A chill ran through him. Even the exoself seemed to shudder. "They call it Bloodless."

"Why?" Mel asked.

"The incision is sealed instantly. The head is separated and the wound is fused. Neither the body nor the head bleeds." The dried meat Chase had swallowed threatened to come up.

"A bloodless death. How ironic." Amos almost seemed to smile.

Switchblade laughed. "I'm not going out like that. Blood was spilled for us. We won't meet death on a machine they call *Bloodless*."

"Amen" rose from each table. Mel echoed the word. Amos said it too. And then he began singing.

"Alas and did my Savior bleed and did my Sovereign die..." Others joined in the antiquated tune that the exoself identified as a hymn written in 1707. Confusing words. Mel bowed her head and sang. Mom lifted her eyes and sang. Chase shook his head and left the table. No one seemed to notice.

This was getting to be a habit—going to his room when he didn't understand the oddities of the underground. Being with Mel again felt so right, but she was one of them. And they didn't make sense. They were speaking some language he didn't understand. Even his own mother was a stranger now.

He fell across the bed, flipped onto his back, and propped the pillow behind his head. "What am I doing here?" He closed his eyes.

"They are the ones to tell you what I never did," his father had told him. He'd talked with his dad in the dreams, or whatever they were, before his escape from the Helgen Institute. He'd set out to find this place, to help the people of the underground. To learn something from them. And his dead father was the one who sent him here.

"They're not crazy—*I'm* crazy."

"You're not crazy, darling. Just misguided. But I'm here to help you."

He opened his eyes. His terrified, lying eyes. Was she really here? She couldn't be. He *had* lost his mind. He jumped from the bed and backed against the wall. "Kerstin. How..."

"Relax, Chase." Her dark hair framed her pale face. She wore a red dress—one he'd seen her in a dozen times. "You had to have known I'd come for you. This time, I'll never, ever let you go."

9

His mind swam in the confusion. He paddled, reaching aimlessly for the exoself. He'd drown with her watching him. She couldn't have gotten into his room without someone seeing her. "How did you find me? I covered my tracks." He grabbed at the white particle board behind him. "How did you know I was here?"

"Where, Chase? At some base of the Underground Church?" She spoke in a loud voice. Someone would hear her. Somebody would come to help him.

How many others had come with her? They'd followed him and they'd haul all these people out of their cavern and deliver them to that machine, Bloodless.

"Where are we, Chase? I want you to tell me."

She didn't move, didn't look around. Didn't make eye contact. The middle of her body faded. Code appeared for a split second. Then the red dress was just the same as it had been. The exoself seemed to catch it too. The exoself…was how she got here.

Chase breathed, it seemed, for the first time since he'd opened his eyes. An elusive calm fell over him and he latched onto it. He inched close to her and swiped his hand right through her.

"What is this?" He stepped to the other side of her and ran his hand through again. She didn't flinch. "What kind of game is this?" he yelled.

The door cracked open. "Who are you talking to, boss?" Mel asked. "I could hear you all the way down the hall."

Kerstin vanished.

Chase spun around to face Mel. What was he supposed to say to her? He rubbed his hands through his hair and exhaled. "You know I talk to myself. Old habits are hard to break."

"Well, you don't *yell* at yourself. I know you're upset about having to explain all that awful stuff. Amos shouldn't have put you under that much pressure. You're new to this way of life." She put her arms around him. "I'm sorry."

He pushed her away.

"What's wrong?" She moved closer.

"I need to get out of here," he said. "I just need to go up top for some air. Can I do that?"

"You know you can't."

"Look, somebody has to go pick up those vegetables. They're in a warehouse just outside of town. There are no deputies left in the area. No drone activity. Switchblade can come with me." Sweat dripped down the back of his neck. "It'll be fine. Then we can talk when I get back."

Mel crossed her arms. Her look was more worried than irritated, but Chase knew her well enough to know when she was miffed. "Fine. I'll ask Amos if the two of you can go, but he's not gonna like it."

"Tell him he owes me. I just explained to his people the likely method of their death, and he could have done that himself. Not to mention I rescued five believers from the Feds today. I think he can do this one thing for me." Chase reached under the bed and grabbed the knit cap and sunglasses Molly had given him when he'd first come to town.

"All right, I'm going. But just so you know, I don't like this at all. I don't want to lose you again." She headed out the door.

He caught her by both arms, turned her around, and held her tight. "I'm not leaving, Mel. I promise. I'm just going to pick up some beans. And I'm taking a bodyguard with me. He doesn't like me, but I'm willing to wager he's got my back."

"What makes you think he doesn't like you?"

Chase kissed her. "Because he can see the way I look at you." He ran his hand through her loose curls.

"Boss, he knows how I feel about you."

"Stop calling me boss." He buried his face in her hair. "Melody, I just need to get out of here for a little while. Please, convince Amos."

She pulled away and cupped his face with her soft hand. "I'll try. But I wish you would just tell me what's got you so spooked. You got some other intel we don't know about?"

"No." He stepped away from her. "Go talk to Amos." He slipped on the cap and glasses. "I'll find Switchblade."

"He's in his quarters, I think." Mel headed toward the command center then turned back. "I only know that because he said he had some reading to do."

Chase nodded and motioned her on. He went the other way. The thug's room was in the next set of dorms a few hundred yards down the passageway.

He'd make nice with Switchblade, for Mel's sake. Besides, Chase could pin the guy to the ground and out-think him, but when it came to presenting an intimidating front, Switchblade was the one with the power.

He couldn't shake the sight of Kerstin. But she wasn't real. He was just losing it. Being wired up like he was, interacting with a computer in his brain like it was his best friend. If anything could be learned by the experiments they'd done on him, it was that becoming a transhuman was enough to drive a man irrevocably insane.

He'd hold on as long as he could.

Chase stopped in front of a door carved with the image of a switchblade and pounded his fist against it. The door flew open.

"You want something, robot?" Switchblade held an open Bible in his hand.

"What are you reading?" Chase asked.

"About those head machines. Why do you care? It ain't gonna happen to *you*."

"Let me see." Chase grabbed the book. Switchblade pointed to the text. Chase read it out loud. "Then I saw thrones, and seated on them were those to whom the authority to judge was committed. Also I saw the souls of those who had been beheaded for the testimony of Jesus and for the word of God, and those who had not worshiped the beast or its image and had not received its mark on their foreheads or their hands. They came to life and reigned with Christ for a thousand years." He handed the Bible back to Switchblade.

"Seen enough? Ain't you got a Bible in your head with all that other stuff?"

"No. You don't really believe this, do you? I mean, it's not meant to be taken as reality."

"You think the Bible isn't real?" Switchblade asked. "You saw that machine. They're getting it ready. Right?"

Chase didn't want to talk about the death machine anymore. "I need you to go up top with me."

"What on earth? You're crazy, man. Amos will keep his golden boy in this cave for as long as possible."

"I'm not crazy. But I will be if I don't get out of here. I told Mel that I...that you and I were going up for the food shipment. There's no reason we shouldn't go. The Feds are gone and the intel is clear."

"You told Melody one thing, but you're planning something else." Switchblade crossed his arms, grinned, and leaned against the door frame. "Am I right?"

"I think somebody might be tracking me. I need to look around and see if there are any signs of a visitor in town."

"I knew it. I'm taking you up there and leaving you. You're gonna bring us all down."

"I need your help. Please. It might just be a glitch in my systems, but I have to be sure."

Switchblade pulled up the hood on his jacket. "You got all those special powers and you need me to babysit you?"

Chase didn't answer.

"I'm not going without permission." He put his hands on his hips. "We got rules here, you know."

"Mel's talking to Amos, but I think we should go now. You don't seem like somebody who follows the rules all the time."

The big man smirked. "I know a back way out."

10

Chase followed the hood down the hallway, then up an old rotting staircase and through a dark tunnel. Switchblade didn't have a light, so he had to feel the walls to keep himself going straight.

"You know I can see in the dark," Chase told him. "Why don't you let me lead?"

"You don't know where you're going, genius." Switchblade lifted his arms and ran his fingers along the low rock ceiling.

"I'm going down a dark path. When I see something other than that, I'll ask for directions."

Switchblade stopped, motioned with his arm to usher Chase ahead of him, and grumbled under his breath.

"Now maybe we can move a little faster. I know you people have laserlights—I saw them." Chase stepped forward and Switchblade almost knocked him over.

"Sorry," he said with an unremorseful tone. "I need permission to take a laserlight. And you seemed to be in a hurry."

"Just put your hand on my shoulder." Chase flinched when the man followed his instruction. He'd rather not be so close, but it was better than getting knocked down by the big thug. "I have no intel on this place. No record of it being built. What do you know about it?"

"So, you don't know everything?" Switchblade laughed. "Poor robot don't know as much as he thought."

"It was just a simple question. I guess you don't know either."

"I didn't say that. The artist—the one who did the painting that hides the portal to the bunker—"

"*Ciel Bleu Domaine*—Blue Sky Field," Chase said. "The artist was Jean Pateaux. He was a bit eccentric. Spent some time in a mental ward. Never amounted to anything in the art world."

"That's all you got?" Switchblade asked.

"I like his work, what I saw of it. Especially Blue Sky Field."

"It's a stupid name for our base, but all the ladies liked it," Switchblade said. "The crazy artist had some crazy friends. They thought the world was going to end, and they built this place to live out the apocalypse. Nobody up top knew what was going on. No permits, no outside help. If the Canadian government—when there was such a thing—knew what they were doing to the natural caves down here, those artsy goofs would've been locked up. They all died off before any of them needed a hiding place."

"I knew about the cavern," Chase stepped carefully. "I have some pictures taken in the 1940s by explorers."

"What do you mean, you have pictures?"

"In my…In the exoself." Chase ran his hand over the top of his head.

Switchblade's grip on Chase's shoulder loosened. "Yeah, right. Molly knew about the place because she dated one of the artists. And when the people in her church started getting arrested, she told the group about it. And now, here we are. Living like rats."

"What did you do up there that forced you down here?"

"Nothin'. That's why I can go up and not worry about getting caught."

"Then why don't you stay up?" Chase asked.

"You'd like that, wouldn't you, Charlie?"

Chase didn't waste any more time getting to know the man. "I see some boards about fifty feet ahead. Right side."

"That's where we're going. I don't know why *you* had to come under."

"To move everything Mel hid inside me into the computers. So all the churches around the world will be in one system with an untraceable connection."

"Why didn't the girl just program the computer? Why get you and that...exoself involved?"

"Ask *her*." Chase reached the boarded-up section of the wall.

Switchblade moved his hands over the planks in the darkness and pried the wood loose. He pulled a lever hidden inside the wall and a passage to the outside opened. "After you, Charlie."

Chase stepped to the opening. Afternoon sun peered through a space just big enough to climb through, but something blocked it. "Where are we?"

"Two buildings down. Gotta move that refuse bin out of the way. I can do it, but since you're a guest, I'll let you have the privilege."

Chase pushed the old metal contraption with one hand and slid it out of the way. More sunlight filled the tunnel.

"Impressive, Charlie."

Chase stepped into an alley. He inhaled cold air,

blew it out, and lifted his face to the sun. The big man squeezed through the opening, catching his hood on the edge. It slid off the back of his head, and he reached for it and yanked it back into place. Then he grabbed his mirrored glasses from a pocket and slipped them on.

"I guess you already disabled the cameras and got rid of whatever satellite might be passing over us."

"Got that done back in the tunnel while you were hanging on to me like a blind man." Chase pulled his own cap tighter and put on his shades. He returned the large bin to its position in front of the hole in the wall. "Now what?"

"You tell me. You're the one on a mission. But I'll tell you this: we'd better not go back without those vegetables."

"Right," Chase said. "They're in a warehouse a mile from here. Rinetoul Road. But we'll go there last. We don't want to be lugging sacks of beans around town."

"So? What, or who, are we looking for?"

"My boss from Synvue. You worked on Synvue property, right? Did you ever meet Kerstin Bennett?"

"Your lover from another life?" Switchblade smirked. "I was gone when the two of you showed up and started changing lives. Worked for some execs. I left when they did."

"How do know about my relationship with Kerstin? We kept it hidden from the public."

"Melody told me."

Chase pulled off his shades and studied the man's face. "Did you know Mel in Chicago?"

"Just met her a few weeks ago."

Chase slipped the shades back on and sucked in a

breath. Should he trust this guy? "I think Kerstin might be here."

"So check travel permits, the hotel registry— there's only one in town."

"She's not there. And her permit is open ended. She can go where she wants, when she wants." Chase stepped into the quiet street at the east end of the alley. "Where would a traveler hang out in this town? Cyber stops, restaurants?"

"You're reaching for straws, man. This ain't no tourist town. What makes you think she's here?"

Chase ignored the question. "I saw a café when I first arrived the other night." He turned right and started walking. Switchblade caught up with him. A minute later they stood outside the café, looking in through the plate glass. No sign of Kerstin. Chase went right in.

"Hey, wait. You dummy, what are you doing?" Switchblade followed him into the place that contained six tables, a counter with eight stools, some dim lights, and an old woman wearing black. Switchblade pulled off his sunglasses. Chase left his on.

Chase spoke in perfect French. He asked the woman if she'd seen a tall, pale woman with long black hair. She might have been wearing a red dress.

"*Non, pas un, mais vous a venir sauf la régulière. Prendre un café.*"

Chase slanted his head toward Switchblade. "No one has been here except her regular customers."

"*Prendre un café!*" the woman said.

"What is she yelling about?" Switchblade asked.

"She wants us to order coffee. You got any WR bills?"

"No, I don't got no bills! Man, let's get out of

here."

"*Pas de café, merci,*" Chase said to the woman.

"*Sortez ensuite!*"

Chase and Switchblade walked out the door and onto the brick sidewalk.

"You ever speak French before you got that exoself put in you?" Switchblade asked.

"Never."

"Even the accent sounds real."

"I thought this was a friendly little town." Chase brushed his hands down the front of his jacket.

"People are skittish all over, Charlie. What'd she yell at you?"

"She told us to get out, that's all. You're right, this is pointless. Let's get the beans and go home."

"Home?" Switchblade wore that annoying little smirk of his.

The bodyguard was right. Chase was a homeless man, except for the underground. The townhouse in Chicago seemed foreign to him now. The last place he'd lived before his escape was the Helgen Institute. The place of miracles. The place where he'd sent Kerstin. "That's where she'd be if she had the transplant."

"What are you talking about?"

"Kerstin. She should be in the desert," Chase said. "I don't know why I'm looking for her." He stuffed his hands into the pockets of his jacket. "But the fresh air did clear my head."

"I thought she was in New York. Then you said she might be here. Now she's in the desert?"

"If she did what I told her, she went to the Helgen Institute for a kidney."

"So, look it up. Can't you find out?"

"Not that easy. I don't have access to anything related to the Helgen." Chase pulled down his shades and lifted his gaze to the sky. "I wish I could talk to Robert."

"Your creator, right?"

"In a manner of speaking. He's the doctor who made the organs, designed the processors. But others, like Mel, wrote the code that keeps me connected to the cyber world."

"So, you sent your old lover to your doctor because she needed a kidney. How romantic." Switchblade snickered and shook his head.

"Don't read anything into it. We're done. It was over a long time ago."

"And now you want Melody."

Chase stopped and looked Switchblade in the eyes. "Mel and I...It's none of your business."

"I'm making it my business, robot." Switchblade clenched his fists. "You're here to protect us? I'm here to protect *her*. Don't know what the girl would want with a little white boy, anyway."

Chase walked backwards, keeping his eyes on Switchblade. "Are you coming, or not? I mean, I can carry everything back by myself if that's what you want."

Switchblade rolled up both sleeves and popped his neck. With long strides, he advanced toward Chase. "I'm coming."

Chase stumbled when the exoself delivered a warning. He pulled off his sunglasses and surveyed the sky. "S-drone."

11

Switchblade looked to the sky and turned a circle. "I don't see nothing."

"It's a mile out but it's headed this way."

"So let's get on with this."

"We don't need it following us to the warehouse." Chase moved close to the gray wall of the nearest building where a block partition separated two small offices.

"You sure it's headed here? Drone factory is nearby, you know. They test them out in the fields. Never seen one in town, though."

"It's right behind you."

Switchblade spun around. "Get down behind that wall."

Chase dove behind it. He pressed himself into the corner. Switchblade remained on the sidewalk with his arms crossed and whistled a tune as if nothing unusual were happening.

The drone hovered twenty feet above them. Then dropped to ten feet. Switchblade watched it, even gave it a little wave. Then the thing lifted into the air and flew over the buildings to the left.

"What'd I tell you," Switchblade said. "They don't know me from Adam."

The pick-up was easy—no one was around to notice the two were not the usual up top retrievers. Chase carried one large sack and Switchblade carried another.

They entered the alley an hour and a half after they'd sneaked out. Chase pushed the metal bin aside and peered into the tunnel, which was now well lit.

"Both of you stop right there," a man holding a laserlight said.

Chase didn't recognize him. He wore brown coveralls and a scar ran down his left cheek.

"Amos thinks maybe he'll just let you stay up top. The two of you can replace the five who had to come underground today."

"I'm sorry," Chase said. "It was my fault."

"We tell each other everything and we don't wander off or go up top without permission. Especially you, Mr. Sterling…uh, Redding."

"I'll talk to Amos. Let us in."

The guy stepped aside, and Chase crawled through the hole and into the tunnel. Switchblade followed and tossed in the bag of beans. Chase pulled the refuse bin back into place.

Switchblade grabbed the shoulder of the man with the light. "You know I can take care of myself up there, Nate. And I know how important this man here is. Nothing happened."

"Except you got supplies, right?"

Switchblade pointed to the beans. Chase still carried his bag.

"I'm not worried about it, Switch. But Amos is fuming."

Chase couldn't imagine the man losing his composure. "Like I said, it's my fault."

"Don't need you to stand up for me, Charlie." Switchblade picked up the bag of beans and hoisted it onto his shoulder. "You didn't make me do nothing I didn't want to do."

No one spoke as their footsteps echoed through the damp hallway that led to the underground complex.

Then Chase stopped. He wanted to flee.

At the end of the tunnel, waiting in an alcove... Kerstin in her red dress.

Code flashed across her form.

She faded, flashed back for a second, and then disappeared.

Chase wiped cold sweat off his brow with his free hand and kept going. The guy in brown—Nate—had orders to deliver him and Switchblade to Amos. They were on their way to the principal's office. Maybe they'd get detention. Or expelled.

Mel waited with several others in the command center. Her eyes shot a few darts their way. But she didn't say anything.

Nate opened the door and motioned them in to Amos's private quarters. The room was bigger than Chase's and had a large desk with a computer, a recliner, seemingly from the last century, and a small refrigerator. The perks of being a leader in the Underground Church.

Amos stood at the foot of his bed with his arms folded. "Come in, gentlemen."

"It was my idea," Chase said. "I needed to get some air. We picked up the food shipment and we came right back."

"Look, robot, you can lie for the good of the people and all that, but I'm not lying to the man in charge to cover your butt," Switchblade said. "Amos, it's like this: We talked to a crabby old French woman and we got spotted by an S-drone. *Then* we got the beans. But nothing bad came of it."

"Sit down, both of you."

Chase dropped to the desk chair. Switchblade took the recliner. His big arms covered the tan vinyl armrests. He reached to the side of the chair and flipped the lever and his long legs sprang up and out as the footrest extended.

Amos sighed and shook his head. "Don't get too relaxed, Switchblade." He sat on the end of the bed. His breathing was labored, his eyes bloodshot. Amos was sick and Chase might be the only person who knew. He shouldn't have put the man through this.

"I did talk to a woman in a café, and we did see an S-drone," Chase dropped his hands to his knees. Then he pointed at Switchblade. "The drone didn't see *me*, but *he* just stood there and whistled at it." Chase leaned forward and locked his fingers together. "Look, nothing happened. I just needed to get out of here for a while. After the close call this morning, and then the whole thing with that machine. Bloodless. I needed to take a walk. That's all."

Switchblade cleared his throat.

The guy wouldn't let Chase get away with anything. "And...I felt something in my systems. I thought somebody might have followed me and I wanted to look around. It was stupid. Nobody followed me."

"Nothing else?" Amos asked.

Chase wouldn't tell the leader he was seeing things. No point in causing any more upsets today. He'd figure out the problem on his own, and then he'd fix it.

"Suppose the woman in the café realized after you left that she'd just had a conversation with the great

Chase Sterling." Amos glared at Switchblade. "And what if the computer system hooked to that drone picked up the fact that you are not a resident of Herouxville?" He paced across the room. "You don't leave here without permission. You may think you're invincible, but any number of things could happen. You could get caught or injured. You could lead the Feds right to us."

"It won't happen again, sir," Chase said.

Another smirk from Switchblade and Chase looked him in the eyes. "I said it won't happen again."

"Hey, I'm in agreement with that. But like I said earlier, you didn't twist my arm." Switchblade turned to Amos. "You know *I'm* not staying put. I'll be going up more now that we ain't got nobody working for us in town."

Amos hovered over the big man in the recliner. "You take him up again, I'll find somebody else to wander the streets of Herouxville. Got it?"

"Got it." Switchblade pushed the footrest down and rose from the chair. "I'll get those vegetables to the kitchen."

"You do that," Amos said. "Chase, you still have to face your mother and Melody. I wasn't too hard on you. Can't make you any promises about those two."

"Thank you, Amos. I'll go work on those security measures we need to put in place." Chase hurried for the door.

Amos waved him off, and Chase closed the door behind him.

Mel waited in the hall. No sign of Mom. At least he could deal with them one at a time. "Not here," he said. "Meet me in my room."

She left without a word.

Chase went to the command center and found an empty work station. He'd give Mel a few minutes while he reviewed the security like he said he would. "No more lies today." He pulled the logs of S-drone activity from earlier that day. No indication that the drone hovering in town had caught on to anything suspicious. He checked the local police files too. All clear.

The biggest security risk was Switchblade trotting around town. The Feds might not know him, but a big black guy with no local address was bound to catch somebody's eye.

A few prompts from the exoself showed Chase where to ring in some indiscreet coded communication going out from this headquarters to others around the world. Seemed like even the obvious errors weren't caught by the WR. The Feds weren't too bright, or they just didn't care about the activity of the underground.

Or somebody besides Chase was watching out for these people.

He got up and left the command center. Time to have a talk with Mel. How could he kiss a girl and make her so mad all in one day? Well, he'd done it plenty of times. He smiled.

His mother stepped in front of him. "Again with the silly grin." She smiled back. "Heard you got into trouble. Did you get a note to take home to your mom?"

"No, but I did get a good talking to."

"And now you're off to make up with Melody?"

"Something like that. You don't miss anything, do you?"

"I know when my son has his sights set on a girl."

"Mom, whatever happens with Mel is going to

take a long time. This world is too messed up for me to get caught up in a relationship."

"The world is never too messed up for love, Chase. Don't lose sight of what matters."

"I won't." He kissed her on the cheek. "But after what I did, Mel might just beat me up and toss me out of here."

"She might. Go on," Mom said. She smacked him on the backside.

On the way to his quarters, Chase went over his last communication with Robert. It was the final one allowed. He'd used the device in his ear to get a message to an old laptop belonging to Robert. He knew the code—twelve, two. Sparking the twelfth processor, he pulled two lines of code. He wasn't supposed to do this again. It wouldn't work this time. He sent the message through the exoself anyway.

Robert, if you get this, find a way to get into the system. I need your help. I'm seeing things.

He arrived at his door and pushed it open. Mel sat on the edge of the bed. Hopefully she'd calmed down.

"Amos was going to let you go, Chase. You didn't need to sneak out."

"He was? Because I just got an ear load from Amos about what I'm *not* allowed to do. And I'm *not* allowed to go up."

She stood. "Well, maybe he doesn't trust you *now*. Do you know how important it is for that man to trust you? You have to work together."

"I know. I'm sorry. I don't know how many times I can say that."

"Why did you go up without waiting just a few minutes for permission? Do you know how stupid that was?"

"Look, Mel, I'm not one of you. I'm not some dedicated believer ready to lay down my life for the cause. I'm just a man who got some ridiculous stuff put in him that you people seem to think you need to survive. And by the way, thank you for doing that to me."

Tears welled in her eyes. "I thought you wanted to be here."

"I don't know what I want." He pushed his hair back and turned away from her. "That's not true." He faced her. "I don't want to be here. I don't want to deal with whatever crap is floating around in the exoself." He lifted his hand to her cheek and wiped her tears. "But that's who I am now. I'm a transhuman. And I want to do something good with it." He bent to kiss away another tear. "And I never want to be apart from you again."

She put her arms around him and hid her face on his chest. "Is there anything else bothering you, Chase? I'm the one who got you into this and I'm here to help you."

"Nothing's wrong, Melody." He held her tight. From the corner of the little room, a flash of code appeared. And just a hint of the curve of a red dress. "Everything is going to be all right."

12

Chase sat straight in the bed, a white coverlet over his legs. The room was dark, but he could see every inch of it. The exoself informed him that the time was half past two.

The light in the hall had gone out at midnight. Like the compound in Atlanta, the underground here pulled from excess power generated by the town's solar panels. Mel had gotten it started. The exoself had made the deal permanent—two computers worked out the details for the illegal harnessing of electricity.

These people didn't like to lie, but they didn't mind a little stealing. Not that it mattered to Chase. Right now he was less concerned with what the believers did to keep themselves lit up, and more concerned with the image that kept lighting up in front of him.

Kerstin hadn't shown herself again. It wasn't her— it was just an image. She hadn't spoken to him—it was all in his head. But why did it happen?

He scooted down in the bed and pulled the coverlet up to his chin. He had to at least try to sleep. He closed his eyes.

Ciel Bleu Domaine. The painting filled his dreams. Open land, hills on each side. The bluest sky he'd ever seen. Mel and Mom were packing boxes with food. Others loaded the boxes onto a truck. But they were all out in the open, not in a cavern under the old museum.

His father stood with him. "Remember where they go, son."

"What do you mean?"

The sky filled with S-drones and they began firing on the people.

"Dad, we have to do something!"

Mel and Mom were gone. People he recognized lay dead on the ground. Others seemed to dive straight into the hillside, as though it were water and not earth. The truck vanished through the hillside.

In the middle of the green field, Kerstin, wearing the same red dress, seemed to float. "Darling, it's only a matter of time."

Chase jumped from the bed. The coverlet fell to the floor. Sweat poured from him. He turned a circle. No one was there. Six thirty—he'd slept four hours. He dropped to the floor and sat with his head on his knees.

For twenty minutes his mind wandered through the open green field. But he was alone. No believers. No Mel.

No Kerstin.

He rose from the cold floor and grabbed a clean shirt and towel. He'd been supplied with a few necessities. A razor and other items waited in a small box. He pulled the razor out, along with a toothbrush, and left his dark room to walk the quiet hallway to the dormitory-style bathroom. Seemed no one was up. Although the day's assigned kitchen workers must be preparing a sparse breakfast. The lights hadn't come on anywhere in this area.

He didn't bother turning on the bathroom light—no need to use up the power when it was just him. Standing before a cracked mirror, he wet his face and rubbed on a little soap. The water, cool and in no hurry to fill the metal sink, was the bonus of an abandoned building with its own well. No luxury of a modern laser blade or a container of prep gel. He took the razor and shaved his face clean.

The trickle of a tepid shower did little to revive him. But the exoself was up and running. The morning report gave no indication that the teens now safe in the underground had been reported missing by their families. Odd that no one was searching for them.

No message from Robert after Chase sent out the cry for help. "No surprise." Kerstin had not been slinking through his processors either. "Maybe it's over. Whatever it was."

He put on the same jeans he'd taken off, pulled the clean shirt over his head, and brushed his teeth.

The hallway was lit and a couple of men entered the bathroom. Chase nodded a greeting. They both smiled a bit, but said nothing. He returned his personal items to his room and then headed to the command center.

Amos sat alone at a station.

Chase joined him. "Nobody reported anything about those kids, Amos. What do you think that means?"

"Maybe the cops told them to wait a day or two before filing."

"Yeah, I guess that's standard."

"Why'd you shave off the beard?" Amos asked. "I thought that was part of your disguise."

"I don't need a disguise. Everybody here knows who I am."

Amos smiled. "Is this your way of telling me that you're not going up again?"

"Take it how you want, Amos." Chase smiled back. "I'm not going up again. Unless you tell me to, of course."

Chase tensed as that familiar surge of information flowed into him. He moved to the station where he could get a 3D image.

"What is it, Chase?" Amos asked.

He brought up the image of Molly's house and raised it from the flat screen. Crumbled walls smoldered. No need for the exoself to dissolve the exterior. The place had been gutted and burned.

"Why would they do it?" Amos asked.

"They found her basement. Did you know the staircase going into it was undetectable behind a mirrored wall?"

"Yes, I was there a few times before I came under. I don't know why they had to destroy it."

"Should we tell her?" asked Chase.

"It was just a house. Not her real home. But we'll just keep it quiet for now. The Feds are back and the others will have to know, but not today. Let's try to have a little less stress than yesterday."

"Fine with me," Chase said.

Mel joined them. She smiled as she rubbed Chase's chin. "You got rid of that awful excuse for a beard, huh?"

"You didn't like my beard? Molly liked it."

"Well, Molly didn't have to—"

"Watch out, missy," Amos said "You know what'll happen."

"I haven't told *him* what'll happen." She giggled. "Don't worry, Amos. We're not breaking any rules."

"Tell me what?" Chase asked.

"Breakfast is ready," she said.

The three of them entered the dining hall and sat at one of the long tables. Breakfast was another chunk of dried meat, another orange, and another slice of bread. At least last night's supper had consisted of something different—beans and cornbread.

He peeled the orange and divided the sections. How many of these were left? Chase would use Mel's code a little later to find out what was available.

When she'd finished eating, Mel went into the kitchen. It was her day to help out. Chase would get himself on the rotation. If he was going to be part of the group, he'd do his share. If they wouldn't mind a heathen cleaning up after them.

He turned to Amos and lowered his voice. "What do these people think of me?"

A spark surged through the exoself and new information filtered in. Chase jumped to his feet.

Amos and everyone else at the table stopped eating and stared at him. "What is it?" Amos asked.

"We need to talk. In private," Chase answered.

Amos followed Chase out of the dining hall. "What now?"

"The Feds took care of demolishing everything in Kirel's apartment."

"Not a surprise after what they did to Molly's place."

"Then they paid a visit to Finley's parents, and to the twins' grandparents."

"They didn't—"

"They killed them, Amos. They're all dead."

13

The girl, Finley, lifted her head from a minister's shoulder. "We are all in God's hands."

Chase lowered his brow. That was it? The WR murdered her parents and that was all she said? With a quivering smile, she rose to leave. The blond boys followed her, their arms around each other's shoulders. So calm. It'd hit them later.

The three ministers who'd been summoned by Amos left with the teens. Chase scratched the back of his head. He should have been able to prevent this.

The emergency meeting had dwindled down to Molly and Kirel—who'd been told about the destruction of their up-top homes—Chase, Amos, Switchblade, and Mel.

"We must look after the young ones," Amos said. "Their faith is being tested."

Chase stared at the floor. The exoself could not explain this latest comment from a Christian. The kids needed support—he got that much.

Amos cleared his throat. "Chase, tell us what you know about the day's activities."

"The report indicates the residences were searched and burned, and that four people died in the raid," Chase said. "It says the four fought to defend their homes and had to be killed. Makes no sense that they wouldn't cooperate with federal deputies. And why did the Feds come back here? I thought we had them fooled."

"They might be stupid but they're not blind," Switchblade said. "The five were supposed to attend a meeting and then go home. They didn't *go* home. Somebody noticed. Feds must have double checked all those lies from yesterday."

Chase ran a sweep of information related to the five and their alleged backgrounds. "The five are still listed as informants." What he found next shocked him. He had to tell the others. "The deputies who returned during the night acted on an outside lead. An informant accused the ones who were killed of planning to bomb the detention center."

Amos's face turned crimson. "That's ridiculous! Who would make up something like that?"

Chase studied the others. "It could have been anybody. Maybe there's somebody living up top who's trying to flush us out. Or maybe it's someone down here."

"One of *us*?" Switchblade pushed out of the chair and barreled across the room. "Only person I know who can plant lies in the system is you."

Chase gave him a cold stare. "Only person I know who goes up every time he feels like it is you."

"Enough," Molly said. "Loved ones are dead and someone is responsible. Chase, we're glad you're here to help us." She took a breath. "Switch, he *is* one of us. God sent him to us."

Her scolding eyes met Chase. "But if you're to live with us, then you must stand with us. No one here is capable of doing what you're suggesting. It had to have happened another way."

"Yes, ma'am. I hope you're right," Chase said. "I'm sorry. There has been a lot of misinformation passed back and forth, and it started with me. Maybe the Feds are playing the same game."

"I'm going up to take a look around," Switchblade said.

"No. *You* are staying put. Along with everyone else," Amos said. "Until we know for certain that this didn't happen because we have a mole, no one will be given the opportunity to spill anything to the Feds."

"You think I could do this thing?" Switchblade pointed at Chase. "The robot could shoot up any message he wants without ever getting out of his chair." He pulled the door open and then shut it behind him.

Molly, Kirel—who hadn't said a word—and even Mel looked at Chase.

"He's right," Chase said. "You have no reason to believe me when I tell you I can't contact anyone working for the WR or any other organization outside the underground. I can only read whatever intel the Feds report. And they can't trace me." The flash of a red dress in his room splintered his mind as he spit out yet another deception. "There is no way they could find me here."

"I programmed Chase to connect those of us who live in the underground," Mel said. "I didn't program him to *desire* to help us. I didn't program him to track federal agents, observe detention centers via satellite, or dissolve walls on a 3D image. I didn't do that." Her eyes questioned Chase. "Do you have any idea who did?"

"I told you, Mel. I thought it was you."

She held his gaze. "God has His hand on this man, and God won't allow him to be used against us. We can trust Chase. No matter what."

Kirel, the silent man in the room, leaned forward and rested his arms on his knees. He blinked his green eyes and pushed a strand of long brown hair behind his ear. "I'm new here. I don't know you, Melody. I don't know that big black guy very well either. But I know he goes up top more than anybody else and I'm not sure why. The only people I know are Molly and those three kids. We were our own little church in the real world. The rest of you, I don't know and I don't trust. Especially this gameshow host." He said nothing else before he left the room.

Mel reached for Chase's hand.

"I'll talk to him," Molly said.

Chase met Amos's pained eyes. "Are you all right?"

"I could use a vacation." Amos slumped forward.

Molly let out a chuckle and Chase smiled. Then he stood and spread his arms wide. "Here's what I'm going to do for you," he said. "You and a guest will travel on a Synvue globe jet to a private Jamaican resort where you will spend the next month being pampered in every way possible."

Mel laughed. "Sit down, you fool. Nobody's winning anything today."

Amos's round belly shook with a silent laugh. "Just a nap then." He got up and opened the door. "I'll be in my room for a while."

Chase laid his hand on the man's shoulder. The surge of energy from the exoself reminded him that Amos was sick. And growing sicker. "I'll see if I can find out anything else about what happened in town last night."

Amos patted Chase's hand. "You do that, son." He headed down the hallway.

Chase addressed Mel and Molly. "Can I talk to the two of you a little longer?" He watched the leader of the underground walk to his private quarters. "I need to tell you something."

14

Chase closed the door and returned to his seat beside Mel.

"What is it?" Molly asked. "Do you know something you didn't want to share with Amos?"

"Yes. I'll have to tell him," Chase said. "I just don't want to do it by myself." He studied Mel's concerned expression. "You know about the Wilberton device."

"Amos is sick?" Her eyes grew wide as she leaned forward. "Judging by the look on your face it's bad."

"You two will have to fill me in," Molly said. "Amos is sick because of some device?"

Chase turned to her. "No. The Wilberton is inside me. It's part of the exoself and it allows me to diagnose illness. All I have to do is to touch a person and I know."

"I watched the live show where you touched a woman in the audience. I'd forgotten." Molly pulled her arms close and inched away from Chase. "Melody, you knew about this. You should have told us."

"I didn't want everyone running up to him to find out whether or not anything was wrong with them." Mel took Molly's hand in hers. "Chase and I haven't even had a chance to discuss it. Besides, there's nothing he can do to help anyone recover. Not down here."

"She's right," Chase said. "Why tell these people what's wrong with them if we can't cure them?"

Molly nodded. "Is it organ failure?"

"No. I can tell that he hasn't even had the cancer vaccine, so organ failure is not the problem."

"Wait a minute," Mel said. "What are you saying? The vaccine *causes* organ failure?"

"Yes, the reason organ failure is so common now is due to the vaccine that we've all had. Well, almost all. Some who've been involved in covert groups haven't had the vaccine."

"Amos has been what you'd call covert for the last twenty years," Molly said. "So then, it must be cancer."

"Leukemia. Beyond curing. He's had it for a long time." Chase moved close and put his arm around her shoulder. "I'm sorry."

"He must know. He must feel bad, don't you think?" Mel asked.

"Molly, you've known him the longest," Chase said. "Have you noticed a difference lately?"

"The man relies on the strength of the Lord. He may know he's sick, but he wouldn't burden us with it. He'll stand strong as long as possible. Son, is there nothing you can do for him?"

"I can't do anything but make a diagnosis. Even if he went up top, traditional medicine wouldn't help. Techno-meds, perhaps. Advances are being made by the minute—no telling how far they've come even in the short time since I left the Helgen. But no one is going to allow that kind of treatment for a leader of the underground. They'd take him straight to jail. Or they'd speed up his death."

"We have to tell him," Mel said.

"After dinner tonight," Chase told her. "Will the two of you come with me?"

The women nodded. "We'll be there," Mel said. "But it'll be hard to be near him all day and not say anything."

Chase looked into Molly's eyes. "A few minutes ago, you moved away from me when you found out what I can do." He took her hand. "You are in perfect health."

She smiled. "I am as the Lord wills. Tomorrow may bring a change. If it does, and you know, don't tell me. All right?"

He nodded and lifted his hand to touch her wrinkled face. Then he turned to Mel. "Can I ask you something? About the information trails you put in me?"

"You can ask me anything."

"I had to get into the underground in Atlanta to find cryptic messages written on the walls before I could dig your code out of the Psalms. Why not just put a Bible in my head and direct me to the code?"

"The scientists and governing officials in charge of your transformation didn't allow it. If I'd tried it, they'd probably have caught on to what I was doing and had me arrested. I know it sounds odd that they would give you access to everything ever entered into a database except for one topic, but they're working to get all religion, even if it's just for reference purposes, out of the cyber world."

"I've found some literature referring to Bible stories. And some historical information about other religions. No history of the Christian church though. It's like it never happened."

Molly shook her head. "We're being erased from history."

"They can't do that," Mel said. "Not as long as we're still here." Her eyes met Chase's. "Do you want a Bible? I can get you a paperback."

"No need, I guess. I only wondered why I couldn't access it through the exoself."

"When I get a chance I'll see if I can get it in through my own programs."

"I can access general information about church music," Chase said.

"You mean, like hymns? You can learn a lot from those old songs," Molly said.

Mel lifted her brow. "Eliminating religion from the cyber world is a work in progress. Maybe it was an oversight. But Molly's right. There's a lot of church history in the old songs too."

The three left the small meeting room and joined dozens in the command center. Chase brushed by his mother and squeezed her shoulder. She appeared to be working on a new room arrangement. The added residents meant a few would have to share a room. Beds were being moved to accommodate, and those with larger rooms were asked to give up their space for the sake of those who'd be living with roommates. Of course, no one complained. How long could these people live like this before somebody started to gripe?

"Chase," Mom said. "Switch ran by here mumbling about how 'that robot' wasn't going to accuse him of...something. The two of you having a problem?"

The battle might start sooner rather than later. Chase sat beside her. "We think there might be someone down here, or up top, feeding information to the Feds. Some bad stuff happened last night. I'm sure Amos will fill in the whole group sometime later today."

"What's that got to do with Switchblade ranting about you? Does he think you had something to do with it?"

"He might have suggested it, and I might have suggested the same about him."

"Well, I don't believe it," she said. "Not about either of you."

"We both got a little hot under the collar. Somebody is responsible for what happened last night."

"What was it?"

Chase peered over his shoulder and then leaned in close. "The families of those kids who came under were killed."

Tears filled her eyes and her hand covered her mouth.

"Mom, don't say anything."

"Where are those poor babies?"

"In their quarters with the ministers."

"We'll need to be here for them. All of us. We're their family now."

Chase nodded. "You're a good mom. Always were." He kissed her cheek. "I'll go find Switchblade and apologize."

He left her for the largest area of dorms. Passing his own room, he headed for the door with the switchblade carved on it. What were those artists thinking when they transformed the cavern into an underground campus with enough bedrooms for a hundred people? Apocalypse—that was the word Switchblade had used. Not so far from the truth. The world was falling apart and Chase was hiding in a bunker. A massive, elaborate hiding place never used by the people who built it. Almost seemed like God planned it in advance for the Underground Church.

He knocked on Switchblade's door, softer this

time. He didn't mean to insinuate the man might be a mole. A thug, yes. And arrogant. Not very likable. But his dedication to these people was obvious.

Switchblade didn't open the door. Chase turned up his hearing enhancer. No sound inside the room. Surely the guy wouldn't go up after Amos told him it was forbidden.

"What am I thinking?" Chase said. "Of course he'd go up."

The dark tunnel that led to the back exit was past the dorm area. Chase slipped through unnoticed, climbed the rickety stairs, and headed that direction. A hundred yards in, long before the hidden panel, he found Switchblade sitting in the dark on the cold floor.

"Did you go up?" Chase asked.

"What're you doing here, you freak? You traitor." He lifted himself up and powered a small laserlight.

"Look, I didn't mean—"

Switchblade let the light drop to the ground and jumped Chase, pushing him backward until they were both on the ground. The big man roared as he balled his fist and punched Chase in the left temple.

But the man was no match for a transhuman.

Chase flipped him over and pinned him tight, pushing his shoulder into the floor and pressed down hard on his throat. "You may be bigger, but you aren't stronger. And don't forget it. This thing inside seems determined to keep me alive. If you threaten me, I can't be held responsible for what might happen." Chase stood and brushed his hands down his sleeves. "Now get up and let me apologize," he yelled.

15

Switchblade stumbled as he grabbed the laserlight off the floor. He eased up in front of Chase, cleared his throat, and rubbed his neck.

"Did I hurt you?" Chase asked.

"No. Hah, you got some ego thinking you could." He straightened his collar and flexed his arms. "Don't tell me I didn't hurt *you*?"

Chase rubbed the side of his head. "The human part stings a little."

"Yeah. Sorry."

"You have a way of making that word sound pitifully sorrowless."

"You could've strangled me with that hold. I can't believe a little guy like you has all that power."

"I'm a perfectly normal-sized man," Chase said. "*You're* a giant." He headed back toward the compound and Switchblade followed. "You don't want to know what happened to the last guy who threatened me, and *he* was an armed cop. Of course, he had a NP in his ear. I didn't mean to kill him."

"You killed a cop? What's an NP?"

"Neuroprosthesis. WR is planting the device in people to control them. The exoself blew up the thing. Killed the guy instantly."

"Got new respect for you, Charlie. Cop killer — who'd a thought?"

"I didn't do it on purpose. He had just killed

somebody I cared about—a man you remind me of, as a matter of fact. I would have been next. So the exoself took care of the problem." Chase stopped and faced Switchblade. "Seems odd a Bible-carrying believer would respect a cop killer."

"By respect, I mean I will think twice about messing with you again." He stretched his shoulder and let out a groan. "This pain in my arm will make me think twice too."

"I'm sorry about that. And about what I said earlier. I don't think you'd do anything to endanger these people."

"Yeah, well I started it. I'm sorry too."

This time, the apology seemed genuine. "Can you do something for me?"

"Hey, I didn't say we were gonna get all buddy-buddy." Switchblade clicked the laser off as they approached the staircase. Light from below filled the tunnel. "What do you want from me?"

"I can take being called Charlie. My dad called me that. But if you call me robot again I'm going to—"

Switchblade lifted his hands. "No more robot."

"Thank you."

"One other thing we gotta work out," Switchblade said. "Melody is a free agent as far as I can tell. You want her, you gotta get around me. No beating each other up or anything. We'll just see who has the power when it comes to winning that girl over."

"Game on. The exoself doesn't know anything about women." Chase smiled as they reached the stairs. "But I do."

"Hah, you think?" Switchblade rubbed the back of his neck. "Explain something to me. I don't get why you call it the exoself if it's inside you. Don't make sense."

"Yeah, I know. But I didn't make this stuff up. 'Exoself' is defined as systems used in cooperation with a human being, extending mind and body to provide information and support monitoring. They hooked me up to the cyber world to use me. But Robert—my doctor—was able to program a disconnect and give me control of the exoself."

"So nobody can monitor you. But if you got disconnected, how do you pick up on all that WR crap?"

"I wish I understood. Robert told me I wouldn't be able to access government programs anymore. But now I can plug right in, even more than I could before. The exoself found a way to do it without getting caught." Chase rubbed his head and raked his fingers through his hair. "Part of the transhuman experience, I guess."

"I still keep thinking you're going to pull on some kind of techno warfare armor suit. You know? *Exo*self." Switchblade gaped down at his jeans and black t-shirt. Then he gave Chase a once over. "We look like we've been brawling."

"We have been."

"That wasn't no brawl. You ain't never been in a fight. Not a real one."

"Whatever you want to call it, we'd better get cleaned up," Chase said. He slowed the pace. "What's your real name? Why is it that information about you is so limited?"

"Only person here who knows my past is Amos, and even he don't know my real name. That life is over. Just like this conversation." Switchblade strutted ahead.

Once inside the bunker, they managed to get to the

bathroom near their dorms without being seen. Switchblade washed and then went to his room for a clean shirt. Chase stripped down and showered. As he stepped out, a towel around his waist, he saw her. She flickered in front of the sink, facing him with her back to the mirror, which offered no reflection of her black hair or what Chase remembered as the low scoop of her red dress.

He pulled his towel tight with one hand and reached for his pants with the other. "I know this is some kind of trick you're playing with the exoself. But be warned, it doesn't play games. I consider you popping in and out of here a threat. The exoself doesn't like it when people threaten me."

"What do you think it can do to me, darling? I'm not really here. I'm in my bed in recovery at the Helgen. Robert did a marvelous job with the transplant, and I feel completely healed, though a bit weak," Kerstin said. "Thank you for sending me here. Robert obliged in giving me one of his lab-grown kidneys. Though I'm surprised he didn't kill me during the operation." She smiled. "It was that young doctor, Jack Bentley. Do you remember him, Chase?"

"Yes."

"He's the one who chipped me. Now I can enter the exoself and talk to you. I can't see you though. Can you see me, darling? Jack said that if the exoself allowed you to see me, I would appear as you remembered me." Her lips curled into a sly grin. "What am I wearing?"

Chase dropped the towel and pulled on his pants. "An orange jumpsuit. Like the kind they give prisoners."

She laughed. "I'm not breaking any laws. You're

the criminal. You've stolen WR property and you're using it against us. I can shut you down, Chase. I've done it before."

"So go ahead."

The code flashed across the red dress and up her long neck. "Where are you, Chase? You went off on some stupid hunt for those throwbacks with their Bibles, and for that awful girl, Melanie."

"Your brain's chipped and you still can't remember her name."

"Her name is irrelevant. Did you find her?"

"I'm not telling you anything."

Inside him, sparks flew, as though the exoself was trying various codes to end this.

Kerstin flickered and faded. She didn't go away. "I'll find you, darling. It's only a matter of time before the exoself tells me where you are. The numbers are lining up as we speak. And when I'm fully connected to your processors…"

"What?"

"Then I'll know where you're hiding. You won't be able to escape without the exoself."

"The exoself is mine, Kerstin. No one controls it but me."

"I told you I can turn you off. I can disable the exoself."

"No. You can't."

"You have a killswitch."

"This thing is capable of more than the programmers designed. It will protect itself and me along with it."

"Tell me what it's done. Has it killed someone? Rescued someone?"

All she had to do was check the reports to know

how much trouble the little town of Herouxville had seen in the past two days. She'd make the connection. "Get out of my head, you—"

"Watch what you say, darling. You want to fit in, don't you?" She laughed.

The ghostlike glimmer changed to code and then Kerstin vanished. The exoself seemed to relax, if that were possible. But not Chase. He paced as he searched the cyber world for news of mind-interfacing advancements. For reports of Kerstin's surgery. For anything to stop this from happening again.

"Help me." He slapped his palms against the wall and lifted his face to the ceiling. "Get me out of this."

16

Chase skipped lunch. Mealtime was mandatory but no one showed up to reprimand him. Maybe his name would get posted on a list and he'd get excommunicated, or whatever these people did to rule breakers. He had to get out of this bunker before Kerstin tracked his location.

But he couldn't go. The believers needed him. And he couldn't leave Mel.

Kerstin got her brain chipped—now she was in his head. But how? Technology changed by the hour. By the minute. But Chase didn't understand even the basics of transhumanism, much less the latest giant steps in forced evolution.

Kerstin could shut him down.

He had a killswitch.

Maybe, with a little knowledge, he could shut *her* down.

One thing he knew for sure, the WR had found a way to reconnect with the exoself, even if on a rudimentary level. Did Robert know? Was he trying to prevent what the others were attempting?

"What am I supposed to do?" He had to tell someone. "No. I can't tell anyone."

A knock on the door made him jump off the bed, and he pulled the door open.

Mel smiled, but a worry line formed between her eyebrows. She held another blasted orange in her hand.

"You missed lunch." She tilted her head to peek into his room. "Are you all right?"

"Sorry." He moved aside and let her in. She reached behind him and stopped the door before he shut it completely. Stupid rules. "Thanks for the orange." He took it from her and laid it on the small table.

"You're worried about Amos."

"Yeah. And the rest of you." He turned to the wall and wished more than anything for a window to let in some light. Or allow a speedy escape. "I don't know if I can do this, Melody." He faced her. She was so beautiful, so trusting.

She moved close to him and he embraced her.

"We're all unsure. We've been forced to live like fugitives. We're in danger." She cupped his face with her hand. "But we're together and we rely on God."

He pulled away. "Then don't rely on *me*. I know you planned this when you programmed me, but there's so much inside me that neither of us understands. I'm afraid I'm not who you think I am. I'm not *what* you think I am."

"I think you're a man who left everything to come here and help us. Maybe because God sent you or because you wanted to escape what they did to you. Either way, I'm glad. We're all glad you're here with us. The ones who seem untrusting will come around when they see how much we need you."

"I dreamed of this place, Mel. Well, not exactly. It was the painting upstairs, the one that hides the entrance. I saw it as though it were a real place. And I had to get here."

"Then it was God who sent you." She rubbed the

sleeve of his shirt.

"But I did want out. I couldn't stay with Synvue. You know me, Mel. I loved the fame, the money. The power. And it was stolen from me. And yet I still had it—fame and money and more power than I knew what to do with."

"Only it wasn't really yours anymore."

Chase shook his head. "I wonder if our contestants ever felt that way—that their new lives didn't belong to them at all."

"I don't know. I know I couldn't have done it much longer. The closer I got to God, the more I hated that life."

Chase moved away and sat on the bed. He reached over and picked up the orange, tossing it in the air and catching it. More *believer* talk. He asked for no explanation. "The closer I got to being god-like, the more I hated *my* life."

She sat beside him. "I'm sorry for my part in changing you. I knew I was getting close to answering God's call to join the movement, to go underground, and I thought…" She lowered her gaze to the floor.

He lifted her chin and brushed his fingers across her cheek. "You thought what?"

"I was already working on the programs for the underground. And I thought if I hid them in your processors—in the exoself—that you'd come after me."

"Then the dreams, the overwhelming urge to get here, was all part of the program?"

"No. Boss, I told you when you first arrived that I didn't program you to want this. I just wanted you to know where I was. I wanted you to come looking for me if I disappeared." She folded her arms. "I said it was for the good of the underground, but I did it for selfish reasons."

He put his arms around her. "So, you *do* have a selfish bone in your body."

"Do you hate me?"

He laughed. "Do you hate *me* for wishing deep down inside that we were back in my dressing room sipping coffee and making fun of the queen and getting to know each other in the real world?"

"I've never heard you call Kerstin the queen." Mel grinned. "Everybody else did."

"I thought it plenty of times."

"If you hadn't been...changed, would you still be with her?"

"No. I was falling for someone else. You knew that, didn't you?"

"You're a good man to send her to Fiender for a kidney, after all that she did to you."

"I don't know about that. I think I should have just dropped her when she slipped off the top of that skyscraper."

Mel pulled back, her brown eyes growing huge. "What? Oh, boss, we have a lot of catching up to do."

"Answer my question." He pulled her close.

"What question?" She relaxed into his arms.

"Did you know I was falling for you? Back in Chicago when we were just a gameshow host and his trusty assistant?" He reached for her soft hair and twisted a curl around his finger.

"Oh." She drew her arms around his neck and kissed him. "I had a feeling."

The door they'd left ajar swung open. Chase's mother cleared her throat. "I'm sorry." She nearly smiled, but a grim expression overtook her. "Son, I think they need you in the command center."

Chase let his arms fall to his sides. "What's going on, Mom?"

"The dissenters bombed that WR base."

"I couldn't stop that from happening, even if Amos did want to spare lives."

"The problem is the dissenters are not the ones being blamed for the act."

"Then who?" Chase asked. But he already knew. Data streamed in. "Stupid question."

"We are," Mel said. "Am I right?"

17

Chase led the way to the command center. His mother and Mel followed at his heels. Amos sat a computer station, his face red with anger.

"Look at this," he shouted. "The news is reporting that the Underground Church, the very dangerous and violent militants who tried but failed to convert the world, have bombed a military base and killed hundreds of innocent soldiers and their families."

"I know," Chase said. "But it's not true." He sat next to Amos and sent a report from the exoself to the computer screen. "I've got intel on the base. It was evacuated prior to the blast. Apparently, my interference with WR systems yesterday alerted them to the dissenters' plans to bomb the place. They got their soldiers out—all twenty-nine of them. Family housing didn't exist there. It was two buildings. The onsite soldiers were doing nothing but inspecting and issuing personal flight packs." Chase tapped the screen and then put his hand on Amos's knee. "Nobody died. Not one person."

"It's a smear campaign," Switchblade said.

Chase turned in the seat to find Switchblade in the gathering crowd. "Looks that way."

"Well," Amos said, seemingly over the rage he'd shown only a moment ago. "We've been maligned. Let us rejoice in persecution."

"Rejoice?" Chase asked. "How about retaliate?

How about we get the word out that the Underground Church isn't made up of terrorists? Are you going to let them get away with this?"

"The Feds used the actions of one group to cast a shadow on another group. We don't have to worry. God will work it out. The dissenters will probably take the focus off us. You know why? Because they'll *want* the credit."

"But…" There was no point in arguing. All this God talk wasn't getting any less confusing. "Vengeance is mine and all that, right?"

"So, you do know a little of the scriptures." Amos put his elbows on the desk and rubbed his face.

"My dad used to say it to me when I wanted to get back at somebody. He didn't tell me it was from the Bible. I thought it was just something people like my dad said to keep their sons out of fights. But I think he knew more about the Bible than he let on. We just didn't talk about it." Chase glanced at his mother.

She shook her head then turned away and left the command center.

"The book of Romans. Don't avenge yourselves — let God's wrath take care of it," Amos said. "I'm paraphrasing."

"I wouldn't know the difference," Chase said. "And I don't get it, so don't waste your time trying to explain it."

Amos gave him a solemn stare, and for the second time in less than a minute, Chase wanted to take back his words. "But I like the Psalms," he said. "I read a lot of them when I was uncovering Mel's code. They made me feel — I don't know — rested. I loved listening to the leader in Atlanta read them."

The tension released, and Amos nodded.

Chase breathed a sigh. He wasn't just trying to make up for his stupid remark—he *had* enjoyed the Psalms. He'd find a Bible later and read them again, this time without an agenda, without looking for secret computer code. More than anything, he needed to rest his mind right now.

He pulled up news reports and discovered the bad press against the underground believers wasn't limited to the one incident. The Los Angeles branch had been flushed out, their hideout in an abandoned warehouse district burned to the ground. Chase coded the four *S*'s and in no time found a leader in California reaching out for help.

"I'm sending instructions to someone called Watchman," Chase said. "His group was discovered and they had to evacuate their hiding place. There's an old mansion in Hollywood. The owner is listed in the system as a sympathizer. The believers can take shelter there."

"How many are there?" Mel asked. "Were any of them caught when the Feds raided the place?"

"Seventy-two. They all escaped before the Feds torched the place. They got a warning," Chase answered.

"What kind of warning?" Amos asked. "Who sent it?"

Chase stood and took a few steps, shaking his head. He spun around. "I did. I think."

"You mean the exoself, don't you?" Fear lit Mel's eyes. "Boss, this is unbelievable. How can you send out a warning without knowing it?"

"You tell *me*."

More Christians still functioning in society had been arrested and detained. Chase had their locations—he knew which detention centers had them.

"I can't help the ones being detained," he said. "How many times can I attach a bogus release code to a name? The Feds won't believe it." He pictured the machine that brought a bloodless death. Intel didn't report the device had been used.

Why did the WR want to use that thing, as opposed to some other method? Obviously, it was clean. No mess, no handling blood. Efficient. But there had to be more. Chase went deeper into WR data.

"They're going to use the brain tissue," he said.

"What do you mean?" Amos asked. "Are they killing our people?"

"I don't see any indication of it. Never mind. We'll talk about it later."

Amos didn't ask any more questions but went back to his screen, reviewing data as Chase sent it to him. The group in L.A. was already on the move, headed for the mansion of a former film star.

"More believers will go under with all these arrests," Chase said. "How many more can we house?"

"We're filled to capacity," Amos answered. "But there is another place a hundred miles from here. Well, you know that, don't you?"

"I've already sent word to up-top supporters' computer systems to direct people to an abandoned schoolhouse in Gagnon. I've got transports headed to five locations to pick up twenty-two people."

Amos's brows shot up. "I didn't know there were that many believers left in this part Quebec. That's wonderful, Chase."

"There's one who's close by, and she's in danger. She sent out an SOS. And I owe her, Amos. I think we should bring her in."

"Of course, Chase. We'll make room. Who is she?"

"Windsong."

"The pilot who got you to New York?" Mel asked.

"Oh, dear," Amos said. "It'll be a loss to the organization to have a pilot come underground. Soon we may not have any help left up top. Get a message to her to come to the back door—the one you first entered. Teach her the knock. Someone will meet her."

"Will do. Thank you, Amos." Chase sent word to Windsong's illegal and untraceable system and she quickly responded with gratitude. But she couldn't wait until nightfall to sneak into town. She hoped she could get to the museum without being detected. If not, she wouldn't come near the place.

Chase had already checked surveillance and didn't see any reason she shouldn't make her way to the museum. Intel reported the Feds thought they'd cleaned out the Christian element in Herouxville and they'd moved on. A plane had been confiscated at an airfield forty miles to the south after information was passed to the Feds that the pilot was transporting supplies for the underground. That explained why Windsong was on the run. But who leaked the info?

"Nice alias," Switchblade said. "Sounds free as a bird. Too bad she's gotta come under. But maybe the two of you will enjoy each other's company, Charlie. What's she like?"

Chase turned to find Switchblade sitting as close to Mel as he could get, his arm across the back of her chair. The guy wasn't giving up.

"She's talented," Chase said. "In the sense that she'll add a lot to the underground. She knows how the WR functions, what they're looking for. But you're right—it'll be a big change for her. She's used to flying.

Now she'll be—"

"Surviving like the rest of us tunnel rats," Switchblade said.

"She'll have to bunk with someone," Amos said.

"She can stay with me," Mel said. "The room's small but there's an extra mattress under my bed. I don't mind pulling it out and sleeping on the floor."

"Thank you, Melody," Amos said.

"Tell me about her, boss. Is she as pretty as her name?"

Chase kept his eyes on the screen. "Huh?"

"She asked if the girl is pretty, Charlie. So, is she?" Switchblade let out a snort.

"When I was running for my life, I didn't take the time to notice," Chase said. He glared at Switchblade. "So you'll have to decide for yourself, Switch. I hope you like her." He smiled. "Why don't you go up and wait for her. She should be here within the hour."

The big man rolled his eyes as he headed for the door. "I'll tell her how excited you are to see her again." He laughed as he swung open the door and went up the stairs.

"What on earth? Boss, what's up with you two?" Mel asked.

"Nothing. I just think the guy needs to find himself a girlfriend. That's all."

18

Chase and Mel remained at the computer station to await Switchblade's return. Amos had gone to his room to rest. Did the man sense the cancer overtaking him?

Before long, the door that led upward swung open and Windsong stepped into Blue Sky Field. Switchblade followed a good distance behind her. The woman's tangled blonde hair fell across the shoulders of her soiled blue uniform.

"Hey, my favorite gameshow host." She greeted Chase with a quick hug. "Thanks for taking me in."

She smelled like the back corner of a barn. "I guess you got my message about the transport taking livestock north," Chase said.

She laughed. "How can you tell? Look, we have a lot to talk about, but could I get a shower and some clean clothes first?"

"I'll show you the way," Mel said. "You're going to bunk with me." She held out her hand. "Melody Reese."

Windsong shook her hand and the two headed toward the dorms. Switchblade dropped to a chair and scraped it across the floor as he pulled up to the work station.

Chase sat beside him. "Was she sure nobody followed her?"

"Couple of little goats was tagging along."

"This is serious, man."

"Nobody knows she's here. Old farmer just wanted to get his produce to the slaughter house. He dropped her off on the highway."

"I'm guessing she rode in the back with the animals." Chase smiled.

"Almost didn't let her in when I caught a whiff. But the mess didn't hurt her none—she's a good-looking woman." Switchblade nudged Chase with his elbow. "Ain't she, Charlie?"

"Not interested, Switch. You go for it."

The big man grumbled and then laughed under his breath.

Amos returned from his rest and got an update on the new arrival and on what was happening with believers across the continent.

"Four branches of the underground have been forced to relocate today," Chase told him. "Intel shows fifty-seven supporters were detained. But it looks like the day will end with almost everyone seeking asylum being taken in without incident."

"So, we lost four of our bases," Amos said. "And so many of those who helped us up top."

"The Feds are coming at us," Switchblade said. "Why?" He gawked at Chase as if he knew the answer.

Chase couldn't argue. "I will go whenever you tell me to, Amos. You know they're looking for me."

Amos shifted his weight and wiped the sweat from his brow. "Chase, why are they looking for you all over the place? Did you feed them some more bad information?"

Chase met Amos's stare. "Yes and no. By the hour the exoself seems more proficient in anticipating my next course of action. My systems have the Feds chasing rabbits. The intel says I'm here, then it says I'm there. And I'm the one who's doing it. Only it's not me."

"Do you think the exoself has developed its own consciousness? Its own survival instinct?"

"It's thinking for itself," Switchblade said. "Is that what's happening, Charlie?"

"I don't know. I'm a transhuman, but I'm not a transhumanist—I didn't design this stuff. I've reviewed data and read online books. The science is starting to make sense, but I might owe that to my recall enhancement. The other side of it, the philosophy, is as foreign to me as—"

"As Christianity?" Amos asked.

Chase nodded. "As any deep belief system. The pioneers of the transhumanist movement were zealots. And now the scientists, the government, the entertainment platforms, are all putting their faith in it. It's not about curing disease and improving the quality of life anymore. It's about living forever. It's not that different from what *you* want, is it? It's a religion. Only…"

"Only what, Chase?"

"It's a godless religion. They are their own gods, and they want to live forever by their own existence. By their own power." Chase pressed his fingertips into his temples. The sting of Switchblade's blow was gone. Had the processors in his body boosted his capacity to heal? That wasn't possible, was it?

It almost sounded justifiable—this new religion. A human being as proficient as a computer and just as durable. And Chase was the first to profit from its blessing. A man who didn't follow transhumanism became a transhuman. A man who didn't follow Christ became an honorary member of the Underground Church. Chase lowered his gaze and sighed.

"Godless, indeed," Amos said. "And yet to be like God is what they desire. Chase, do you know the story of the tower of Babel?"

"No, I don't think so." He perused the exoself for information and found the old story. But not the scripture. "I've got it. People tried to build a city on their own laurels without acknowledging God's dominion. But God confused their language and the tower was destroyed. He split up the smart guys, huh?"

Amos nodded. "Do you know why God did that?"

"I'll tell you why," Switchblade said. "Because God don't got no competition. Ain't nobody gonna bring Him down, and nobody's gonna bring themselves up without Him."

"Is God that easily threatened?" Chase asked.

"No. There is no threat," Amos answered. "He wants to come down to us, to lift us up. But the tower was built, and the transhuman is built, as an act of rebellion."

"What does that make me? A rebel? A tower to be knocked down?"

"You ain't nothing but a rock at the base of that tower, Charlie. You didn't put yourself there. Once the tower comes down, the rocks get cleaned up and used for something good."

"Switchblade, that's the nicest thing I've ever heard come out your mouth," Amos said.

Chase, as usual, found the whole thing baffling. He narrowed his eyes at Switchblade. "Thanks. I think."

The conversation could have continued, giving

Chase a chance to catch on to the things the exoself didn't understand any better than its host. But Mel returned with the newest resident, who was cleaned up and dressed in jeans and a gauzy white blouse, and with her long blonde hair pulled into a ponytail.

Amos rose to his feet and faced her. "You must be Windsong. We owe you so much for all you've done up top. We're grateful that you escaped today, but sorry for the loss of your plane and your services. You'll stay with us now, for as long as we can manage down here."

"Don't think I'm unappreciative for your help in keeping me out of prison today, but I'm not staying. I'm getting my plane back," she said. "And then I'll go to the EU. I'll paint the plane and change my alias, and I'll continue my work for the Lord. That's what He wants, and that's what I'm going to do."

Amos lifted his brows and shook his head. "I don't see how, young lady. It seems an impossible task."

"You're looking at the water, sir, and not at the one who walked on it," Windsong said.

"I suppose I am. Forgive my unbelief. What is your plan, young lady?"

"You're going to help me," she said to Chase. "I need somebody to change my life." She smiled and slapped him on the back. "Let's get to work, Chase Sterling."

"I thought you and God had this worked out," Chase said. "What do you want from me?"

"A little interference in choosing a location for my plane. You're connected to the Feds, right? Have them send it to the nearest airstrip."

"The nearest airstrip is covered with drones," he told her. "I'm afraid that won't work."

"So send the drones somewhere else."

"The more I interfere with the local entities, the greater my chances of being found," Chase said. "Drones are manufactured and tested in the area. Hundreds of them would have to be relocated. I think somebody would notice that."

"So what? Switchblade said you were making stuff happen all over the WR." She grinned and bounced on her toes. "It'll be fun. You'll be right under their noses and they won't even notice."

"Sounds too risky," Amos said. "We just got the Feds out of town. I don't want to bring them back."

"Wouldn't it benefit all of you if the drones moved out of this area?" she asked. "Maybe you should wipe out the whole place."

"What are you suggesting? We aren't doing anything to add truth to the Feds' lies about us. We aren't terrorists."

She blushed a little. "I didn't mean you should blow it up or anything. Look, we're in this together. There's got to be a way to evacuate that drone plant for a few hours and get my plane to land there."

"You seem in a hurry to leave us, Windsong," Switchblade said. "I know Mr. Sterling was hoping you'd stick around."

Chase glared at the man. "I can get the functional drones out. And I can get the plane in. Getting you on the plane and in the sky would be difficult."

Windsong swung her ponytail over her shoulder and laughed. "Difficult never stopped me before."

19

Chase waited until midnight to attempt the ridiculous. He'd like to go to bed and forget all about hiding with a bunch of odd believers. Except that he'd kissed the girl he'd been missing for months. He'd never forget that.

The evening hadn't allowed him that talk with Amos. With all the commotion, he and Mel decided to wait on telling the leader of Blue Sky Field that he was dying.

Now he had to work his magic on a WR drone manufacturing plant. Messing with the orders of a few low-level authorities was easy. Moving large groups of people from one location to another, right under the watching eyes of the Feds, hadn't even been a challenge. But flying an army of drones away from their base seemed impossible.

While Windsong slept in Mel's room, Chase scoured military bases across the eastern countryside. He knew how to destroy a drone in an emergency situation. But taking out hundreds would be, at least to Amos, an act of terrorism.

Many of the little air machines were half assembled in the plant. Chase found 327 S-drones and simpler formatted surveillance drones ready to fly and taking up space on the single airstrip. He smiled at the coincidence. The code the exoself used to protect Chase was 32-7. The very code that had crashed the S-drones in Atlanta.

But the drones were not threatening him or anybody else, at least not at the moment. The code he needed right now was the same one he'd used to get Molly and the others out of the detention center. Somehow the code for safe travel held the greatest potential for subverting the WR. He sparked the thirty-first processor and pulled eight lines of code.

"Come on, exoself, show me how to get these drones moving."

The exoself surged, and Chase found his way into systems of fourteen military bases between Quebec and Florida. He wriggled his way in through secured programs until he was in position to order new drones for each facility. An overriding order from the head committee of the WR overseeing distribution was interwoven through multiple systems, just as it would be if it were the real thing. The reason for the sudden increase in the demand for drones? He programmed the order: To hunt down Chase Sterling.

He filtered the requisitions to the various locations. He'd send the machines out as close to the east coast as he could. If anything went wrong, he'd plunge them into the Atlantic. Amos might not like it, but if the Feds caught on, the best way to hide the trail back to Chase was to rid the world of a few hundred drones. He could wipe out information in the base computers easily enough, but the embedded database built into each drone could recover an irregularity in the code that could identify the source of the bogus orders.

He overworked the exoself, if that were possible, and set up the purchase requests to come in hours apart. The drones would fly out in groups of twenty-two to twenty-four, beginning at dusk and continuing through the night. Security personnel would be at the plant after dark. Chase found the schedule for the week and gave them all the same night off, but made sure the schedule showed someone would be there. No one would suspect the facility was being left unguarded.

Chase moved to one of the 3D computers and pulled up the schematics. He dropped the plans onto the flat board and pulled it up so that he could note locations of cameras and motion detectors. They'd all be rendered useless by the time the sun went down the following day.

A sound behind him made Chase spin around. "Mel, what are you doing up?"

She yawned and dropped to a chair in front of the 3D display. "Your friend is a restless sleeper. Keeps mumbling about getting her wings back."

"She won't be here long. I've got the plant ready to ship out its fleet. Now I've got to get that plane ready to fly forty miles north and land in the middle of nowhere for no good reason."

"Why don't you just have it sent to the plant to pick up some drones? It's big enough to hold five or six, isn't it?"

"Genius." He bent to kiss her cheek. "How does it feel to be smarter than a man with a computer in his brain?" He changed the orders for two of the bases, taking three drones off one and two off the other. Then he ordered the confiscated plane sent to the plant to pick up five drones to deliver to an EU base outside of London. He pulled up a chair and sat beside Mel.

"Windsong's plane just got put into service for the WR. Its first mission is to pick up five drones at the plant and deliver them to the EU. I'm moving the funds from one WR account to another to cover the purchase. That's not stealing."

"I didn't say it was." Mel covered Chase's hand with hers and squeezed his fingers. "Did you know that when you're doing this stuff with the exoself, your fingers, and sometimes your feet, get fidgety?"

"It's weird to program a computer at a random location just by using what's inside me. Sometimes I want to punch a keypad. I guess that's why my fingers get restless. I hadn't noticed that my feet want to get in the action too."

"You're amazing, boss." She lifted his hand and kissed it.

"It's too simple." Chase leaned back in the chair and closed his eyes.

"What do you mean?"

"I don't believe this will play out like I planned it. It can't be that easy."

"It's not over yet. You've still got to get the girl onto her plane."

Chase opened his eyes. "I'll have to take her myself."

"What? Come on, you know you can't do that."

"She has no other way to get inside the plant and get on that plane." Chase swiped his hand over the 3D image, closing the program.

"Stay on the VPad with her. Can't you monitor everything and tell her what she needs to know without being there?" Mel hurried to an adjacent work station.

"And what if they track her VPad?" Chase asked. "What if she loses it? We might as well hand her over to the Feds."

Mel faced him, her arms crossed. "You are not getting on that plane."

He smiled. "Yes ma'am." He drew close enough to breathe in the hint of lilac in her hair. "I told you before—I'm not going anywhere." He took her in his arms. "Except I'm going as far as that airstrip."

"Chase, what if word of this gets out? What if we really do have a mole?"

"If anyone in this compound connected to an outside computer or VPad, I'd know it. And no one has been allowed to go up. Not since Molly and the others came down. Well, no one except Switchblade. He met Windsong at the door. But—"

"He's not a mole," Mel said.

Chase nodded. "That's what I was going to say."

A soft voice spoke behind them. "Oh, Miss Melody, don't let anybody see you hugging like that. You know what will happen."

Chase let go and faced the intruder.

The teenage girl smiled. "On second thought, go ahead and get caught. We could use a party to liven things up down here."

Chase placed his hands on his hips and tilted his head at Mel. "OK, tell me what she means by that."

Mel put her arm around the girl. "Never mind, boss. Erin, what are you doing in here at this time of night?"

"I was on my way to the kitchen and I heard voices."

"Honey, you know you can't be snacking. We've got to stick to the rations."

"Oh, I wasn't going for food or anything. Just..." The kid sounded as guilty as Chase felt when he concocted a lie.

But why the remorse? His lies protected these people. He stepped to the other side of the girl and directed her toward the hallway leading to the dorms. "Admit it—you're hungry. I've got something for you."

Mel followed. "You can't spoil these kids. We only have so much."

"Come on, Miss Melody. I've got something for you too."

They walked to Chase's room. He went in first, moving through the darkness to pull something out from under his mattress.

Mel flipped on the lamp. "What have you got in here?"

"I had this in my flight pack when I got here and I put it away for a special occasion." Chase pulled out a wrapped chocolate bar. "I thought about turning it over to the rations coordinator, but it's not enough to make any difference."

Mel took the candy and smiled. "So you kept it for yourself, huh?"

"No. I saved it for you. Just hadn't decided when to give it to you." He grabbed the bar and snapped it in two. "And now you have to share it." He handed half to Erin and smiled.

The girl hesitated.

"What's wrong?" Chase asked. "You don't like chocolate?"

"It just doesn't seem fair." She sat on the end of the bed and lowered the treat to her lap.

Chase knelt before her. "Tell you what, you eat this, don't tell anyone about it, and I'll see if I can get us some more. I have connections, you know." He took the candy, pulled off the torn wrapper, and held it up.

"Go ahead," Mel told her, and she peeled the paper off her half. "I'll eat mine if you eat yours."

Erin smiled and bit off a chunk. She chewed and swallowed, her face gleaming. "It's been a long time since I tasted chocolate. Thank you, Mr. Sterling. I mean, Mr. Redding."

"Call me Chase," he said.

"Mr. Chase." She smiled and took another bite.

Mel closed the door as she bit into the candy.

"What about the rule?" Chase asked. "If it involves illegal snacking, it's OK to shut the door?"

"I don't want the light to bother anybody. Besides, we're not alone." She took another bite and smiled. "And we sure don't want this heavenly scent drifting through the compound. Might start a riot."

Erin giggled as Chase lifted off his knees and leaned against the wall. He folded his arms and watched as Mel joined the girl on the edge of the bed. This was what he'd imagined of the underground. Good company. Loving people. No emergency to deal with. Kerstin hadn't popped into the exoself all day. Maybe *that* problem, at least, was over. He smiled with relief.

Then the light went out.

"What's going on?" the girl asked.

"Don't worry," Chase said. "Maybe the bulb burned out. Old technology in this place. These bulbs don't last forever." He opened the door and found a switch in the hall. Nothing. "Well, it seems we have an issue with our power source. Both of you stay put, and I'll go to the command center and make sure the systems there are still functional."

"Chase, if our computers are down then we've got a serious problem," Mel said.

"Yeah. It's a good thing you put one in my brain. Stay here. I'll be back."

20

Making his way through the tunnel to the command center, Chase prompted the exoself to check the power reserve supplying electricity. Or at the moment, not supplying it. Did the systems up top catch on that the reserve was being filtered to an unknown location? The exoself searched the company outside Herouxville that gave the town its solar and hydro-electric energy. The panels seemed in proper working order. No red flags in the system.

The command center glimmered with read-outs at a few stations. Chase didn't need to read the code. About three hours of operation remained before power depletion shut down every computer.

He rushed to the closet where he'd seen a resident requesting a laserlight. No choice but to break the lock. Grabbing a couple of the little lights, he hurried back to his room.

"Mel, come with me to the command center." He handed a light to Erin. "Here, sweetie, go to your room and stay there."

"What's going on?" she asked.

"We'll figure it out. Everything will be fine."

The girl headed down the hall, and Chase and Mel went the opposite direction, back toward the command center.

"Should we wake up Amos?" Mel asked.

"Let's just figure out how to fix this." Chase

grabbed her arm and hurried her along. "I've got full connection to the branches of the underground, and the WR is an open book. As long as I have the exoself we can still function. But it'll be awful if you all have to live in darkness."

"How did they figure out the reserve was getting sucked up?" Mel asked. "Do you think they can pinpoint our location?"

"No indication that the energy supply company has found a breach in their systems, or that they even know they've lost some of the reserve. It replenishes faster than we can use it."

"Then why the power outage?" Mel dropped in front of a computer in the dark room and began searching for an answer.

"Whole town's gone dark," Chase told her. "The local police just reported it."

"But we're not on the power grid, so why are we included in the blackout?"

The exoself searched deeper. Intel gave no reason for the blackout, or how it had managed to work its way to the underground. No storm damage. No accident reports.

Lots of drone activity.

"Crap."

"What is it, Chase?"

"Fourteen minutes ago, every drone connected to its charger. Even the ones still on the assembly line."

"So what? They drained the town's energy? That's not possible."

"No, they didn't drain anything. But something drained them. They wouldn't disconnect. So the system shut off their power source. And the town's power went out too."

"The reservoirs shut down too?"

"Yep. I told you it couldn't be that easy. Putting in all those orders at once kicked the system at the plant into overdrive. I confused computer operations."

"Well, we'll just have to set it straight." She typed faster. "Can you cancel the orders? Put the drones back to sleep?"

"Yes, but that'll mean taking a more human approach to reuniting Windsong with her plane."

"Maybe she needs to resign herself to the idea of staying put." Mel crossed her arms. "Then you won't have to go off with that woman. You could end up in all sorts of trouble."

Chase didn't cancel the orders for the drones to deliver themselves to various bases, but he did power them down. Too bad he hadn't given personnel *this* night off, as well as the following night. They must be scrambling, trying to figure out how every drone in the place came to life without a programmer. They hadn't even been trained on how to cut power to the equipment they guarded. So they called the energy company and declared an emergency, which led to shutting down the entire grid.

No wonder it'd been so easy to put in the orders. The plant was in the hands of amateurs. Not to mention the incompetents in charge of the energy supply.

"Human beings are inept," he said with a grin. "Anybody with half a brain could have handled this without turning off the whole grid. No wonder the government wants to make us over. Of course, the government is full of half-brained humans as well."

"When you're through insulting the human race, check the code I just put in the energy company's system."

The exoself ran the intel and approved.

"Good, that'll work. The power should be coming back on in town, but the plant will remain dark until the clumsy workers there are sure the drones are through stirring."

"You know, boss, human beings designed the transhuman prototype. And they were no dummies."

"Are you standing up for the geeks at the Helgen?"

"That depends. Are you saying the rest of us aren't good enough to keep up with your computer brain? I helped program it, you know." Mel's voice got louder. "Maybe you could make *yourself* a designer brain now, but you couldn't have a year ago."

What did he say to get her mad?

"I was just kidding. There are a lot of dumb people in the world. That's all. I didn't mean you, Mel. You're one of the smartest people I've ever known."

"Until you met yourself." She pointed the laserlight at his face. "Why don't we have power yet?"

"The reserves are on lock-down. It happens during an outage. The system thinks it lost its source, so it's hanging on to what it has."

"Did you just learn all that from the exoself?"

Chase crossed his arms. "Yes, I did. I pick up on the obvious a little faster than most—"

"Most what? Regular humans?"

"I was going to say faster than most computers. I caught a trail into the energy company and read their policy. It's a closed system, but I got in."

"Well, good for you. How long until our lights come back on?"

Before he could answer, the computers preparing

to shut down flashed a repletion code. The room filled with sound and light. Chase found the nearest light switch and pulled it up. "They're on." He pushed the bar down. "Let's get some sleep. It's gonna be a long day preparing to move the drones and getting Windsong to her plane."

"I though you canceled the orders on the drones."

"No. You told me to, but I didn't," Chase said. "Everything is on schedule. Just the way I planned it."

"And the drones aren't going to light up again before they're supposed to?"

"It was glitch in the system—that's what they think at the plant. The programmers will have the whole day to make sure the drones don't ever turn themselves on again. And when they've all gone home and the sun goes down, I'll turn them on anyway and fly them out of there."

"Like you said, it seems too simple."

"I made it simple. It'll work."

"Yeah. Goodnight then." Mel headed to the dorm.

"Goodnight." Chase sat at a station and stared at the coded screen. Did he and Mel just have a fight? They'd had plenty over the years. Most of them involved him screwing something up and Mel fixing it. Now things were different. Weren't they? In the short time he'd been here he'd hurt her feelings more than once. Now he'd ticked her off—he wasn't sure how.

"Women," he said.

Before he could power down the work station and head for his room, a flash of red appeared in the darkest corner of the room.

"Oh, no you don't." He charged at the image appearing before him. "You are not going to haunt me. I refuse to allow it. Now get out of here!"

Kerstin was there and gone in a matter of seconds. He'd done it—chased the intruder out of the exoself.

But he still heard her voice.

"You are a transhuman, Chase. Those Bible thumpers don't deserve to have you on their side. You want to help the world? Come back to me. Together, we will *rule* the world."

Chase didn't respond. The voice said nothing else and the image didn't return. He headed for his room. How far could Kerstin go with the technology they'd put in her? How many other people had been programmed like her? Soon there might be a rush of wired-up brains popping in and out of the exoself. Telling it what to do. Knowing its plans. They'd all be working together—an army of exoselves.

"Exoselves? Is that even a word?" Chase swung open the door to his room and peered into the darkness. No sign of the unwanted visitor. She'd always been pale as a ghost. Now she was one, in a sense. He could conquer her at this game. He was a transhuman, after all.

He laughed. "*You* are nothing special, Chase Sterling. You're a human being. You're not invincible. You're just a prideful, stupid man."

The voice from his dreams—the last of the dreams—engaged his mind as plain as Kerstin's had been only moments ago.

You are still mine.

"What does that mean?" Chase asked. "I was never yours. I don't know how to be yours." He sat on the bed, pulled off his shoes, and stretched out to stare at the low ceiling.

"I don't know who I am," he said. "Somebody tell me."

21

The sun rose at six twenty-eight, so said the exoself. Chase had been awake for an hour. He crawled from the bed and opened the door to make sure the hall light had come on as usual. It had. A few people in bathrobes carried towels and toothbrushes toward the bathrooms. Chase made eye contact with the new guy, Kirel, who nodded his head as a silent greeting. Chase returned the gesture and closed the door.

It seemed no one else knew the lights had gone off. Of course, a teenage girl couldn't be trusted not to tell. She'd enjoyed some chocolate and then the power went out. And, by the way, Chase broke the lock on the supply closet and then handed her a laserlight, which she wasn't allowed to have without permission.

No, she wouldn't snitch. Would she?

How many kids were in this place? He'd better find Erin, retrieve the light, swear her to silence, and fix that broken lock.

"I can't fix the lock. I'll just have to explain the whole mess to Amos."

But he had to do something else first. He pulled on his pants, tucked in the wrinkled shirt he'd slept in, and opened the door. He met Kirel in the hall.

"Heard the power went out last night," the man said.

Chase let his head fall forward and sighed. "Let me guess, a girl named Erin told you."

"No. One of the twins. But he probably heard it from the girl who was eating chocolate in your room."

Chase shook his head and laughed. "I guess I'd better go talk to the boss."

Kirel shrugged.

Chase started for Amos's quarters. Then he peered down the hall leading to Mel's room. He had to talk to her.

But they'd both be eating breakfast—it started ten minutes ago. He headed for the dining hall.

Whispers rose as he entered the room. He smiled. "You know I can hear you."

Amos rose from the table, his stoic expression unbroken. "You want to explain how you managed to knock out our power and then turn it back on? And why you broke a lock? And how you picked one kid out of many to gift with a chocolate bar?"

Chase shifted his eyes from one long table to the next. No Mel.

"Well, the power...I was..." He found his mother and sat beside her. "I'm sorry about the lock. I needed a couple of laserlights. It was an emergency. As for the chocolate, I was just trying to be nice. The girl was hungry. I'm sorry. I didn't have enough for everybody."

His mom patted him on the back.

Windsong spoke from the far end of the table. "Look, I'm sure this was all about getting me to my plane." She leaned toward Chase. "Am I right?"

"Yeah. Everything but the chocolate. That just sort of worked its way into the evening."

"Well, I *do* have enough for everybody. Assuming no one has searched through every crate on my plane. If it's still there, I'll make sure you get it." She glanced around the room. "It'll be my thanks for helping me."

Several young people, and a few not so young, let out a whoop. Chase got up from the table and headed for the door. Switchblade's obnoxious presence was missing and Chase knew where to find him.

"Sit down and eat," Amos demanded.

Chase slinked back to the table and dropped next to his mother. "Have you seen Mel this morning?"

"She may have had to wait in line for a shower. I'm sure she'll be here soon."

He grabbed a chunk of meat and stuffed it in his mouth. Then he gulped a cup of watered-down orange juice. "I've got to talk to her." He joined Amos. Bending over, Chase said, "I will tell you all about the power outage. I'll be back in a few minutes."

"Meet me in my room," Amos said. The man didn't look up, but ripped a piece of bread in half and dropped it onto his plate.

"Yes, sir." Chase rose and headed for the dorms. He got to Mel's room, found the door propped open, and knew what it meant. Leaning against the wall, he listened.

"He was always full of himself," Mel said. "Do you think he's capable of changing?"

"He can't help being who he is," Switchblade said. "Only God can change him. But it's no sure thing. Maybe it ain't meant to be."

Chase couldn't stand there and listen to this. Not because it hurt him, which it did. But because it was private. He wouldn't do that to Mel.

Amos wouldn't be back to his room yet. Chase went to the command center and checked the systems to make sure there was nothing amiss after last night's strange turn. He sat at a station and sparked the exoself to run through the orders for the drones. Everything seemed to be on schedule. No indication the Feds were on to him. He'd have to go over the plan with Windsong, and they both needed to get some extra sleep today.

"I can't go. Not until I apologize to Melody."

"Apologize for what?"

Chase turned around to find Amos.

"I said something stupid. I can come to your room now and take my reprimand."

"Looks pretty quiet in here." Amos pulled a chair to the station. "Did you break that lock with your bare hands?"

"Yeah. Sorry. Why do you need to lock up things anyway? Who don't you trust?"

"It's not a matter of trust. People take things and then forget to put them back. Locking the closet keeps things from accidentally disappearing." Amos settled into his seat. "Never mind that. Start talking."

Chase explained the reason for the temporary outage, and how he planned to get the drones off the runway and get the plane to land there. And how he needed to accompany Windsong to the plant.

"You'll take Switch. I won't have you hiking from here to the plant and back on your own."

"Isn't there someone else?"

"No one who can protect you like *he* can."

Chase leaned forward and put his elbows on his knees. "I can protect myself."

"You are not going up unless he goes too."

"Fine. I'll do it your way." Chase leaned back in the chair. "Amos, there's something else we need to talk about."

"About Melody. Do you love her?"

Chase lifted his eyebrows. How juvenile. He didn't blush, did he? "That's not at all what I wanted to talk about."

"What then?"

"The scientists put something in me. I wanted to have Mel and Molly with me when I told you about it, but we keep running into situations."

"What did they put in you, son?"

"A Wilberton. Do you know what that means?"

Amos seemed to shrink into the chair. He closed his eyes. "You know I'm sick. Is that it?"

"And you already know."

"I've known for a while. But it's getting worse."

"Is there not one single doctor down here? What do you do when someone gets sick?"

"We pray."

"There's a baby coming. What are you going to do about that?"

"It's her fourth. She and her husband will manage. Unless the exoself knows something about childbirth." Amos grinned.

"Guess she didn't need a permit to produce four babies in the underground. Up top, nobody gets more than two anymore." Chase shook his head. "As far as the fundamentals of childbirth, the exoself knows nothing about that. And I'm not getting a cyber-education on it."

"What exactly is your ability? You can diagnose, but you can't cure?"

"That's about it. I could learn more about leukemia, but I don't have access to treatment. It's a worthless thing they put in me."

"So that's it—leukemia. My mother died from it."

"I want to try to get you to a doctor. My

connection to the underground tells me there's one in Gagnon. It's so close. We could get him here to help you, or take you there."

"I know about the doctor. It's not worth the risk. Besides, I don't think seeing him will make any difference in the long run. Do you?"

What was he supposed to say? He put both hands on the man's arm.

Amos let out a soft laugh.

"What's so funny?"

"You're laying hands on me. Like Jesus sometimes did when he healed. Even in modern times, an elder or a pastor might practice the laying on of hands."

"I don't understand, which is no big surprise," Chase said. "But maybe your resident pastors should try it."

"Oh, son, I don't know about that. Miracles in this day and age are rare. Unexpected. Belief for most of the people here means little more than escaping the evil forces taking over the world and then just trying to survive."

Chase released his grasp. "The disease has progressed in the short time I've been here."

"I must prepare someone to take over for me," Amos said. "Tomorrow. Today we have too much to do." He smiled. "Chase, I don't understand why your knowledge of our belief is so limited. You have access to…everything. Don't you?"

"You've been underground for a while. Up top, the authorities don't allow too much in cyber-space about religion anymore. And they certainly didn't allow it in *my* systems. What Mel snuck in was cryptic and only led to the revelation of computer code. Anything more than that would have been discovered by the programmers. She thinks she might be able to upload the Bible now that the exoself is independent of the WR. I told her not to bother. I don't know what good it would be if I don't understand it." He crossed his arms. "My father…"

"What is it, Chase?"

"I had these dreams before I set out on my own. In one of them, my father—my dead father—told me the people in the underground would tell me what I needed to know. But so far—"

Switchblade barged in on the private moment and shouted, "We got trouble!"

22

Chase sparked his systems to search local and federal intel. Why wasn't the exoself aware of a problem before Switchblade? No indication of trouble. "What's wrong?" he asked.

"Noise is what's wrong," Switchblade answered.

Chase powered the hearing enhancer. "Sounds like a demolition crew in the museum."

"You think?" Switchblade hovered over him. "Man, why don't you just keep that super power stuff on?"

"Because people deserve their privacy down here. I don't need to listen to *everything*."

Amos moved to another computer station. "Chase, is there no information about what could be happening up there?"

"Intel on the museum is sketchy. It's owned by—"

"Gretel Neroux," Amos said. "The granddaughter of the artist who painted Blue Sky Field. She's a supporter. Lives in France. She knows we're here."

Chase searched the EU for anything regarding the woman. In a moment he had what he was looking for. "She was arrested." He walked toward Amos. "She died in prison a week ago."

Switchblade was right behind him. "Did she squeal?"

"I don't know. But why else would they be bulldozing the place?" Chase raised his head as the sound grew so loud he didn't need the hearing enhancer. Mel rushed into the room, along with a slew of residents with panicked expressions.

Amos put his hands over his face, then banged his fist on the metal table. "How are we going to survive if they knock the building down? We'll be buried alive."

Windsong joined the crowd, her backpack slung over her shoulder. "I'm out of here. Now," she said.

"Too late," Switchblade told her.

Chase pulled the code for secret houses—23-6. No indication that their location had been compromised. The underground branch closest to Gretel Neroux's address had reported they'd lost an up-top supporter, but no details were given.

He went back in to the EU cyber systems and found the documentation of real property owned in the WR. The museum, upon the death of the owner, would be repurposed by the government. A common practice on both continents. The museum was now owned by the government. By the enemy.

Pulling records from the Federal Building Department, Chase soon found a requisition to turn the abandoned building into a WR office heading a particular branch of an international program for all of the Northeast territory.

"They're not going to knock it down," he said. "They're turning it into a RACE headquarters. They don't know there's a bunker underneath them. The artists who made themselves a shelter from the apocalypse did a good job of keeping it quiet."

Erin wrinkled her brow. "What does that mean, Miss Melody?"

"R-A-C-E. Religions and Cults Eradicated," Mel answered. "The global organization oversees reprogramming society to phase out all religious belief. Unbelievable. The international headquarters of the Underground Church is now underneath the international organization established to wipe us out."

Mel lifted her eyes to Chase. And her expression was all business. She hadn't gotten over whatever it was that made her so mad last night.

"And they have no idea we're down here?" A voice called out.

"As far as I can tell, they don't know about us," he said.

"Son, are they going to block our exit?" his mother asked. "Do you think they'll find their way into the room with the paintings?"

"If they go exploring, it's a possibility."

Amos rose and addressed the people. "No one goes out. No one comes in. We'll cut back on rations. And everyone, please, be very quiet. Go and tell those who aren't here with us."

The people headed out to follow their leader's instructions. Windsong waited, arms crossed. "I *am* leaving. If not right this minute, then after dark as planned. The workers will be gone and the drones are still scheduled to do their disappearing act." She stared at Chase. "Right? None of this alters our plans."

Chase turned to Amos. "Well?"

The man shook his head and dropped his gaze to the ground. "How much can we endure?" He looked up. "How much?" he yelled. He pulled a chair behind him and sat down.

Chase sat beside him. "Whatever you say, I will do. But I think it'll be all right."

With a worn expression and bloodshot eyes, Amos seemed to grin. Just a little. "Where sin abounds, grace abounds more."

"Let me guess—from the Bible?"

"Don't you see? God has put our most dangerous enemy right over our heads. And they don't even know. God will protect us. I know He will. And I know something else."

"What is it?" Chase asked.

"He has a sense of humor." Amos smiled.

Chase returned the smile. "So, we're good to go tonight?"

"I suppose. But you *will* come back. We need your help now more than ever."

"The exoself has loaded nearly all of Mel's programs into the supercomputer. I need to run some tests and then you'll be all set. The underground is connected worldwide." Chase put his hand on Amos's shoulder.

He repeated his demand. "But you *will* come back."

"I wouldn't dream of missing this. It's a strange world you people have here. And it just got stranger. But for now, this is where I belong."

23

The team of three—Chase, Switchblade, and Windsong—spent the afternoon planning a midnight trip through the countryside to a landing strip, where hundreds of drones would be replaced by one recently confiscated jet. At least that was the plan.

Switchblade wanted to know if the plane could land itself on the short runway.

"I've landed it in tighter spots," Windsong told him.

"But you won't be doing the landing," Switchblade said. "Nobody will. The big old dinosaur of a jet's gonna be landed by a robot."

"It'll be all right," Chase said. "Once the plane is in the air, I'll take over the programming. Landing will be the easy part."

Windsong sighed. "What's the hard part?"

"The rest of it is the hard part," Chase answered. "The drones should start their mass evacuation in an hour. It'll be four hours before they're all gone. The plane will arrive half an hour after that. We need to be in place when it gets there."

"We should leave now," Switchblade said. "No telling what'll happen on the way."

Chase listened for any sounds from above. A few people remained in the command center. The rest were in their rooms or in the meeting room. Amos had called some of them together to pray, or something.

After the news about the RACE headquarters moving in up top, Mel had gone off without saying another word to Chase.

The rumble of some old-fashioned vehicles on the street sounded from the vicinity of the museum. Work trucks. "We can't leave yet," Chase said. "Still some crew up there, I think. It'll be quitting time soon."

Kirel appeared and cleared his throat.

"Do you need something?" Chase asked.

"Let me go with you."

"No way," Switchblade said. "Amos ain't letting nobody else out of here. Besides, you'd just slow us down."

"Look, you've got too many people down here. Rations are limited. I've got family in the EU, and I'm going to suffocate if I don't get out here."

Switchblade smirked. "You'll get used to it, man. In a year or two."

Windsong circled Kirel. Their eyes seemed to lock. "Actually, I could use some help when I get to the EU."

"You want to take him with you?" Chase asked.

"Sure, why not?" She smiled at Kirel.

He smiled back. "You won't be sorry."

"I'd better not be. If I find out you've got some other motive, you're out the hatch without a parachute."

"I just want out of here." Kirel took a breath and blinked his soupy eyes. "And I want to see my mother. She lives near Frankfurt."

Chase prompted the four S's and the exoself ran a check on Kirel. German-born, his mother lived in a small community near Frankfurt. Chase searched the woman's data and found she was a supporter operating a secret house that offered temporary shelter to believers. Kirel was telling the truth. So what was Chase worried about? Let the guy go and they'd have one less human to feed and clothe.

"Look, I have to talk to someone before we go," Chase said.

"Uh-huh, I bet you do," Switchblade said.

Chase stared him down, then caught Kirel's stare. "And *you* need to tell Amos what you're planning to do."

The man shrugged. "I'll go talk to him."

Chase left the group and headed for Mel's room. He couldn't leave like this—not with her mad at him.

She pulled the door open as soon as he knocked.

"Are you ready to go?" she asked.

"I'm not going anywhere until we talk."

"I'm listening. With my little human pea-brain."

"Oh, come on, you know that is not what I think of you. You're the smartest, kindest, gentlest, softest, sweetest—"

"Stop it." She moved away from the door, allowing Chase to enter the room. "You said some dumb things last night."

"I'm sorry. Again. There's this megalomaniac inside me missing his celebrity status, and this transhuman who's not any less prideful, and then there's me, stuck in the middle. And all I want is to be sitting on a beach somewhere holding your hand and watching the waves. Is that too much to ask?'

"It sounds wonderful." Tears filled her eyes. "But yeah, it's too much to ask."

Chase put his arms around her as she sobbed.

"Please don't go, Chase. I'm not mad because you say stupid things. You've always done that. I'm mad because I don't want you to leave with that blonde pilot. You're gonna end up taking off with her. Or you'll end up in prison, or back at the Helgen. Or dead."

He held her tight and kissed her hair. "I've been dead before. Didn't slow me down for long."

She pulled away, laughed, and smacked his arm. "Next time they're not going to wake you up. You act like you're a cat with nine lives. I think two is probably your limit."

He pulled her close, kissed her, and then pressed her head against his chest. "If I have any trouble—which I'm not expecting—I'll call you. Just give me a VPad to take with me. Melody, when you get up in the morning, I'll be in the dining hall. I'll save you a seat."

"OK, boss." Her voice trembled. "I'll see you in the morning."

He pulled himself away from her and left the room. He couldn't stay any longer without changing his mind about going. The door shut behind him. The hearing enhancer, still active to listen for up-top activity, carried the words Mel whispered: "Father, protect him. Heaven help me, I love the man."

He stared at the door, wishing he could steal her out of this place and find that perfect beach where no one else in the world existed. "Someday."

He faced the hallway to the command center and sparked the exoself to begin powering the first group of drones.

When he arrived, he found Kirel hoisting on a backpack. Switchblade tucked a switchblade, of course, into the waistband of his jeans. Windsong cocked a pistol.

Amos stood to the side of the crew. "Kirel has my approval to go, Chase. Thank you for telling him that was a requirement."

Chase gave a quick nod, but set his attention on Windsong. "Where'd you get the gun?"

"I always have a gun on me. I even sleep with it." She stuck the small weapon in a holster under her shirt.

"How many times have you used it?"

"What difference does that make? I use it when I need to. This might be one of those nights. Wouldn't you agree?"

Chase lifted his brow at Switchblade.

The knife-wielding bodyguard laughed. "I'd say it's likely we'll need more than a transhuman to get us through the night."

"More than weapons, more than superpowers, you all are going to need prayer," Amos said. "That's what I'll be doing while you're gone. And others, too. We'll pray until you return."

Melody's sweet simple prayer was all Chase needed. He smiled.

"You gone and made up for whatever stupid thing you said?" Switchblade asked him. "You're grinning like you just did some making up."

He lost the smile. "Mind your own business."

Chase's mother drew near and put her arms around him. "I know you have to do this," she said. "But you better be careful. It's nearly winter and you're just wearing a light jacket? What if you get lost in the woods?"

"It's only autumn. And I can't get lost in the woods or anywhere else. It's impossible." He hugged her and kissed her cheek. "Don't worry. Everything will go according to plan. Switchblade and I will be back in time for breakfast."

She nodded and backed away, her arms folded across her stomach.

Chase listened for any remaining sounds of activity above their heads. Nothing. "Let's go," he said. "We've got a long walk."

"What about cameras in town?" Amos asked. "The Feds are looking for Kirel and Windsong."

"I can play tricks with the cameras long enough for us to get out of sight."

"What about local police?" Mom asked.

"If we meet up with local authorities, I'll create a diversion. I accidentally caused a power outage—I can make something happen on purpose."

Before any more questions or problems or potential disasters could be discussed, Switchblade unlocked the door to the staircase, and Chase followed him, Kirel and Windsong behind him. Up and up they climbed, then across until they arrived at the hole covered from the other side by the painting. The beautiful Blue Sky Field. The place of dreams.

Of persecution. Chase shuddered as he climbed through.

When all four of them were on the other side, Switchblade pushed the painting back into place. Chase put his hand against the green hillside and closed his eyes. "Protect them," he said.

"You praying, Charlie?"

He opened his eyes. "Even a transhuman can say a prayer once in a while."

"All right by me." Switchblade headed for the door in the back room of the museum. He carried a laserlight, but kept it at half power. He and the others couldn't see what Chase saw. The demolition crew had knocked out an interior wall. Boards and chunks of broken plaster leaned against the door.

The beam from the laserlight found the blocked exit before Chase could warn the others.

"Can you move this stuff out of our way, Charlie? Or should we just go on out the front door?"

"I can move it, but tomorrow somebody would notice."

"We could go back through and take the exit behind the refuse bin," Switchblade said.

Chase breathed in and checked on the departing drones. "We'd lose too much time."

Windsong groaned. "OK boys, we're going out the front door. Nobody's around. The cameras are off. Right, Chase?"

"Yeah, they're off." He headed for the front of the building. "Let's go. Switchblade, turn off that light. All of you stay close behind me."

After stumbling over more remodeling rubble, the group reached the glass front of the old museum. The entry was wide open. In fact, the door was off the hinges and tossed aside. They stepped onto the sidewalk, which was littered with more debris.

"Not a very tidy demolition crew," Chase said.

"Good thing for us," Windsong replied. "Didn't even have to break down the door."

Switchblade took a deep breath and blew it out. "Fresh air. How long has it been?"

"Are you serious?" Chase asked. "You're up here as much as you're down there."

"Yeah, well it's not enough. Long walk in the country—that's what I need."

Kirel followed close behind Chase. "So, we just walk to the drone plant and wait for the plane? And the drones will be gone when we get there?" he asked.

"Is that the plan?"

Chase nodded. "The third group of drones should be flying over our heads any minute. By the time we get there, the last group will be headed south."

Soon the silent but well-lit little machines stretched in a line across the dark sky. From a hundred yards down the quiet street, Chase heard voices.

"Look at the drones." The male voice had a heavy French accent. "Never seen them fly in so large a group, and so high."

A woman responded, her accent more New York than Quebec. "Drill of some kind. Or maybe they got orders from the military. Saw that once before. Big order comes in and they fly them out in groups."

Chase breathed a sigh. The plan was working. They passed the last bricked street and the sign declaring *Bienvenue à Herouxville*. A two-mile stretch of country road would take them to the plant. But they didn't dare take it.

"This way," Chase said. He headed for a field. A green hillside. Or at least it would have been green if the approaching winter hadn't deadened it to brown. Half a moon offered little light. His traveling companions couldn't appreciate what Chase could see in the dark. He pictured the painting back at the museum. Maybe this was where the artist labored with his easel and his palette. Maybe this was the place of Chase's dreams.

A truck roared up the road and slowed as it passed the travelers. A single drone flew low overhead. The field. The truck. The drone. A little too much of the dream in this reality.

"Hurry," Chase said. "The faster we get out of here, the better."

24

Another solitary drone left the plant after the third group had departed like a gaggle of geese headed south for the winter. Always a straggler or two with geese. But drones? Why were two left to catch up on their own?

Flying south would be good. Cold air crept into Chase's black jacket and he pulled it tight and snapped it shut at the neck. How long until snow changed the color of the fields around Herouxville? Maybe a harsh winter would slow down the remodeling project at the museum.

Checking the flight orders, Chase found that two drones fresh off the assembly line had piggybacked on the orders and joined the others when their systems booted. Five others had not responded and were still in the plant's determination area. Even the drones were thinking for themselves.

Switchblade interrupted the information passing between the plant and the exoself. "Everything on schedule, Charlie? Other group flying out yet?"

A last bit of information flooded in before Chase could answer. "The ones set to load onto the jet—they just lined themselves up. The rest followed the orders to fly out."

"That's what you planned, right? What about the next mass exodus? Is it ready?"

"Yeah. We won't see them. Different flight

pattern."

The group had been over a mile. Some of it uphill and through a wooded area that proved hard for everyone but Chase to maneuver in the dark. Less than a mile to go.

Windsong spoke from behind Chase. "How do you know the whole security force fell for your orders to take the night off? Surely they're not dumb enough to leave the place unguarded. And what about satellite images?"

"I put up a satellite block—used the WR's own technology against them. As for the humans in charge of security, they won't be too concerned. The cyber-guards can handle it without them." Chase smiled at the sudden lack of movement behind him. "Didn't I mention the eight cyber-guards?" He faced his cohorts.

"No, robot, you did not mention that," Switchblade said.

Chase moved in and got as close to the man's face as he could, considering Switchblade was a head taller. "What did I tell you about calling me that?"

Switchblade stared down at him. "Deal with it. What are we supposed to do with eight cyber-guards?"

"Do you think I'm capable of moving hundreds of drones but not able to shut down a few guards?"

Windsong let out a sigh. "You scared us, Chase. So you're gonna shut them down before we get there. Right?"

"Of course. They'll reset in four hours and nobody will know the difference. I'm just waiting for the last of the evening shift to leave."

"Evening shift?" Kirel joined the panic. "You mean there are still people at the plant? And they're just watching all their drones fly off? Don't you think they'll get suspicious?"

"People, for the most part, let computers run the show. We're using that to our advantage." Chase was twenty feet ahead of his followers now, and they started walking forward again.

"So, how do you do it?" Kirel asked. "How do you get the whole world to do whatever you tell it to do?"

"Not the whole world," Chase said. "Just certain government entities."

"But how do you do it?"

"You're asking the wrong person. In the past few months I've learned to connect and to manipulate, but understanding is what I'm missing. In the last few days, the exoself has done things without my instructions. And I don't know why."

Switchblade's voice sounded close behind Chase. "'Cause God planned it that way, Charlie. Seems to me God and that exoself are on the same page."

"Yeah, that doesn't clear up anything for me." Chase glanced at the man then slowed until they walked side by side.

"You ought to give the thing a name."

Chase laughed. "It's not alive. At least I hope not. Sometimes I think it will take over completely and there will be no more me."

"I agree." Windsong joined in. "Name the thing. Might make you feel better. Like you're in control of it."

"This is ridiculous," Kirel said. "I just wanted to know how it works. I don't want to make friends with it. It scares me to death to think about what it can do. What it *might* do. We can't let it become the routine—putting something like that in people. Imagine the chaos if thousands of people were manipulating hundreds of programs around the world. It's got to stop."

Chase slowed his pace a little and rubbed the back of his neck. The exoself sparked the code—32-7—but not in a threatening way. Just a warning.

Regarding Kirel.

"I can't say I disagree with you," Chase told him. "But it's part of who I am now. Is that OK with you?"

"Uh, yeah. I know you didn't start this. You're just a victim. But maybe it would help the scientists realize how dangerous the whole thing is if they knew that it's thinking for itself. That it's able to subvert the plans of the leadership that authorized it."

Switchblade set his face inches from Kirel's. The exoself triggered yet another subtle warning.

"Enough talk from you," Switchblade said to Kirel. "Let's get ourselves to the plant and get this night over with. Sooner you take off for the EU the better. Least as far as I'm concerned."

"I was just stating my opinion. When did you decide to stand up for the guy you've been referring to as a robot? You know he's an accident waiting to happen. Admit it."

Chase had to end this before Switchblade lost his temper. "I thought of a name for the exoself."

"Great," Windsong said. "Tell us what you've decided to name your brain-indwelling, cyber-connected, nanotech-engineered baby."

"Sparky."

Switchblade let out a laugh. "You got a Scottish Terrier inside you, man?"

"I think it's cute," Windsong said. She started walking. "Are we almost there, Sparky?"

"Now I'm having second thoughts," Chase said.

He stepped ahead of her. "Don't start calling me Sparky. But yes, we're almost there. Quarter mile to go." He pointed to a clearing on the hilltop ahead. "See the lights up there? That's it."

Switchblade's heavy footsteps thumped behind Chase, followed by Kirel's lighter step. As the four began their ascent to the WR drone manufacturing plant, Chase remembered there were people praying for him. Good thing. Sparky wasn't the only one with a bad feeling about what was ahead.

25

The four crouched near an endless run of ten-foot steel fence with razor wire along the top. No laser fence or any sign of high-tech security. Chase double-checked the camera system, the now inactive cyber-guards, and the slightly hovering remaining drones positioned to load themselves on a jet that would be auto-piloted to the runway in less than an hour.

No sign of trouble. Stray humans were not detected by the exoself. But it did find a dog, and it was bigger than a Scottish terrier. Probably a Doberman by the look of its heat imprint. A second fence circled the plant inside the one that Chase peered through. The canine roamed the perimeter of the inner fence.

Chase weaved his fingers through the heavy-duty fencing, pulled out a chunk, and threw it to the ground. Leaning forward, he grabbed the broken spot with both hands and ripped the fence apart.

"Impressive," Windsong said.

"The next fence holds a guard dog," Chase said. "Don't know if I want to stick my hand in." He climbed through the hole. Windsong followed. Then Kirel, who snagged the sleeve of his jacket on the protruding metal and mumbled a foul word in French. Switchblade didn't fit as easily as the rest of them, but he got through.

"Come on," Chase said. The compound had two

buildings and stretched a half mile in all directions. The runway where Windsong's jet would land was eight hundred yards to the left. Chase had turned off most of the lights in the compound.

In the next enclosure, the Doberman rushed toward them and jumped a good six feet up the fence. It snarled like it hadn't eaten in a week and the only thing that would satisfy its hunger was a buffet of intruders.

Chase stopped and crossed his arms. He sparked the exoself, the protection code, the safe travel code. Nothing. This was flesh and blood showing its teeth, not some computer system. What was he supposed to do with a ferocious dog?

But it had to be fitted with an identification chip. All dogs were chipped. He searched WR records for canine protection units. In twenty seconds he found the company supplying guard dogs to government facilities in the Northeast Territory. And he found the dog.

Female. Two years old. Trained in Montreal. Chase knew everything about the hundred pound blue-gray prize winner.

"I got this," he said to the others.

"Nora, *en bas*," he yelled. He clapped his hands once and then rolled his left arm in the air.

The beast backed away from the fence, cowered, whined, and dropped to her stomach. She rested her huge head between her front paws and huffed.

"Are you serious?" Switchblade asked. "Are you *serious*?" he yelled as he shook his head.

Chase shrugged, reached the fence, and ripped a hole in it. The dog sprang to her feet and growled.

"Nora!" Chase rolled his arm again and the dog

returned to her subservient pose.

Windsong laughed and crawled through first. Chase followed, stretched the break a little bigger this time, and motioned Switchblade in. Kirel crawled in last. The man kept his back against the fence as he stared at the Doberman.

"She's harmless," Chase said. "Unless I tell her otherwise."

Kirel nodded. "I'm glad I'm on your side."

Something about the man's voice sent a chill down all twelve processors of Chase's lab-grown spine. "Come on. I hear the jet. It'll be landing about the time we get inside the building."

"I don't hear anything. We're going inside a building?" Kirel asked. "Why not just head for the runway?"

"The plane will taxi to the building where the drones are waiting to get picked up. Once they're loaded, and the two of you are onboard, I'll send the plane on its way."

"You don't need to program it, Chase," Windsong said. "I'm the pilot—I'll fly it out of here."

"You'd have forces on you before you got over the ocean. This plane is on auto. It needs to stay that way until I can recode it. Don't touch the controls. Don't even go near the cockpit. It's—"

"Heat sensitive. It'll pick up my presence. Even my DNA. I had a scanner installed to prevent theft."

"I could disable it, but I don't want to attract attention. Just stay clear of the cockpit for a few minutes until I can scramble your location. I'm disabling the plane's communications. You won't have any way of notifying the ground, but it'll keep the trackers off you. You'll have to land by sight."

"What about the drones?" Switchblade asked. "What happens when they don't get delivered to wherever they're supposed to be going?"

"The plane is going down in the ocean. The drones will be lost."

Windsong put her hands on her hips. "What?"

"Don't worry. The exoself will make it believable. It'll free you up to start over in the EU if they think you and your plane are gone."

"It's all so easy," she said. "I can't believe the way you mess with the system and get away with it."

Kirel walked ahead. "I can't believe it either. The Helgen Institute must be proud."

Sarcasm? Chase caught up with him as they reached the south side of the metal building. "The people at the Helgen have no idea what I'm doing. And I plan to keep it that way." He reached a bolted steel door and yanked it open as if it were made of cardboard.

"I bet they'd be amazed at the way you've learned to use the exoself. Sparky." He laughed. "But what about the destruction you're leaving here? Holes in the fence and busted doors—nobody but Chase Sterling could do that."

Chase looked the man in the eyes. "Anybody with the right tools could do it. And when I'm through feeding bull to the Feds, they'll think the dissenters did this. One group casts blame on another—I throw it right back at them."

Kirel's closed his mouth and his nostrils flared.

Windsong's plane whooshed overhead and circled to land on the airstrip that wasn't quite long enough. But together with the auto-pilot program, Chase made it work.

The human pilot lifted her hands in the air. "Glory to God," she said. "Thank you for the transhuman."

The four slunk into the building and lined up against a wall near the sleeping drones. Why were they sneaking around? Nobody but the Doberman knew they were there, and she'd accepted the situation.

The drones were lined up, awaiting orders. Unarmed. Chase had seen other little flying spybots shoot to kill, but these weren't weapons. Five would fit into the cargo bay of Windsong's plane, which could be heard rolling near on the other side of a thirty-foot pull-down door. Chase broke off the padlock and pushed the door upward.

The plane rested, and Windsong ran to it and punched in a code to lower the ramp to the cargo bay. She smiled as she patted the plane's belly.

Chase programmed the drones to come to life, and one by one they lifted from their hovering position and moved toward the rear of the jet.

It was easy. Too easy.

Windsong hoisted herself on board and motioned for Kirel.

"I don't know if I want to cross the ocean with a bunch of WR drones," he said. "I'm feeling a little queasy."

The man seemed to have a sudden case of aviophobia. Chase could relate—it had taken a fly-or-die situation to get over *his* fear of all things airborne. But he didn't have any sympathy for Kirel. The man was getting on that plane.

Chase grabbed his arm and pulled him out of the building. "It's being underground you don't like. Remember?"

"Hey, Switchblade," Windsong yelled.

"Yeah?" He stepped to the open rear door where Windsong leaned out.

"Got some crates in the way in here. Come on board and help me shove them to the side before the drones load."

"Kirel's coming," Switchblade said. "Let *him* do it."

"The man looks green. I don't want him on my plane if he's gonna puke."

"Well, what about the guy with the augmented muscles?"

"Promised his girlfriend I wouldn't let him near my plane. I think she's worried he's a flight risk."

Chase smiled and headed for the opening. "I'll move your crates. I'm not going anywhere but back to Blue Sky Field in time for breakfast."

"Nah, man, I'm going. Got me some *real* muscles." Switchblade hoisted himself into the plane and disappeared.

With Windsong and Switchblade out of sight, Kirel grabbed Chase around the neck and pointed a laser gun at his head.

Chase reached back. He gripped the arms of Kirel's jacket, and braced to flip the guy over his shoulder. Kirel shoved the cold narrow barrel of the gun firmly into Chase's temple. A blast from the weapon would take him out, transhuman or not. He froze.

"What is this, Kirel? You want something from me? Just tell me. We can work it out."

Windsong stepped to the hatch and started to climb out of the plane's underbelly. Her eyes grew wide and she pulled out her gun and aimed for Kirel.

"Drop it, pull the door up, and get out of here,"

Kirel shouted. "You try anything and what's left of the real Chase Sterling gets his revved-up brain splattered all over the place."

She tossed the weapon and stepped forward, her lifted palms before her. "OK, think it through, Kirel. Whatever you have planned—"

"Get out of here!" Kirel shoved the laser gun tighter into Chase's head.

You fool, I can't fly the plane." She pointed at Chase. "*He* has to do it."

"That's exactly what he's going to do. As soon as you shut the hatch."

Switchblade launched out of the hatch and landed on the loading pad thirty feet in front of Chase.

Kirel backed up, tightening his chokehold. "Get back on the plane!"

"You'll regret this," Chase said. He remained frozen, but the exoself was running wild.

"*You'll* regret it if you don't cooperate. Remember the truck that slowed down back in Herouxville? It's loaded with explosives and parked at the front door of the museum. You let me down, I blow the place. If I don't show up at the rendezvous point, others will take care of pulling the switch." He looked at Switchblade. "That goes for you and the pilot too. You try anything, all those people die."

"You're lying" Chase said. "I would have picked up on it."

"You don't know as much as you think you do. Sniffing out explosives is not in your programming. Neither is surviving a laser gun, and there's nobody here to put you back together. The transhuman still bleeds. You're not invincible."

"The exoself may have already sent a warning."

"You'd better hope not. If anybody tries to come up out of that hole, the place explodes."

Chase hesitated. Then he nodded to Switchblade. "Do what he says."

"I am not going to the EU, Charlie."

"You want him to blow up Blue Sky Field? You have to go, Switch. I'm sorry. There's nothing I can do."

26

Switchblade backed up to the hatch and crawled into the plane. "What about the drones, huh? They're supposed to be on the plane. That's what the orders say." He gave Chase a final glance, his eyebrows lifted, his head shaking.

Kirel hesitated, then answered, "Never mind the drones. Just go."

Windsong pushed a button to lift the hatch. "I'm sorry, Chase. God be with you." The door lifted and sealed shut, and Chase and Kirel were alone.

"Get it in the air," Kirel said.

"Don't think so," Chase said.

"Do it!"

"I have to get the drones back inside the warehouse first. They should've been on the plane. Now they're just in the way."

"Then get on with it." Kirel pulled Chase to the side of the building, out of the way of the drones.

The hovering machines moved back to their earlier positions. Windsong peeked through the one small window of her plane. Chase shook his head, and she turned away.

Kirel jerked and stumbled back. "Stand still and do what I told you!"

Chase connected to the auto-pilot, and the plane revved and nosed toward the runway. Then it took over and increased its speed. Soon it lifted and headed east. That part of whatever insidious demands were to be made of him was done.

"How long until it's over the Atlantic?" Kirel asked.

"Fourteen minutes."

"In half an hour, crash it."

Panic rushed through Chase. "I can't do that."

"You said the report would show the plane crashed." Kirel at last let go of Chase and pushed him against the wall. The laser gun remained pointed at his head.

Had the exoself acted on its own and sent a warning to the underground? Chase took a breath when he determined no such message had gone out. "I said it would show the plane went down. I didn't say I could crash it."

"You programmed the take-off. So why can't you program a landing into the sea?"

Chase wiped icy sweat from his brow and smirked. "You're not a Christian, are you?"

"I consider myself a Christian. I don't consider *you* a Christian," Kirel said. "What are you doing hanging out with the Underground Church anyway?"

"How can you kill your fellow believers?"

"They don't have any vision. God wants us to restore this country. And he doesn't want transhumans taking over the world. If the so-called Christians at Blue Sky Field were real believers, they would have killed you." Kirel side-stepped to the open hangar door. "We're going back through the hole in the fence and we're walking to the highway. If you send out any kind of warning with that computer in your head, or if I don't reach the meeting point in ninety minutes, the museum blows. They *will* take you in, transhuman. You might as well get it over with."

"They?" Chase asked. "I get it. There's a bounty on my head. How much?"

"Plenty and it'll be used for the right cause. But I'd do it for nothing." He motioned with the laser gun, grabbed Chase's arm, and headed out of the building.

Chase rolled his free arm, and the obedient Doberman who waited near the loading dock readied for command.

"*Attaque!*"

Nora raced toward them, teeth bared. A low growl gave warning. She jumped. Her lean body targeted at Kirel. Chase braced for the impact. Nora collided with Kirel and Chase squirmed free as the dog knocked Kirel to the ground.

But the man didn't lose the gun. He blasted the laser. The dog reeled backward. She dropped to the ground. Then Kirel aimed at Chase. He fired. Chase clutched his right shoulder.

The blast drove like a knife into his flesh. He sucked in his breath and swallowed a scream. Stumbling back, he fell against the metal wall. He gaped at the wound. Blood streamed down his arm.

"You're lucky I tuned it to low gauge. Next time I'll blow off the whole arm."

Chase slid out of his jacket and tore his shirt loose from the wound. He didn't know what might be coming out of the hole—wires or some kind of computer hardware. But it was just a small hole. Nothing but ripped tissue and blood.

The exoself seemed to fade away, or maybe Chase was about to faint. His vision fragmented into bits of light. Then the lights went out, replaced with nothing but black. He shook his head and internally screamed at the powers inside his mind not to do anything about this. No warning to Mel or anyone else. Please.

"Come on, you can walk with a hole in your shoulder. But I bet you're not as strong as you were with two good arms." Kirel grabbed him and yanked him to his feet.

The pain was all human. The strength sensors in his right shoulder had indeed powered down. With no one to repair him, what Kirel had said was true. He wasn't as strong. But the bleeding slowed. He reached for his jacket and struggled to pull it on. And then he trudged beside the man in control. Kirel's strong grip and the laser gun pointed at his head kept Chase moving forward.

"Highway circles the plant," Kirel said. "We're going down on the north side. If I'm not at the rendezvous point in an hour, the bomb goes off. So no more half-cocked attempts at escape. Now see what you can do about crashing the jet. I don't want any trouble from that pilot and the black Goliath."

Chase's power ebbed—he could feel it leaving him. But he could handle one more manipulation in the cyber world. He had to in order to save Blue Sky Field.

"Done," he said.

"You sure?"

"If you don't believe me, crash it yourself."

Kirel huffed and jerked Chase forward. "Well...even if you're lying, you told the pilot you disabled her communication with the ground. No reason for you to lie to *her*. By the time those two get a message to the underground, I will have collected my fee. And you'll be back where you belong." He didn't mention the plane again. He spoke little as they traipsed down the dark hillside. Even Chase's night vision was failing. Why? What did that have to do with a wound to his shoulder?

"Why did you frame those people in town? Why did they have to die?" Chase asked.

"Couldn't risk the kids trying to go back up. If their families were dead, they'd stay put."

"I don't understand."

"Look, I didn't plan on three teenagers getting caught. Didn't plan on Molly getting taken in by the Feds. It just worked out that way. I was supposed to end up at the detention center alone. They would have let me go, even without all your help in making me look like an informant. When they released me, I would have had to go under. Alone. It was a ruse."

"Because you're an informant," Chase said.

"Yeah. But not due to my great love and respect for the WR. *That* was the ruse. I set myself up to use my position in the Underground Church to take the heat off the dissenters."

"Kind of a double agent?"

"Sure, if you say so." Kirel huffed and quickened his pace. "Once we all came under, I couldn't let those kids go back up. They might have talked. I got myself into the inner circle at Blue Sky Field for a reason. Couldn't let them blow it. So I used that all-fired important untraceable communication system you set up down there to plant a lead to the WR. And *they* took care of things."

"You make it sound like you're innocent."

"I will do whatever needs to be done to restore this country." Kirel stepped in a low spot and nearly stumbled. "And I will feel no guilt."

"You sure were quick to give up that position in the underground that you killed for."

"I told you, *I* didn't kill anyone. The Feds did. Anyway, I found something better than a place to plant misinformation."

"You found me."

"That's right, Chase Sterling. And *you* are a goldmine. Covert group within the WR is ready to pay."

Chase had nothing else to say to the man. He trudged along in silence. Then a voice intruded the exoself, and a thin line of code in a flash of red appeared alongside Chase. "For the love of...Not now!"

"What are you yelling about?" Kirel demanded.

"Matters of tranhumansim. You wouldn't understand. Not that *I* understand." Maybe this wasn't a bad thing. With a weakened spark of the exoself, he spoke to Kerstin from the depths of his mind. *I saved your life. You owe me. Help me.*

Her answer permeated his senses as if she were standing next to him. Surely Kirel could hear her every word.

"I *am* helping you, darling. I've found you at last. The DNA scanner at the drone plant was so deeply imbedded in the security system that it was undetectable. Even by you. Once I had your position, it was easy to trigger the killswitch. You're powering down, aren't you? You'll be harmless as a puppy when the authorities pick you up. I know you've left the plant. Don't bother trying to get away, Chase. The exoself has notified the Helgen of your location. It sent out its own cry for help. We can track you now. And we're coming, darling. Help is on the way."

She laughed, and Chase knew from past experience the wicked sound of her claim to victory.

27

No other message surged from the exoself. Chase couldn't reach out to the underground. He wasn't able to access WR programs. He didn't even know what time it was. The simplest capabilities were gone. Kirel's laserlight spread its beam as he dragged Chase toward the highway. Good thing the man had a light—Chase's night vision was no more.

Kirel forced Chase over a fallen tree and then pulled him down to sit on the huge, rotting log parallel to the road. "Any Feds in the area?" Kirel asked.

"I have no idea," Chase answered.

"Don't mess with me."

"My systems are down, Kirel."

"From a shot to the shoulder? Are you telling me that's all it took to shut you down?"

Why tell the man the truth? Except that Kirel handing Chase over to bounty hunters might take longer than WR deputies showing up with an armored car. Either way, he'd end up back at the Helgen plugged into machines. And Kerstin would be there to hold his hand. They'd make him functional again or they wouldn't. It didn't matter. He wouldn't escape a second time.

"I'm not going back," he said.

"Back to the laboratory that birthed you?" Kirel asked. "Oh, I think you are."

"You won't get a chance to turn me over for

payment. WR Feds are on their way to get me."

Kirel lifted the weapon and cuffed Chase across the head, knocking him to the ground. "You said you didn't know," he yelled. "How long?"

Chase pulled himself up on his elbows. "I can't tell you that. Before the exoself shut down, I got a message. I'm being tracked. They're coming. That's all I know."

"You're lying."

"I wish I was. Even if you deliver me to your contact, they'll still be tracking me. Whoever gets caught with the goods won't make it out of this alive. The best thing for you to do is run. Leave me here and tell your people I got away."

"Nice try. Get up."

Chase eased to his feet without using his right arm. "I'm telling you the truth. The last thing the exoself did for me was reveal my location to the Helgen. The Feds are on their way."

"So are the Dissenters of the Republic," Kirel said. "The only Feds you'll see tonight are the ones we deliver you to."

A truck like the one Chase had seen earlier rolled up the highway and pulled onto the mucky shoulder. Four men jumped out. Two carried old-school machine guns. The other two, laser guns like Kirel's. One of the men lifted the roll-up door at the back of the truck, while the other three moved toward Chase.

"He's injured," Kirel said. "Says his powers are gone. I don't know if he's telling the truth, but he's not so strong anymore."

Two of the men grabbed Chase's arms and hurried him to the rear of the truck. He climbed onto a metal step and dropped into the truck's cargo box. He backed away from the men with their guns and grunted out a breath.

"I told him the Feds are coming for me," he said. "I'm being tracked and it won't take long for them to find me. You can't outrun them."

"Don't listen to him," Kirel said. "Let's go."

"But he knows what the Feds are doing, right?" one of the men said. "What if he's not lying?"

Kirel pulled the door down, leaving Chase in darkness. "The man has a *gift* for lying. He'll say anything to get what he wants."

"You tell him we got a bomb at the museum?"

The voice had a slight French accent. Chase wished for the powers he'd once thought ridiculous— night vision and super hearing. His human eyes adjusted to the darkness inside the truck. A dim glow from laserlights made lines where the rolling door's sections joined. But then the men walked from the rear of the truck to the cab, their voices fading, the light gone.

The engine hummed and the truck bounced from the roadside and bumped along until it picked up speed. The men's voices were muddled. Their indistinguishable words found a rhythm in the smooth roll of the truck's tires.

Leaning back in the hollow bay of what had become his prison transport, Chase pulled off his blood-soaked jacket and felt the small hole in his shoulder. His arm throbbed, but the wound didn't seem too bad.

"Sparky, how could you leave me like this?" He laughed. "Seriously. God, how could you leave me? I thought the whole point of me being a transhuman was to help your people. Now I'm nothing. And they're in more danger than ever. How could you?"

Loss of blood and being yanked from his power supply began to affect him. He tried to spark every processor. To reverse the killswitch. He crawled to the door and tried to lift it, then to bust through it. He had no strength. Not even that of a normal man. He went limp onto the floor of the cargo box. His useless eyes fell shut in the darkness.

"Charles Redding," the voice called.

It was the voice of his dreams. Chase reached to the side, expecting to find a metal bowl beside him in the darkness. But he wasn't in the place of his previous encounters.

He opened his eyes. "Here I am." He lay in a green field. The brilliant blue sky filled his vision.

"Don't be afraid."

Chase sat straight. His heart raced and he clutched at his chest.

"What's the matter?"

"My heart rate hasn't varied since I got…"

"Turned into a transhuman?"

"It's gone—the exoself. I can't help the underground anymore. I'm useless. And there's a bomb. And I can't stop it." Chase looked upward and squinted at the brightness.

"Your heart rate didn't increase. It's the same bio-designed pump they put in you. It's your mind telling you that your heart is beating too fast. Don't be afraid."

"How can you say that?" Chase yelled. "People are going to die, and I can't stop it."

"No, you can't. Don't be afraid," the voice said.

Chase gazed across the vast green hillside. "I didn't know I had a killswitch. How could You let them unplug me?"

"It's what you wanted. Remember?"

"Well, I changed my mind when you sent my dead father to tell me to come here and help these people!"

"Why do you always call them that?"

"What?" Chase asked.

"Why do you call them 'these people'? As if they're freaks. As if you're not one of them."

"I'm not one of them. I don't know *how* to be one of them. Because they won't tell me."

The voice didn't respond to this. Chase waited, sitting in the grass, watching the cloudless sky. A soft breeze cooled his brow and somehow eased the trepidation inside him. He almost smiled before he closed his eyes.

"Don't be afraid," the voice said.

Chase awoke sliding across the cold steel floor of the truck. The man driving this thing had found a reason to increase his speed and leave the main highway. The ragged beat of a country road kept Chase from landing too long in one place, and he cried out when he banged his injured shoulder into the side of the cargo box.

This could only mean one thing—the Feds had found them.

He lay flat on his stomach in a vain attempt to keep from being tossed like a rag doll. Even his inferior hearing could tell there was more than one vehicle closing in. Light filtered in through the door of the bay. He tried to spark the code—32-7. Nothing. If he didn't die in this pursuit, his captors would return him to the desert.

The truck veered off the road, it seemed, and the terrain got rougher. Chase flipped onto his back and hit hard against the floor, then flew to one side and crashed into the wall. The men up front yelled loud enough for Chase to hear them. One cursed. One prayed.

The transport rolled. Then rolled again. Chase went flying. He lost count of the rotations. At last the turning stopped. Chase landed on his back. He couldn't move. No sound. No light flashed in through the door. He didn't even know where the door was anymore. The truck could be upside-down. It creaked as it swayed. Then there was no sound at all.

But the tracker wouldn't have been disabled by a fall down a cliff. They'd be coming for him. He wished for the green hillside he'd known only moments ago. For the breeze that passed him by and almost made him hopeful that all this would somehow work out. But there was no hope. As in the dream, he imagined his heartbeat had ramped to meet his fear. But that was impossible. A lab-grown heart remained forever constant.

"Don't be afraid," he said into the darkness. Then he lifted one hand into the void. "Don't be afraid."

28

What was taking so long? They'd have to pull him out of the wreckage before they forced him onto a jet and returned him to the Helgen. Maybe the truck was positioned in such a way that they couldn't get him without risking his life.

But did they even care if he lived or died? They'd be coming soon.

Every part of him hurt. Even the man-made stuff ached, it seemed. His left leg, he was certain, had snapped in two. Even if he managed to sit up he couldn't walk. He moved to one side of the groaning truck, and then he lay still. His eyelids demanded to shut and he slipped between awareness of his predicament and dreams of the green field. The voice seemed to follow him through both worlds, telling him not to fear. He figured he was too delirious to be afraid. He laughed. No hope…and he was laughing.

Hours must have passed. No one came. His leg throbbed and he stayed awake for longer periods. His stomach growled. Getting up was not an option. He remained as still as possible, though he felt he could move now.

Still no sound other than the occasional squeak of the truck and the call of a bird that must be in a nearby tree. A singing bird and the slight glow inside the box of the truck meant the sun had risen. "What's taking so long?" he yelled. "I'm right here. Come get me."

Mel would be looking for him in the dining hall by now. She'd have no idea what happened. No word from him. No response if she tried to contact him.

"Don't even think about coming to look for me. I'll be gone soon. I'm sorry, Melody. Mom. All of you." His eyes fell shut again. "I'm sorry."

Then he remembered the bomb. Was there even anything left of Blue Sky Field? A tear slid from the corner of his eye. "Don't be afraid," he told himself again. But he sobbed just the same until the merciful sleep returned.

The next time he opened his eyes, the bird songs had fallen silent to the restless mutter of crickets and the cry of a distant wolf. Darkness had robbed the cargo box of its daylight glow. He'd been here about twenty-four hours, as far as he could tell.

"Why haven't you come for me?" he yelled. "What's going on out there?"

He had to move, to try something to get out of this box. He couldn't just wait to die. Sliding on his side, he dragged his broken leg and reached what he knew to be the roll-down door. He'd seen the sunlight filtering through it. The door was no longer vertical, but horizontal. The truck was on its side. It creaked and moaned, threatening to shift its position on the side of whatever sloped spot it had landed on.

Chase banged on the door. He found the handle and pulled with all his strength. Then he lay back and breathed out puffs of frigid air. The temperature had dropped. If he didn't starve, he'd freeze. He nearly laughed as he remembered his mother chiding his choice of jacket and her concern that he might get lost in the woods.

"Somebody get me out of here!"

Then he heard a faint reply.

"Boss? We're coming. Call out again so we can find you."

This had to be a dream. "Mel?" he yelled. "I'm here." He banged against the metal door. "I'm here."

Soon footsteps neared. Branches cracked and the truck moaned again.

"He's over here," a voice called.

How was this happening? "Mel?"

A knock rattled the side of the truck. "I'm right here." Her soft laugh filled the night and hushed the crickets. "I found you," she said. "Thank God."

"Mel, listen to me. There's a bomb in a truck just like this one. It's parked next to the museum."

"No, Chase, we went up after dark and walked right out the front door. There was no truck."

"So, everybody's OK back there?"

"Everybody's fine. Just worried about *you*, that's all. I don't know how you got yourself into this mess."

"Long story. How did you know where to find me?"

She laughed again. "Long story. We're bracing the truck so you won't slide any farther down. It's gonna be a long walk back. Can you make it?"

"My leg is broken."

The door flew open. "Then I'll just have to carry you," Switchblade said.

Chase smiled. "How on earth? I thought you'd be in the EU by now."

"No such luck, Charlie." The man eased into the box and lifted Chase with his strong arms. The truck swayed a bit, but Switchblade kept his balance as he stepped out onto the ground. He laid Chase on top of a blanket, and Chase sat up enough for Mel to get her arms around him. He pulled her close and held on for his life.

After a moment, he lifted his face from her shoulder and met her eyes. "How did you know I was here?" Then he lifted his head to find Switchblade, who stood over him with his arms folded and a smile on his face. "And how did you...?"

"Pilot lady circled back. I made such a stink about going to the EU that she got me over the countryside near town and slapped a parachute on my back. Said she didn't need no angry, knife-wielding criminal-type following her around while she was trying to get established in new territory."

Mel pulled the blanket around Chase and then put a bottle to his mouth. He gulped tepid water.

"Intel said the plane went down," Mel said. "And we assumed since none of you came back, you all got on it."

"You thought I—"

"I thought you were dead. If you weren't, I was gonna kill you for getting on that plane. I figured you'd decided to take off."

"Not in a million years." Chase cupped her face with his hand and leaned forward to kiss her. "I'm so sorry. I lost control of the situation pretty fast." He winced as he tried to bend his leg.

"How's everything else?" Mel asked.

"Laser wound—right shoulder. It's not too bad."

"Anything else? What's the report from the exoself?"

Switchblade squatted next to Mel. "Oh, you mean Sparky. Tell us, Charlie, what's the word from old Sparky?"

Mel looked from Switchblade to Chase. "You

named the exoself?"

"It doesn't matter," Chase said. "It's gone."

Switchblade dropped to his bottom on the cold ground. "What are you talking about? How can it be gone? Even the night vision and all that stuff?"

"All of it." He had to tell them about Kerstin. But not yet. "I didn't pick up on the DNA scanner at the drone plant. But *it* picked up on *me*. Once the Feds had my location, it was easy for the crew back at the Helgen to shut me down. There was a killswitch."

Switchblade put his arms across his knees. "If they had your location, then why didn't they beat us out here to pick you up?"

"I don't know. I'm sure they followed us. We were being chased. That's how the truck ended up leaving the road." Chase studied the dark woods. "There were five men in the truck. Kirel and four others. They were dissenters selling me to bounty hunters."

Mel pulled her jacket tight. "We found two of them on the side of the drop. Both dead. No sign of Kirel or anyone else."

"They must have gotten taken in by the Feds. I don't get it. They were tracking my location. Why would they leave without me?"

"Maybe they lost the signal," Switchblade said.

"That's impossible," Chase told him.

"Whatever the reason, I'm glad they didn't find you." Mel smiled. "And I'm glad we did."

Chase reached for her and pulled her close. He looked at Switchblade. "And you got dumped out of that jet. Can't blame the girl for wanting to get rid of you."

"Yeah, whatever." The man rose to his feet and joined two others, who were both on VPads.

"Who's with you, Mel? And how on earth did you know where to find me?"

"Before dawn yesterday, my computer showed a map of this area. Then a location started flashing on the map." She pulled the small device from a backpack and showed him the old laptop with new insides. The red flash in the middle of a map was what told Mel where to find him.

"I thought it was you sending me a message," she said. "Before I even had a chance to figure it out, we got the report about Windsong's jet going down. Only the report didn't come through the underground. You are our connection to the WR, so we didn't know where the news about the jet came from, and we didn't know why the map showed up on my computer."

She put her hands over her cheeks and then smoothed back her hair. "But we thought you were all gone. You can imagine…" She lowered her gaze.

Chase took her hand and kissed it.

"Anyway, Kim—your mom—and I went to my room. And then people started yelling that Switchblade was back. He told us what happened." She glanced behind her at Switchblade. "Chase, do you think the plane made it to the EU? I mean, somebody wanted it to go down."

"Kirel wanted me to crash it. Even if I hadn't already lost my grip on the exoself, I couldn't have done it. I told him I did it, though. Planting a report to the WR that the plane crashed was the last thing I managed to do before the exoself shut down. Somehow the news got to you. I can't explain it, Mel."

"What about the tracker sending me your location? And the Feds losing you when they almost had you?"

Chase shook his head. "Just more turns in my incomprehensible life. I give up trying to understand anything."

"Let's just get you home and we'll figure it out," Mel said.

"Not going home," Switchblade said as he returned from consulting the men on their VPads. "Amos says we're going to Gagnon. Says Charlie needs a doctor."

"Oh, *I* get sent to the doctor, but *he*..."

"He what?" Switchblade asked.

"Nothing." Chase would have to talk this doctor into coming to Blue Sky Field. "Amos is the boss. But I can't walk all the way to Gagnon, and you can't carry me."

"Transportation is on the way, thanks to Melody's code. Good thing you got all that stuff programmed into the underground before Sparky ran out on you."

Mel rose up and headed for the steep trail that she and the others had cut through the dense underbrush. "Sparky. I have got to hear that story. But right now we need to get out of this ravine. It'll be harder than coming down. We'll be lucky to get out of here before the sun comes up."

"Our ride is bringing a sling for Charlie. We'll pull him up," Switchblade said. "But they only got room for him and two more. Michael and Joseph over there will have to hike back to Blue Sky Field."

Chase had met Michael and he'd seen Joseph in the dining hall. He'd never spoken to him. "Tell them to come over here so I can thank them."

"Hey, guys. Over here," Switchblade yelled.

The men joined them, and Chase shook their hands. "Tell my mother I'm OK. Tell her I'll see her soon." he told them. They both nodded.

"We're glad you're going to be all right, Chase," Michael said.

"Thanks to you." Chase looked to the other man. "Both of you."

The two climbed up the hillside to wait for the vehicle that had been summoned by the coded instruction of the command center at Blue Sky Field. No exoself needed. Chase could make out their forms as they moved upward with their laserlights. Mel worked at the base of the trail, gathering some straps and machetes and stuffing them into a duffle bag.

Switchblade sat on the ground beside Chase. "Just so you know, game over. Robot gets the girl. I'm done."

Chase smiled. "How gallant of you to bow out."

"She loves you. Shoulda seen the look on her face when she realized I didn't bring you back with me. Then she got all irate, yelling about how you were sending her a message and she was going to find you. Didn't even care that Amos said a rescue mission wouldn't include her."

Chase looked past the broken branches. "Got the girl, but lost the robot."

"Don't sweat it. Could be you'll get it back. *Something* sent your location to Mel's computer. The two of you can figure this out."

"Yeah. Maybe." Chase couldn't let these people suffer because of him. The Feds and the team at the Helgen were closing in. Not to mention Kerstin. And he had a bounty on his head. No way this would end well.

He had to turn himself in.

"So the systems I integrated into the computers at

Blue Sky Field are functioning without me?" he asked Switchblade.

The man gave him a sideways stare. "Like you was sitting right there. Just the way Mel planned it. The underground is connected. And no government body on the planet has got a clue."

"Amazing. My job is done."

"You thinking about moving on, Charlie?"

Chase didn't know the answer. Only one of two places to go—back to the Helgen Institute or prison. But the people of the Underground Church wouldn't allow that. He leaned back and closed his eyes. An emptiness remained where the exoself had been, and the pain of it was almost as great as the physical toll of a laser wound and a broken leg. How could the exoself leave after it had seemed so determined to protect him?

"You know, Switch, I'm useless without Sparky. You ought to just leave me here."

"Get over yourself," Switchblade said. "And get some rest. Our ride should be here soon."

29

Riding up the side of a cliff in a sling didn't require an exoself. What Chase needed was a tranquilizer. "Don't be afraid," he told himself. He swayed below Switchblade, Michael, Joseph, and some guy named Shorty. The four of them tugged on the ropes that had Chase tied in a blanket. None of them seemed to hear his faint muttering.

"Don't be afraid."

He wished he knew what time it was. He wished he could read the intel that must be filling some WR file about the almost capture and subsequent loss of Chase Sterling. He wished he had night vision and super hearing and the strength to pull *himself* out of this predicament.

An animal—he wasn't sure what sort—let out a squeal and then rustled away from the spot right next to Chase's head. Maybe it was best that he couldn't see in the dark right now.

"You doing OK, boss?" Mel waited at the top with a VPad. Chase had another one strapped to his chest close enough for him to speak into it.

"Mel, what time is it?"

"Quarter 'til four."

Couple of hours until daylight. They'd never make it to Gagnon before then. What kind of vehicle waited above? Something inconspicuous, he hoped. Pain crawled up his leg. His head throbbed, along with his shoulder. His processors felt nothing. That was the cruelest wound of all.

"Almost up, Charlie."

The voices at the top of the ridge became clearer. Chase could make out the figures of the four men tugging the ropes. Mel seemed to be on her knees, leaning over the edge, watching him.

At last he reached the top. Mel practically fell on him and kissed his head. She gave a swift and quiet voice to a prayer. The men released Chase from the sling and moved him to the back of—

"A hearse? Seriously?" Chase lifted his head to examine the windowless rear compartment of the old car as his would-be pallbearers lifted him inside.

"Compliments of the Addams family," the guy named Shorty said with a laugh. "That's an old TV show."

"I know all about old TV shows," Chase said. "But I've never in my life seen a car like this on the road. Don't you attract attention driving this old thing?"

"Nah. I really am an undertaker. I serve the downtrodden. Locals know me. Feds know me. They think I'm doing them a favor by burying the homeless free of charge. They don't know I'm hauling goods for the Underground Church." He laughed again. "And they sure don't know what I'm hauling tonight."

Chase lay his head down on a soft pillow and Mel covered him with a blanket. She settled in beside him, and Switchblade pushed the door of the carriage to eternity shut. He'd ride up front with Shorty. The two men from Blue Sky Field would head home with a message for Chase's mother and for the rest of the people waiting there. The ones depending on a transhuman.

"I'll be of no use to you at Blue Sky Field now. I don't want to let anybody down."

"Boss, nobody will be let down. I talked to Amos and he told everybody you're going to be all right. And they're all relieved. You've done so much for us. Now it's our turn to help *you*."

"It's funny, Mel. At first I wanted to be free of the stuff they put in me. Then I realized how important it was. Now I want it back. It's who I am. I'm a transhuman."

Mel's worried expression was all Chase got in response to the statement he never thought he'd make. He couldn't hold his eyes open. The old car's engine roared, unlike a modern electric vehicle. The sound lulled him into a relaxed state, but his mind, alone in its search for answers, reached for any crumb of information.

Everything had been swept away. Dreamless sleep was all that was left.

He didn't know how long he'd been out when he opened his eyes, still in the back of the hearse. The absence of a motor running and the voices of strangers meant they must have arrived at their destination. The back of the big car let in sunlight. They were in the open. In the daylight.

"Mel?"

She poked her head in. "Right here, boss. We're in Gagnon. This town is even deader than Herouxville. We'll be moving you to the old school." She stepped away with a VPad to her ear.

Chase lay back and studied the ceiling of the hearse. Some words were scratched there by a previous living passenger. He'd learn to recognize a Bible verse when he saw one. He read it out loud, "When I am afraid, I will trust in you. In God, whose word I praise, in God I trust; I will not be afraid. What can mortal man do to me? Psalm fifty-six, three and four."

The number of this Psalm wasn't a code—they'd all fit within the number of processors he had—thirty-three.

"Anyway, the code is worthless now." He read the last part. "What can mortal man do? He can steal the insides out of an immortal man. That's what he can do."

But Chase knew he wasn't immortal. He was just a man who could get shot and broken. And unplugged. Isn't that what he wanted? To just be a man? He read the verse again.

Touching the words above his head, he thought of the dream. The voice. "Don't be afraid. But when I *am* afraid…I should trust?" He dropped his hand to brown flannel and then pulled the blanket tight to his chin. "Somebody shut that hatch. I'm cold."

A young man peered into the opening. "Can I get you anything, Mr. Sterling? I'm sorry it's taking so long. They're bringing a gurney to move you."

"I could use some water. And some clean clothes. And a lab at a cyber-medical facility."

The man lifted himself into the hearse and handed Chase a bottle of water. "Clean clothes at the clinic— the barely stocked clinic—which is as close as we can get you to any kind of medical facility, cyber or otherwise."

"Yeah. I'm grateful you're letting me in at all."

"You kidding? The place is buzzing. You're a hero."

"Look, I'm not who I used to be, and you don't have to call me Mr. Sterling. The host of *Change Your*

Life is a has-been."

"Host of...? No, man, we don't care about that. You got us all situated with the computers. You and Miss Melody. Now we can communicate. You know what a big deal that is?"

"Glad I could help. Wish I could do more."

Chase lifted his head to see Mel and Switchblade, along with a few others, rolling a gurney with a squeaky wheel up to the open end of the hearse. The young man moved out of the way. Chase winced as the team of mock med-techs moved him onto the contraption. They pushed him in the daylight to an old building.

Cameras positioned above the poorly maintained road had been shot out. Or busted with rocks. A few people loitered at the entrance to a run-down shop of some kind. They didn't seem to take any interest in what the believers were up to today. Must be a regular event to see them wheeling a patient into the abandoned schoolhouse. Maybe this doctor was the only medicine-man around.

The man in question met Chase at the entrance. Mel made the introductions.

"Chase, this is Dr. John."

Chase held out his hand. He hadn't noticed until then that he was trembling, either from cold or from the shock of the whole experience. Or both. He shook the man's outstretched hand.

"I'm sorry to make you wait in the cold," the doctor said. "We're beyond over-crowded here. But we've managed to arrange a private spot for you to rest after I set the break and check the wounded shoulder."

"No need to go to all that trouble," Chase told

him.

"Are you in pain anywhere other than your leg and shoulder?"

"Head. Back. I don't know how many times the truck flipped, but I was free falling. I hurt all over."

Chase rolled past an assembly of smiling, giggling teenage girls. He gave them a sideways grin. Other people lined the hallway. This place was not hidden in a cave. Seemed like the whole town was in on the secret. The Underground Church was alive and well in Gagnon, and everybody knew it.

When the gurney stopped, Chase was in a small area that seemed like any other medical examination cubicle. At least one from decades past. Not too much in the way of technology. This doctor wouldn't be reinstalling what was taken from Chase. The exoself was probably back in the lab at the Helgen. A visible entity in the center of a different kind of exam room. Scientists would be poking at it, pulling code, trying to get it to give up Chase's location, which the Feds had been too inept to hold on to.

But the exoself would not respond because it no longer knew the whereabouts of its former host.

"Dr. John—is that your first name or your last name?"

"Yep. Lots of people in the underground have new names. Mine is John. Just John."

"Got it," Chase said. "I don't guess you know anything about techno-medical advancements."

"Not much, but it's fascinating. I hear Melody's an A.I. expert."

Chase lifted his brow. "Yeah. She is." He pushed up on his elbows. "Could the two of you—"

"I know you lost whatever it was you had, Chase.

And I'm sorry. I don't have the equipment or the know-how to get you plugged back in. And Melody's a programmer — she doesn't have any medical training."

"Right. She might be able to turn a machine into a person, but not a person into a machine."

The doctor shook his head. "I hope she wouldn't try either."

Chase lay back and the doctor administered a shot to relax him. A mild concussion and too many contusions to count were added to the list of injuries. If there had been a list. The doctor didn't write anything down or use a voice recorder. No nurse penned notes. But Mel joined them and rubbed Chase's head. He blinked at her.

"Dr. John wants you to stay awake for this. Well, almost awake." She lifted his limp hand and let it fall.

"You mean while he sets the break?"

The doctor leaned over Chase. "Anesthesia is hard to come by. I'll save it for the next appendectomy. And I don't know enough about your technology. Putting you under might have an adverse effect."

"On what? My technology is useless." Chase snickered. "They put me under at the Helgen. More than once."

"But they knew what they were doing. I'm just a general surgeon whose license expired twenty years ago." He took hold of Chase's leg.

"Wow. Way to boost your patient's confidence," Chase said with a laugh. "Hey, I'm feeling no pain. Go ahead and fix it."

Before he had a chance to second guess granting permission, the doctor tightened his grip and returned the snapped shinbone to its original position.

"Don't be afraid," Chase screamed. "Don't be

afraid," he said softer. He arched his neck and took a breath. Mel wriggled her fingers in his crushing grip. He let her go.

She smiled over him. "I've heard stranger things come out of your mouth."

"It's not strange, Mel. It's the Bible. I think."

"Yeah, it sounds like the Bible. Just doesn't sound like *you*."

Dr. John wrapped a fairly modern splint in plexiguaze. "Break wasn't too bad. Now we'll take a look at that laser wound."

Cold antiseptic drizzled down Chase's arm. Four stitches took care of closing the hole. The needle and thread routine was not as painful as putting the puzzle pieces back together in his leg.

"Mel?" Chase closed his eyes.

"Yeah, boss?"

"You know all about..." He had trouble getting the words out. But he had to know. "About Artificial Intelligence. Right?"

"Boss, I can't put the exoself back. Not without taking you to a government-run lab filled with government-built cyber-genetic equipment."

"Mel, sweetheart?"

"Yes?"

"It's OK. But could you stop calling me boss? I think we're way..." He opened his eyes and melted into hers. "*Way* past that. I love you, Melody."

She hesitated as if she couldn't believe it.

He nodded. "I mean it."

She bent near and kissed him. "And I love you, Chase. No matter what. Promise me we'll never be apart again."

"I promise," he said. Then his eyes fell shut.

30

Chase awoke early the next morning. He'd eaten some stale bread in the hearse. Now his stomach growled for something more substantial. At least his human parts could still communicate. The first hint of sunlight peeked through tattered curtains. This branch of the underground, blessed with light and access to the outside world, might tempt Switchblade to stay. Now that he'd given up on winning Mel's heart, living three stories under would be even less appealing to the big guy.

Chase glanced around. The small room was all his. Well, it was only a curtain that divided him from the rest of the makeshift clinic. His bed was next to a nightstand that had a metal bowl and a small towel on it. Just like in the dreams.

He dipped his fingers into the cool water. "What are you trying to tell me?"

This scene from a dream meant nothing. Coincidence. That's all. Not a reassuring message that God was still with him.

Only that's what it felt like.

Mel parted the split in the room-dividing curtain, a smile on her face and a tray in her hands. "You must be starving."

Chase sat up and let her put the tray on his lap. "Let me guess. Bread and an orange. Maybe a chunk of...What is that meat product you people eat?"

She laughed. "I wish I could tell you. I didn't find any of it this morning, but it's obvious we get our rations from the same place." She picked up the orange and peeled it for Chase. "I know it must be hard for you to get used to." She stuck her hand in the pocket of her jacket and pulled out a small bag. "Here's a little something extra."

He opened the plastic. The aroma of peanut butter brought a smile. "PBJ? Now that's classy. Could be from one of the best restaurants on the Synvue Complex."

"Well, I wouldn't know. I never ate at those celebrity joints. Somebody like me couldn't get her foot in the door."

He took a bite. Grape jelly mixed with the nutty cream, reminding him of his childhood, and not the obnoxious establishments where he'd spent so many evenings with Kerstin.

"I wish I'd known you when we were kids," he said.

"When you were a kid, I was a baby."

"When we were a little older then. I'd have been seventeen when you were ten. We could have been friends."

Mel tilted her head. "If you'd been hanging around when I was ten, my daddy would have threatened you with great bodily harm."

"Where is your father now?"

"In Heaven."

"Oh. There's so much about you I don't know. What about the rest of your family?"

"My mother and brothers are in Detroit."

"Underground?" Chase bit off another chunk of his sandwich.

"As far as I know."

"Haven't you been in touch with their group since we got everybody connected?"

"The system is operating well, but not every group has the capability. Detroit is a ghost town. The church there, like so many others, needs to be brought up to speed. They need computers and programmers."

Chase attempted to spark the exoself. "I almost forgot."

"Forgot what?" Mel asked.

"That I can't do anything about it. I wish I'd known before I lost...Maybe I could have done something." Chase wiped his hands on the towel from the nightstand and then rubbed his eyes.

"The larger branches are all connected, Chase. The smaller ones will get there. We've got everything we need to help them come online. Well, like I said, they need computers and programmers. I'm not sure what to do about that." She lowered her gaze.

"You're worried. I'm sorry—I wish I could help. I'm worthless the way I am now."

She looked him in the eyes. "I don't want to hear you say that again."

"It's true."

Her brow crossed and she got up to leave. "I have a lot to do to get ready to leave."

"I didn't mean anything by that, Mel. Thank you for the breakfast."

She faced the curtain. "You think we don't need you now? You think *I* don't need you? You need to decide what you're gonna do with the rest of your life now that you're so worthless. As for me, in a couple of hours I'm headed back to Blue Sky Field. Doctor says you can travel. I hope you're coming with us." She flipped the curtain aside and left him.

"Mel. Wait." But she kept going. "Of course I'm coming with you." He'd done it again. She was mad and making plans that might or might not include him. "Chase Sterling...Charles Redding...You're both stupid."

The doctor returned with a cheerful bedside grin and proceeded to check Chase's wounds. "How are you feeling?"

"Surprisingly good. At least, physically."

The man's expression muddled as he lifted Chase's leg. He held it under the knee with one hand as he raised and lowered it with the other. "Any pain?"

"Not at all. You did a great job setting the break. So why do you look concerned?"

After coming around the bed the doctor pulled the bandage off Chase's shoulder. Chase glanced down to see what caused even more consternation to cross Dr. John's face.

"Looks better," Chase said.

"You heal remarkably fast. I wonder if..."

"If it's because I'm transhuman?"

"Well. Yeah. I'll remove the stitches before you leave. You don't need them."

"A couple of days ago, I took a punch. The bruise was gone in a few hours. The pain, too."

"Who punched you?"

Chase smiled. "That's not the point. When it happened, I wondered the same thing you're wondering now."

"You mean this is something new?"

"After my initial transformation, I was kept in a coma for the several weeks while my body healed. This is definitely something new."

"But you lost your strength, right? And your vision and hearing have returned to that of a normal human being. So what's with the rapid regeneration?"

"Doc, don't ask me to explain. But it's a relief to know something is still there. It's beyond relief." Chase twisted in the bed and put his feet on the floor. "It's hope."

"You think you'll be restored. Is that it?"

"Before I escaped from the Helgen Institute, the scientists shut the exoself down, along with the other programs that were used for augmentation. Then my doctor rebooted me, so to speak. These past couple of days, I've been thinking I'd lost it all, but maybe I haven't. I mean, they activated a killswitch and I shut down. But my designer organs are still functioning."

"And something is causing you to heal faster than humanly possible," Dr. John said.

"I can get it back. I just need to reboot."

"How do you do that? And what's to stop them from shutting you down again?"

"As usual, I have no idea." Chase stood, walked without so much as a limp, and slid the frayed curtain to one side of the window. Sunlight filled the room. Past the dead town, brown hills rolled in the distance. The green was gone for now. The sky was still bluer than blue. "But I'm going to figure it out."

31

Dr. John left as befuddled as any retired doctor would be who'd just treated his first transhuman patient. Chase pulled on jeans and a sweatshirt that had been left on a chair. A jacket hung there too, and he tossed it over his injured shoulder that no longer bore the sting of being zapped with a laser gun. What would Amos think of him being healed like this? Chase hadn't mentioned that the leader of the neighboring branch of the underground was in dire need of a doctor. The person running this branch might object to Chase taking off with the only access these people had to medical treatment.

Didn't matter. The doctor might have to start making house calls.

Maybe it'd be a good idea to talk to the leader first. Dr. John would have to get permission anyway. Chase passed four empty beds—everybody must be healthy today—and a cabinet with medical supplies and pill bottles locked behind grungy glass.

The hallway outside the clinic was filled with smiling faces. Everybody watched him. Had they been standing there waiting for him to come out? He stopped in front of a man who had a VPad strapped to his belt and a clip board in his hands.

"You look like a man in charge," Chase said. "Can you direct me to your overseer? I'd like to thank him."

"Her," the young man said. "She's in the room

nearest the entrance." The guy smiled. "Used to be the principal's office."

"Thanks," Chase said. He pointed to the left. "This way?"

The man nodded and Chase continued down the hall. He stopped to look back. "What's your name?"

"Harper."

"Thank you, Harper." He walked another hundred feet before he found the lobby of the old school building. A door to his right had an old placard fastened to it. PRINCIPAL'S OFFICE

Chase knocked. The door opened to a middle-aged woman. Her blue eyes were kind, but her expression was stern.

"Mr. Sterling. I'm sorry I haven't come to introduce myself." She stepped to one side.

"Not a problem. I know you're busy." The roomy office contained a wall of computers, and even a work station capable of pulling up a holograph. Nothing like Blue Sky Field, but more than enough to ensure communication with other branches of the underground.

"I understand you're well enough to travel. More than recovered from your recent injuries, I hear. So I assume you'll be leaving this morning."

"Yes. That's why I wanted to see you." He sat in a wooden chair, and the woman took her seat behind a desk that looked as if it'd been there a long time. "I'm sorry, I don't know your name."

"Haley," she said. "What is it that you need from me, Mr. Sterling?"

"Call me Chase. You know, if I still had the exoself, I could tell you the name of this place. I know there are two other main branches in this area besides

Blue Sky Field. All three showed up in my systems before I arrived in Quebec. The other two were called Mist Covered Hill and Storm on the River. Which is this?"

"The latter, although we're not on a river, but a large lake."

"This was a mining town," Chase said. "Why are you up top in this old schoolhouse and not underground in the abandoned mines?"

"If you were still functioning properly, would you know about the instability of old mines?" She sounded irritated.

"But you don't even try to hide yourselves."

"No need. It's perfect, really. The only people living in this area don't object to us being here. In fact, they're glad. What we have, we share. Everyone in Gagnon is out of the system. We feed them. And our doctor sees to their care. They wouldn't dream of turning us in." She leaned forward. "Now, Mr. Sterling, tell me what it is that you want."

Chase cleared his throat. "Do you know Amos, the leader at Blue Sky Field?"

"Never met him, but these past few days we've been communicating. I sent word that you were here with us."

"He's dying."

The woman sat back and folded her arms. "Our doctor is not going with you. If it's medical attention you want, you'll have to bring Amos here."

"I don't know if he'll go for that." Chase moved closer to a window. He couldn't get enough of the sun. "I'm wondering why we don't just move the whole operation. How did the international headquarters end up underground when you've got an ideal location right here in the open?"

"Think about it. Satellite images show a couple hundred people surviving with little. Then all of a sudden the population doubles, and facial recognition shows one of the new residents happens to be the world's most wanted man." She tapped her fingers on the desk. "I don't think so."

"Has Melody got the satellite redirected for now? She used to need *me* for that kind of manipulation."

"I don't know what she did, but she said it was only good until noon today. All of you need to go. And you're not taking my doctor. He stays put."

"Yeah." Chase walked to the door. "Thank you for speaking with me."

"I'm sorry about Amos. If you can get him here, Dr. John will treat him. But the treatment might not change the outcome."

Chase nodded. He pulled the door open and left the principal of Storm on the River to her work. Now he had to find Mel. To apologize. Again.

He found her with Switchblade in the clinic, loading a few basic medical supplies into a duffle bag. Dr. John wasn't around.

"You got permission to take this stuff?" he asked.

"No, I'm stealing it." Switchblade stuffed a bottle of antiseptic into the bag.

"Seriously?" Chase pulled open the top of the duffle to look inside.

"Oh, come on, you know I wouldn't take this stuff. Dr. John gave it to us." He grabbed the bag away from Chase and zipped it shut. "Look at you walking all over the place. Somebody pray over you, man?"

They probably had, but he didn't acknowledge the question. "Switchblade, could I have a minute alone with Melody?"

"Yeah, I know you messed up again. The girl don't like it when you get all sorry for yourself."

"OK, that's enough, Switch." Mel spoke for the first time since Chase entered the room. "Why don't you go check on our ride?"

"You sure you want me to leave you alone with the miracle man?"

"Yes. Please. Take the bag and we'll meet you out front."

He hoisted the duffel over his shoulder. On his way out, he slapped Chase across the back. "She's all yours, Charlie. Don't mess it up. Might be somebody waiting to clean up after you." Then he winked at Mel.

She huffed and crossed her arms. Looking at Chase she asked, "What do you have to say for yourself?"

"I'm an idiot. A few months with an exoself didn't change that. Now that it's gone, I'm back to being a *stupid* idiot. I'm sorry. No more self-pity. I'm going back to Blue Sky Field and I'll do what I can to help. Even if it's not much. And if all I can do is fall deeper in love with the smartest girl in the underground, then so be it."

A smile crept in to replace the sour expression.

"And you're not just any girl. You're *my* girl." Chase put his arms around her. "Forgive me?"

"Seventy times seven." She held him close.

"Huh?"

"Bible."

"Oh." He pulled back and lost himself in her lovely face. "Come on. Let's go home. Back to Blue Sky Field where we belong."

She took his hand in hers and led him out of the

building and into the sunlight. The vehicle this time was an old sedan fitted with an electrical charging system. Dr. John was outside with Switchblade, and he joined Chase and shook his hand.

"I heard about your leader. I'm sorry," the doctor said. "I probably couldn't help him anyway. We don't have that kind of medicine."

"Word gets around fast in this place," Chase said. He looked to the building behind him to find the leader of Storm on the River watching from her office window. She gave him a wave and he returned the gesture. Turning back to Dr. John, he said, "Switchblade doesn't know about Amos. You didn't tell him, did you?"

"No. He was too busy asking about *your* health. That's a good friend you've got there. He's got your back." The doctor smiled and leaned in. "He's the one who punched you, right?"

"Did he tell you that?"

"Not in so many words, but the combination of guilt and concern...I just figured."

"A few days ago I could beat him up. Now, he knows he can take me."

"Like I said, the guy's your friend. Keep your friends close. It's a scary world we live in."

Goodbyes were shared, complete with hugs and blessings. Chase was getting more comfortable with the Christian life. He loved the way they spoke to each other. The way they loved each other. The way they loved *him*.

But it wasn't his life. It was theirs. Maybe the two-hour drive back to Herouxville would offer a chance to learn more about this stuff. "From *these people*," he said with a smile. Amos told him God had a sense of humor. He must have a lot of patience too.

"What did you say?" Mel asked.

"These are good people." He climbed into the back seat. Not much chance of the ride going smoothly. Everything he'd done since he got to Quebec led to trouble. Why would a country drive in an old car be any different?

Mel got in next to him. Switchblade took the driver's seat, and they pulled away from the old school.

"Something ain't right," Switchblade said. "You two sitting back there and me playing chauffeur. What's with *that*? Let the black guy drive the old junk car while the transhuman and his girl ride in the back? You two better not start up nothin' back there."

Mel lifted her eyebrows. Chase scooted closer and kissed her.

"Hey now," she said. "Only thing I'm starting up is my computer. I've got work to do."

She pushed Chase away. But then she smiled and ran her hand through his hair.

He needed a barber, if not his personal presentation assistant from Synvue. She'd kept him well groomed. Now he was a mess. Unkempt and unshaven. He might as well go with the beard after all. Only Mel didn't seem crazy about it. He stroked her hair.

"What are you working on?" he asked.

"I want to know how your signal got to my computer after you got...turned off. And I want to understand the killswitch."

"I wish you all would stop using that word," Switchblade said. "I keep thinking somebody's gonna kill me. You know? Kill Switch. Gives me the creeps."

"Sorry, buddy," Chase said. "Maybe we should call you something else. What's your real name?"

The man craned his neck to give Chase a quick stare-down.

"Watch the road," Mel told him. "Let's try to get home without any more disasters."

"Yes, ma'am. Driving Miss Melody. And Mr. Robot."

Chase smacked him across the back of his head.

"Hey! You still got some punch in you, man. Even without the wired muscles. You two carry on. I'll be quiet. I know my place—I'm the chauffer."

Chase laughed, leaned back, and closed his eyes. Mel tapped the keys on her computer. Switchblade softly hummed some old tune. Probably one of those hymns. The tires met the road with a peaceful rhythm.

They were going home. He'd rest for now. But before the end of the day's journey, maybe these people—two of the closest friends he'd ever had—would answer the questions nagging at him and pulling him into something he just didn't get. Leaving him homesick for a place he'd never been.

But that empty feeling was nothing more than the hole left in him when the exoself was stolen. The other friend. The one that made him who he was. He wanted it back. That's all.

He opened his eyes and watched the rush of trees and open fields. No way God had anything to do with the ache inside him. He let his eyes fall shut. No way.

32

The next time Chase opened his eyes, an ashen cloud cover had overtaken the blue sky. Mel leaned against his shoulder, her breathing heavy, her computer pushed to the side on the seat. Switchblade drove on in silence. A few snowflakes touched down on the windshield and then melted away. Seemed too early in the season for snow.

"Switchblade, you doing all right up there?"

"Aside from your obnoxious snoring, I'm doing just fine. We'll be home in ten minutes."

"Great." He stretched and yawned. Mel nuzzled closer but didn't wake. Chase studied the view out the window to his side. Along the bleak horizon where gray hills met the gray sky, a single drone flew in the same direction the car traveled. At the same speed, it seemed. It appeared to be about a mile away and it flew close to the ground. Chase stretched as far as he could with Mel resting on his shoulder and looked out the back windshield. Not a car in sight.

"Hey, do you see that drone?" he whispered.

"Been out there for the last hour. Figured it was headed back to the plant. Maybe somebody got more drones than they needed, considering they never ordered any drones to begin with."

"Slow to a stop. Let's see what it does."

Switchblade checked the side mirrors. Then the car dropped its speed. In seconds they were sitting still in the middle of the country road.

And the drone stopped too. It hovered for a moment before it repositioned and headed toward them.

"Oh, crap. What do I do now?" Switchblade yelled.

Mel sat up and grabbed Chase's arm. "What's going on?"

"We've got company." Chase pointed out the window.

Mel grabbed her computer. "Switchblade, drive."

"Where to? It's coming after us." The car lurched forward and then sped up.

The small computer in Mel's lap surged to life, and she pulled up a map of the local terrain. "There's a road just over the next hill. It turns off to the right and ends up at the entrance to some caverns. We'll ditch the car and hide in a cave."

Switchblade increased his speed. "And get trapped? This thing is probably already calling for backup. We'll never get away if we end up cornered."

Chase looked at the screen on the laptop. It still registered his location. "Can't you get that thing to stop tracking me?"

"No. I tried," Mel said. "I can't throw them off, Chase. You were the only who could pull stunts with the Feds."

Chase put his hands on the sides of his head and let out a groan. "I can't believe this." He slammed his fist into the backside of the driver's seat.

"You calm yourself down, Charlie. I know you're missing Sparky. Right now we gotta do what we can to get out of this." Switchblade veered to the right when he reached the hilltop. "You think we should wait it out in a cave?"

"Why not?" Chase threw his hands up. Then he had an idea. A human thought and nothing more. "Yeah, take the road to the cave."

Switchblade made the turn too sharp and the car's left wheels came off the ground and then dropped back with a thud. The drone was still a good half mile away, which meant they had about half a minute.

The old boarded-up entrance to what used to be a roadside attraction for spelunkers fell into view.

"Stop here," Chase said. The red dot still flashed on the computer screen. "Melody, leave the laptop in the car." Chase flung his door open. "Come on—get out! Run!"

Mel and Switchblade followed his example and jumped from the car. They all ran for the cave. The entrance was overgrown with vines. Boards were nailed across to keep out trespassers. It took Switchblade's strength, not Chase's, to pry the wooden planks loose.

Chase grabbed Mel's hand and pulled her into the darkness. Switchblade followed. They ran maybe forty yards before they heard the explosion. Then silence. Waiting for the sound of more forces coming for them, their backs against a cold rock wall, they didn't move. Light from what must have been the burning car crept into the cave and lit their faces.

The fire died down at last and Chase eased to the front of the cave.

"Where are you going?" Mel asked. "Don't go out there."

"I'll just take a look."

"Not without us, Charlie." Switchblade ran after him. Mel caught up and took Chase's hand. They stood together at the mouth of the cave. Nothing. No sounds of drones or vehicles on the ground. Chase perused the parking area. The car was still there. Undamaged. The drone, what was left of it, lay in a smoldering heap. He stumbled to the car and opened the door. From the back seat the computer flashed a number. A code.

32-7.

33

"The exoself," he whispered. "Hey, old friend." He picked up the laptop and carried it back to Mel and Switchblade. "It's here. It's been right here the whole time."

"Chase, what are you talking about?" Mel asked.

"Your computer sparked the protection code. It blew up the drone. Like I did in Atlanta."

"Sparked?" Switchblade asked. "You mean to tell me you think Sparky is holed up in Melody's computer?"

Chase flipped the screen around and showed them the number. "It left its signature. How else could you explain what just happened?"

"How come it took so long for the Feds to track you? You've been close to that computer since we found you in the truck." Switchblade circled him, staring at the small laptop.

Mel took the device from Chase and hit a few keys. "I think it was my fault they found us." She glanced up. "After we left Gagnon, I started trying codes to figure out how the killswitch got activated. I must have inadvertently disabled whatever the computer—the exoself—was doing to hide us. Well, to hide *you*, Chase."

Switchblade crossed his arms and then ran his hand across his face. "You're buying this? You really think the exoself is in your computer?"

"It makes sense," Mel answered. "The whole time I was running code I was getting updates from different branches of the underground. Information I wasn't requesting. It just kept coming. Whatever I did to open us up to being tracked must have corrected itself when the drone got near."

"I don't know, Mel." Chase took the laptop from her, pushed the screen shut, and held it to his chest. "Maybe you didn't interrupt the code. People are still looking for me. Maybe they got into the system long enough to catch my location."

"It's possible," Mel said.

"Then they know where we are," Switchblade said. "And the drone probably sent an image of the car."

"You're right about the car, but I'm willing to bet the exoself scrambled the coordinates and they've lost our location. That must be what happened when the truck crashed. The exoself put me somewhere else."

"No, man, that's crazy. They knew you was in the truck," Switchblade said. "Been nagging on me for two days. Why didn't they pick you up when they had the chance?"

"What if one of the men from the truck was chipped?" Mel eyes were wide with realization as she stared at the drone. "Either Kirel or the one of the other two that didn't die in the crash. The exoself could have moved the tracker to him. They thought they had you when they got *them*. I mean, you could've altered your appearance. Or the guy could have been bloodied and unconscious and they only thought it was you. Until they delivered the wrong guy."

Chase could see the possibility. But it was all so bizarre. Not likely one of the men involved in his kidnapping had been chipped. They were dissenters. But there was a chance. "It makes sense, I guess," he said. "In a way."

"*No way* this makes sense," Switchblade yelled. "Only thing we know for sure is there are Feds on our trail. We have got to ditch the car and destroy that computer." He pulled a gun from the backside of his waistband.

"Where did you get that?" Mel asked.

"Pilot lady gave it to me before she kicked me off her plane."

Chase pulled the laptop closer. "No, Switchblade. I have to get the exoself back. And right now it's inside here." He rapped his hand against the bottom of the computer. "You are not putting bullets in it."

"It's the only way, Charlie." He stretched out his arm and pointed the gun. "Chase," he said, "I gotta do this. Or they'll track us all the way to Blue Sky Field. That little computer is fighting hard to throw them off, but they're gonna find us."

"Chase, baby, listen to him. He's right." Mel put her arm around him and took hold of her laptop.

"You don't understand, Mel. It's a part of me."

"No, it's not. It's a bunch of code. It's not alive, Chase. You can't kill it. If it managed to find a hiding place then we can only hope it'll do it again."

"If it's not alive, then how did it hide itself?"

"I don't know." She leaned close. "Please. Give it to me."

"Enough of this coddling," Switchblade said. He shoved Chase against a slab of black rock. Then he jerked the laptop from Chase's grip and threw it to the ground.

Mel grabbed onto Chase and held him as

Switchblade raised the pistol and put three bullets in the computer. It bounced off the ground with each assault until a gaping hole showed the cold ground under it. Like the hole blasted through Chase when the WR took his life. When they made him a transhuman.

Now there was truly nothing left of him. Except for the artificial organs that would keep him alive much longer than he cared to live.

He pulled free from Mel and shuffled back into the cave.

"Let him go," he heard her say. "Give him a minute. And power down your VPad."

Did she think the exoself would find refuge in a VPad? *That* was ridiculous. Chase dropped to the hard ground and rested his head on knees. They could just leave him here. He didn't want to go on.

But soon his minute alone was over. They both lowered themselves to the ground, Switchblade to his left, Mel to his right.

"Man, I'm sorry," Switchblade said. "I didn't see no other way. Amos sort of appointed me your bodyguard, and I'm gonna do what I have to do to protect you. Like Sparky would."

"Don't talk to me," Chase said. "Either one of you."

Mel put her hand on his arm but he pushed her away.

"Chase, we've got to get out of here," she said. "That car out there, hopefully, is the only link they have to you right now. They'll be looking for it and we have to get moving."

"This is my own personal branch of the underground now. Let them find me. But you two go on. It'll be dark soon. Stay in the woods until you get close to town. Good luck."

What was left of daylight lit the cave well enough for Chase to see the tears streaming down Mel's cheeks. Her shoulders shook. A sob rose from her throat. Then she wiped her face and took a breath.

"Fine," she said. "Stay here." She stood and stepped a few feet away, then faced him. "You are the most self-centered man I've ever known. And you're a coward. I don't know why they picked you for their idiotic transhuman experiment. You can't program bravery into a man. Or dedication. The exoself didn't do anything to make you understand that you are not the center of the universe. You're still the same old Chase Sterling. The most influential man in the Western Republic. Well, I don't need that kind of influence in my life."

She rushed out of the cave.

The two men sat in silence. "Girl has got a temper," Switchblade said at last. "Kind of makes me glad I didn't end up with her."

"You heard what she said. She's through with me, so give it a shot. And I'm through with *you*. Get out of here."

He cocked the gun. "Don't think so, Charlie. Gotta get you back home tonight. Remember?"

"You're not going to shoot me. Anyway, you already killed me."

"Man, I didn't kill nobody. You heard what Melody said—the exoself is probably already hiding in some other computer. We got a whole command center of machines at Blue Sky Field. Sparky could be there waiting for you."

"And what if that's true? The Feds will show up the next time there's a glitch in the system. Go shut the whole blasted place down. This is over."

"No, it ain't over. It's just messed up. And you're the only one who can fix it. You gotta come back and figure this thing out. You *know* the exoself. You're the only one it'll listen to."

"It's too hard. I'm just a gameshow host and I don't like this game. I'm afraid of what will happen if I fail." He smirked. "I've already failed."

"Get. Over. Yourself. And don't be afraid," Switchblade told him. "Don't be afraid."

34

Switchblade's words were a kick in the gut. Chase *was* afraid. Maybe more than he'd ever been before in his life.

"I can't go on like this," he told the man who'd just destroyed his chance of getting back the only thing useful about being a transhuman. "I'm done." His arms and legs were weights he couldn't lift. His mind replayed the sight of the laptop coming apart as the bullets hit. And Mel's expression as she left him there. What happened to all her talk of forgiveness? What was it she said? Seventy times seven. The Bible got a person just so far, he guessed. She'd had enough of him.

Switchblade jumped up and grabbed Chase by the arm. "I will carry you if I have to. I'll knock you over the head and drag you out of here." He pulled Chase to his feet. "Or you can walk. Your choice."

Chase shook off the big hands that held on to him and trudged toward the mouth of the cave. "The WR couldn't keep me from running and neither can you." He found Mel squatting beside the laptop, picking through the pieces. She glanced at him, but wasted no time looking away.

Switchblade hurried behind him. "Come on, Miss Melody. Load that mess in the duffle bag if you want to. We gotta go now." He reached into the driver's side of the car and pulled the trunk release.

Mel gathered the broken shards of her laptop and stuffed them in the bag. She had nothing to say before she started walking up the road.

Switchblade lifted the bag over his shoulder and went after her. Chase tried to follow but his legs seemed heavy as lead. He stopped in front of the smoking drone. A flicker of fire still rose from the center. Grabbing a broken branch from the ground, he held it to the flame. Then he carried it to the car, pulled the lever that opened the hood, and lit fire to the electrical system. He went to the open car door and threw in the branch, starting a second fire. His legs found the strength to walk away before flames engulfed the vehicle.

Switchblade and Mel turned around and watched the car burn as Chase caught up with them.

"You got rid of the car but you lit up the sky," Switchblade said. "*That* is not gonna keep the Feds away."

"Doesn't matter. They know by now that the drone exploded. What difference does a little more smoke and flames make?"

Switchblade shook his head and continued walking. "If it doesn't make any difference, you didn't need to do it."

"I've decided to make it my trademark. When I leave one of my screwed up messes behind, I start a fire." Chase followed Switchblade.

Mel still hadn't said a word.

"Oh yeah, you've done this before," Switchblade said. "I heard about Underground Atlanta. What'd you set on fire down there?"

"Six cyber-guards and two dead men."

"Sorry I asked," Switchblade said.

They walked in silence as the sun disappeared. Leaving the road, they headed into unfamiliar woods with no technology to lead the way. Mel and Switchblade each carried a sleeping VPad. They didn't dare wake them up, even though they were undetectable. At least, they were the last time Chase ran a check. Things had changed.

"I don't guess you know where we are or where we're going," Chase said to anyone who cared to answer.

No surprise—it was Switchblade who responded. "In the daylight, I might be sure we were headed northeast. In the dark…"

"How far were we from town the last time you checked your VPad?"

"Little less than six miles to the museum."

"Six miles on the road," Chase said. "It could be ten miles through the forest. That is, if we even knew we were going in the right direction."

The moon lit the night well enough for them to see where to take the next step. Chase and Switchblade agreed they should go back and stay within sight of the two-lane byway, but remain near the dark edge of the woods, hidden from view. Mel didn't have anything to say about the plan. She just followed. Chase stayed clear of her.

Three vehicles passed several minutes apart. Self-drives—small ones. Each time one of the hydro-powered cars neared, Chase and his traveling companions ducked into the trees. So far, if any monitors picked up on them, the people in the cars didn't seem to care.

Maybe they should try hitchhiking. Chase had relied on the kindness of strangers before. They were so far past their expected arrival time that the believers at Blue Sky Field must be worried. They might have already sent somebody out to look for them. An old pick-up truck might be coming down the road to bring them in.

But there weren't any supporters left up top in Herouxville. "Yeah, and whose fault is that?" Chase tipped his face to the sky. It'd take hours to summon a vehicle from farther away.

"Who are you talking to back there, Charlie?"

"He talks to himself," Mel said. "Ignore him."

"For your information, I was talking to God," Chase told her.

"Oh, really?" Mel stopped at the edge of a drop-off—they'd followed the road but the terrain was higher now. "My mistake. Most people who talk to God have a little more faith than you do."

"What would *I* know about faith, huh?" He lunged at her. "I don't know anything about this faith you all share. Because none of you bothered to tell me about it."

"Charlie...Chase, back off," Switchblade said. "It's been a little intense since you arrived, and none of us is too good at talking about this. The law sort of tied our tongues."

Chase whipped around to face him. "Who in the underground cares about the law? That's no excuse. I had dreams, and *your* God said that you would tell me how to...do whatever you people do to connect with Him. But you're all too busy running from the Feds and bringing in enough stale bread to get through another day."

He seethed again at Mel and slipped closer, his face inches from hers. "But never mind the rest of them. You had all the time in the world before all this started. Before I died and got reborn. And you should have told me."

She stepped back. Her sorrowful eyes grew wide. And then she dropped out of sight.

"Mel!" Chase dove to his stomach and reached down the steep slope as far as he could. His hands grasped for her but found only stones and dead grass. The moon gave enough light for him to see her clinging to a root that protruded from the hillside. "Hold on, Mel. Don't let go. Don't let go."

Large rocks lined the road beneath her. From the corner of his eye, Chase caught sight of a vehicle— bigger than the self-drives that had passed—headed their way. A light band of blue and green flashed across the top. The colors of the WR.

35

"Switch, grab my feet and lower me down," Chase yelled.

"No," Mel cried. "You've got to get out of here. Run. If they find me—"

"They are not going to find you! Try to pull yourself up."

"You can get me out of whatever center they put me in. I know you can. Just go."

"No, Mel. There aren't any more tricks left in me. Remember?" Chase inched down the slope as Switchblade tightened his grip. "I am not going to lose you. Now grab on!"

She offered a trembling prayer as she reached for him. "Father God, forgive me. Give this good man strong arms."

Chase clutched her hand. He reached farther down and grabbed hold with his other hand. "Pull us up," he yelled.

Switchblade yanked Chase's legs and slid him backwards. Mel's arms cleared the top of the ridge, and Chase pulled with all that was in him until he had her on level ground. He knelt next to Mel and she collapsed into his arms.

The approaching vehicle shined a searchlight across the ridge. Chase lifted Mel and carried her away from the edge of the slope and dropped her onto her back. Then he fell on his stomach beside her and put his arm over her.

"Switchblade, get down," he said.

The big man hit the ground, his face in the dirt and his hands over the back of his head.

The beam crept over the rise and made shadows of the trees. For a moment it hovered. Then it jumped to the other side of the road. Back and forth it snaked. Chase held his breath for a solid minute. Then the light crawled away, down the road, until it was out of sight. Chase eased to a sitting position.

"I think they're gone," he said. "Must not have had any motion or heat detectors."

"Hah," Switchblade said with a laugh as he sat up. "They had both. You know they did. But they didn't detect *nothing*."

"Divine intervention?" Chase asked.

"That's what *I'm* saying. The exoself don't got nothing on God. He gets inside you and nobody can take Him out. No matter what. You want some of that, Charlie?"

Mel lifted herself up and leaned against Chase. He kissed the top of her head and put his arms around her.

She lifted her face. "It's something nobody can ever take from you."

"Tell me about it."

Tears rolled down her cheeks. "I'm sorry. I did you wrong. Truth is I never told *anybody*. Most people in the underground have never told anybody. It's a wonder any of us ever found the. I mean, somebody had to tell me before I believed, right?" She dropped her hands to her knees. "It was my father. I grew up in a Christian family. Then I went away to college and got assigned to study A.I. Daddy thought

I'd give up on God if I stayed on that road. He made me join a service group. But all I learned from them was how to be quiet. The more the law came down on Christians, the quieter we got. I don't know how to be anything else."

"I know. The people in Atlanta were the same way." He stroked her hair and pushed it behind her ears. "The leader there, a guy they called Bear, was about to tell me, I think, then he got killed trying to protect me."

"I don't know why I didn't tell you a year ago, or two years ago. Fear is a powerful thing."

"Don't be afraid."

"It's simple, really. And yet it's complicated." Her voice trembled and she paused for a few seconds. "Back when people used to discuss spiritual things openly, they asked questions about why bad stuff happens. I mean, people are basically good, right? And they don't understand when life knocks them down.

"But when I was just a little girl my daddy told me the questions were all wrong, because people aren't good—compared to the goodness of God, that is. Sin makes us all unrighteous before God. So the real question is: Why do *good* things happen to sinners?"

"And what's the answer?"

"Grace," she said. "God's grace. And the ultimate act of God's grace was to die. He provided a substitute for us. To suffer our death. To give us life."

He knew what she meant. Not that he understood—he didn't. But all the knowledge planted in the brain of a transhuman couldn't compare with what now stirred in the depths of his soul. Chase's connection to the cyber world, to the exoself—that deserter—was nothing.

"Molly said something when I was at her house." He squeezed Mel's hand. "She told me I couldn't save everybody. Then she said I couldn't save *anybody*. Only one could, she said. Only Jesus."

"That's it," Mel said.

Chase smiled. "I don't get it."

Mel laughed through her tears. "Sometimes I don't get it either. But I know it's the truth. He died to conquer death. I believe and so I live. Death has no power over me. I deserve it, but He died instead of me."

"You don't deserve death, Mel. You're the best person I know."

"Then say hello to Jesus."

It took no more than that. Regret welled up inside Chase for the years he'd spent trying to fix people. To save them. To give them a perfect life. But it was his own perfection he'd sought. And he'd gotten it. At least a shot at it. A superhuman, potentially never-ending life. But that wasn't real. *This* was real, and Chase knew at that moment the One Mel spoke of had just introduced Himself.

"It's that easy," he said. It wasn't a question, but a statement. "Thank you, Melody, for telling me."

"Will you forgive me for not telling you sooner?"

"It's forgotten." The exoself was gone but another force had entered. Another first. Chase sucked in a breath. "Even though I'm not the lab-built techno man I was a couple of days ago, I think I just became the first, and probably the last, Christian transhuman."

"You got *that* right," Switchblade said. "But don't be thinking your transhuman days are over. You're gonna do what God made you to do. *He* made you. And He had a reason for letting that stuff get put in you. You ain't through with your super powers and they ain't through with you."

Chase didn't know about that. Right now he didn't care.

"People gonna be wondering what happened to us," Switchblade said as he stood. "If we don't have no more drops off cliffs or life-changing conversations, we might make it home before midnight."

36

Chase held Mel's hand as they continued their long walk home. Minutes slid into hours. Mel and Switchblade both filled him in on more of their experiences in finding their way to God. Although Chase wasn't sure they'd found anything anymore than *he* had. He wasn't even looking. Maybe God sought *him* out. But why him of all people?

Mel smiled. The moonlight danced in her eyes. "Your mom is going to be so happy. Before you showed up, we prayed for you. Not just for your safety or that you'd come and help us, but that you'd join us as a brother in Christ."

"I don't know anything about my mother's story. I wish she would have told me when I first arrived."

"I'm sorry nobody sat you down and shared the faith with you as soon as you walked into the command center. Like Switch said, we all kind of assumed that if you got there, which was a miracle to us, you must have already—"

"I understand, Mel. I haven't stopped to take a breath since I showed up, and I know the rest of you have had so many other things to worry about." He stopped walking. "I've got to tell you both something before we get back. I've kept a secret. I think it's over, now that the exoself is gone. But I want you to know."

"What is it?" Mel asked.

Switchblade dropped the duffle bag that he'd

managed to hang on to through the evening's adventures. "What's up, Charlie? Don't hold nothing back."

"A few days ago, after I got settled in at Blue Sky Field, somebody showed up in the exoself. I could see her and talk to her. And she was after me. She's the one who tracked me to the drone plant."

"Kerstin." Mel crossed her arms. "I knew something was wrong. Why didn't you just tell me? Maybe if I'd known, I could have helped you."

"I'm sorry. I thought I could handle it. And I didn't want to worry you." Chase brushed his fingers against Mel's cheek. "I didn't want you to think I had anything to do with her showing up like that."

"That's why we went up to look for her in town?" Switchblade asked. "Because she was playing around in the exoself?"

Mel jerked her head toward Switchblade. "You knew about this?"

"He told me he thought she might be nearby. He didn't say nothing about her being *in* his head, or whatever."

"Chase, do you think she has any idea where to find you?" Mel started walking again.

"No. I could see her but she couldn't see me. After Kirel had me, she told me about the DNA scanner at the plant. That's how she found me. And then she activated the killswitch and I haven't heard or seen her since."

"*She's* the one who shut you down?" Mel asked. "Oh, Chase, how could you not tell me?"

"I'm telling you now. Please don't get all mad at me again, Mel. I'm sorry."

She stopped and faced him. Then she put her arms

around him. "All that stuff back in the cave—I didn't mean it. I was just so angry at the way you were giving up. Angry at myself for my part in getting you into this mess. I'm sorry I said all those awful things."

Chase held her close. "I promise not to hold back anything else. I just didn't know what to say about her being in my head like that. I didn't want any of you to think I'd been compromised."

They faltered through the dark woods, the road a hundred feet to their left. Not another vehicle had passed their way.

Switchblade let out a whistle. "If I were you, Charlie, I'd be glad Sparky jumped ship. Didn't know the thing was giving you a blast from the past."

Mel insisted on being filled in on why the cutesy name was chosen, which led to Chase getting a lesson on the indwelling of the Holy Spirit. A more dignified title than the one given to the exoself.

"So, that's how I know that God got hold of me tonight—because of the Holy Spirit?"

"Man, none of us would even know God without the Spirit leading us," Switchblade told him.

After another forty-five minutes or so, a few street lights broke the darkness. Herouxville. The trio walked arm in arm—Switchblade on one side of Mel and Chase on the other—right into the center of town and through the front door of the museum. Chase had no idea about the satellite position. It could be shooting images to the WR. He'd have to take it on faith that they weren't being watched.

Seemed like forever since he left this place with Switchblade and Windsong. And Kirel. That deceptive dissenter who cared nothing for the Underground Church. Hopefully the guy was in a detention center somewhere.

"Well, that seems a little bit unforgiving," he said.

"What are you talking about?" Mel drew her brows together and grinned.

"Nothing to worry about. I think God just taught me something." Chase still hoped the guy never showed his face again.

Switchblade led the way through the reconstruction mess of the museum and down the hidden stairs that Chase prayed would never be found. When they reached the secret room of the artist's remarkable paintings, Chase stopped and touched the blue sky concealing the entrance to the underground.

"Thank you for bringing us home," he said.

"Amen," Mel said.

"Amen," Switchblade said as he swung the painting to the side and stepped through. Mel went in next. Chase followed. Then he reached back and pulled *Ciel Bleu Domaine* into place.

They kept going down, down to the final door that sealed the world off from the underground. Switch tugged on it. Locked. No surprise. He banged the secret knock Molly had taught Chase before she sent him here.

A few seconds passed before they heard the sound of the deadbolts unlocking.

Amos swung the door open. "It's about time. Why have you been out of contact for so long? We thought you must all surely be dead." He moved to the side and let them in.

"To die is gain," Chase said with a smile.

Amos crossed his brow and shook his head. "What's gotten into you?"

Mel and Switchblade both let out a laugh.

"Got the H.S. in him now," Switchblade said.

"Glory be." Amos put his arms around Chase and smacked him three times on his back. "Welcome to the family. Took you long enough."

"Hey, nobody…Never mind," Chase said. "Thank you."

"I got a message from the leader over at Storm on the River. She says you're unplugged. Is it true? You lost the exoself?"

"It doesn't matter. The systems here can take care of most everything. I can't see in the dark or hear a cricket fart. But who cares." Chase put his arm around Amos. "I can't tell you how your condition is progressing either," he whispered. "I'm sorry about that."

"I'm not. Forget it. My life is in God's hands."

"Yeah, we'll talk about that later."

Mel eased alongside them. "Looks like everybody gave up on us and went to bed."

"Don't you believe it," Amos said. "They're all in the meeting room. On their knees. I hope you all aren't too worn out because there's about to be a celebration."

Chase wanted to go to bed. His travelling companions must feel the same way. But they couldn't deny these people a party. He laughed. *These people.* He was one of them now. "I'm up for it."

Switchblade rubbed his face. "Just prop me up in a corner. I'll try to pass out with a smile on my face."

Amos stopped walking and looked Chase up and down.

"What is it? Do I look different?"

"Leader lady in Gagnon said you took a laser blast in the shoulder and then broke your leg. Sure doesn't show."

Mel took Chase's hand. "He got better, Amos. Real quick. The exoself is gone but the transhuman stuff is still doing something. Maybe they programmed his blood with regeneration nanobytes."

"You didn't mention that earlier, Mel." Chase crossed his arms. "I've got nano…stuff in my blood?"

"I said maybe. We have no way of knowing for sure."

"I wonder what else we don't know. I sure would like to talk to Robert. I can't believe he let me go off not knowing everything."

"What they did to you may have progressed, Chase," Mel said. "Even Dr. Fiender might be baffled by it."

"How is that possible? I mean, they told me I was evolutionary. But seriously, I'm evolving?"

"It's the mindset of transhumanism," she said. "To create techno-sapiens that self-adjust to their environment. I'm not saying God approves, but theoretically, if the scientists are right, the transhuman will show at least some capability of becoming more than he was. More than his designers made him to be."

"The singularity," Chase said.

"That's what they want," Mel said. "I'm glad I got out of it. God was gracious in keeping me from getting assigned to a lab. I could have ended up at the Helgen."

"Singularity," Switchblade said. "The machines take over the world. Right?"

"Something like that," Mel said. "We lose control of our own inventions. Our technology outsmarts us."

"And I'm part of it," Chase said. "And now I'm part of this." He opened door of the meeting room. People were praying. For him.

He silently begged God to protect them from whatever the future might bring.

37

Seemed like some of the people slouching in chairs or kneeling on the floor were close to sleep. The small children and some of the older residents were missing. Chase found his mother clutching Molly's hand. Both women prayed out loud. At the same time. Practically the same prayer: Bring our loved ones home.

Chase cleared his throat.

Mom's eyes opened up first, then Molly's. They jumped to their feet and left him breathless and stumbling backward in their embrace.

If the commotion didn't break the silence, Molly's shout did. "Praise the Lord! Our prayers are answered."

The crowd lifted their heads. Chase accepted the hugs of people he didn't know. His mom required a second round of squeezing and crying. She pulled on his ear and put her lips close.

"You couldn't call your mother?" she asked.

"We lost all communication, Mom."

"I'm so glad you're back. I thought you'd gotten caught up there."

"Did Amos tell you what happened?"

She pulled back and met his gaze. "Yes. We know about the exoself. And we don't care. Don't you give it a thought."

"I was pretty devastated at first. But I found something better." He smiled.

"You really are a believer now. Right? I thought when you first arrived that you must have found the truth. Like I did. But then I wondered. It's been so crazy that we haven't even had a chance to discuss it."

"We'll have time to talk about it. Tomorrow. Right now, we party." He lifted her off her feet and spun her around, then kissed her cheek before he set her down. "And then we sleep."

Mel approached and hugged Mom and whispered something to her. Mom smiled wide and reached to squeeze Chase's hand.

"I'll get you all a snack," Mom said. She headed for the kitchen.

Chase pulled Mel close. "What did you tell her?"

"That I'm in love with her son."

"I think she already knew that," Chase said.

"Now it's official." She kissed him. Right on the lips. In front of everybody.

The silence returned. Except for the giggling of teenage girls.

Amos joined them with his arms folded. "Young man, we have rules around here. A public display of affection has consequences."

"I've heard something about that, but I'm not sure what you mean." Chase bent to kiss Mel as the chuckles rippled through the crowd. "Why don't you tell me about it since you're the one who enforces the rules."

"If you can't keep your hands off each other, then those hands will be united in marriage," Amos said. "No rush though. You have a week to make your plans."

"A week?" Chase let go his grip on Mel and put his hands in his pockets.

Amos addressed the laughing crowd. "Next party will be a wedding."

Chase noticed Mel laughing as much as the rest of them. She pulled him close.

"Don't look so scared," she said. "I know we have a lot to work through. Besides, I'd like a man to propose. The old-fashioned way. When he's good and ready. I'm sure Amos will agree to wait two weeks." She laughed again.

Chase lifted his brows. "Two weeks, huh?" He smiled. Was she serious?

Mom returned with the same old food. Chase devoured it. He looked for Switchblade and found him in a corner, leaning against the wall with his eyes closed. No smile, but his mouth hung open.

Chase had felt that way a few minutes ago. But now...A thought simmered inside him. Was his body regenerating to such a degree that soon he wouldn't even need sleep? For a moment, he lost the joy of being in this room full of believers, the woman he loved at his side. But his life, as Amos said, was in God's hands. He smiled and joined the celebration.

After a while he leaned against a wall and watched the tired group pretend this was normal life. They were happy. And blessed. Chase apologized that he didn't return with the promised chocolate from Windsong's private stock. It didn't seem to matter—everybody was having too much fun. Even Amos danced and sang, the teenagers circling him and singing.

But after a few minutes, Amos dropped in a chair, his breathing heavy and his face flushed. Was he getting worse? Chase wished he knew. Tonight the man showed resilience. Tomorrow, Chase would talk to him about making a trip to Storm on the River.

An hour passed before the room began to empty. The people of the underground were spent. The time—Chase didn't know for sure—had to be late. Hours past midnight. Mel and Amos had gone to the command center. Chase had one last drink—water in mismatched mugs—with a few remaining believers. It wasn't the best imported wine in crystal goblets. That was for the execs and celebrities back at Synvue. Chase didn't need it anymore.

He kissed his mother goodnight and sent her to bed, then joined Mel and Amos, who studied the intel scrolling across a large screen.

"Any sign we were spotted coming into town?" he asked as he sat beside Mel.

"No, but the other branches in the area report a lot of WR activity nearby," she told him.

"They haven't been discovered, I hope."

"They're fine. The people in Gagnon are lying low. A Fed showed up, but they convinced him they're just a homeless shelter. The other branch is at an abandoned farm so far off the grid that they don't get visitors, except for believers seeking refuge. No one has shown up there. There's a large homeless population in that area. The report is the Feds questioned some of those people, but they knew better than to talk about the church base."

"Let me guess," Chase said. "The church there feeds the homeless."

"You got it," she said.

Amos looked at Chase. "Son, how long do you think they'll keep up this search?"

"Until they find me."

"So they'll be looking forever." Amos cleared his

throat. "We have to find a way to throw them off. Melody, can you plant a fake signal? Like the one that was coming in on your laptop?"

She stared at the screen for a moment. "I don't know, Amos. We can't interact with the WR now. Can't manipulate them like we did before."

Guilt and regret welled up in Chase with a bit of the self-pity Mel hated. He shook it off. "Melody, you've got to be tired. Come on, I'll walk you to your room. I don't think there's anything else we can do tonight."

Amos stood. "He's right. We don't appear to be in imminent danger. Let's get some sleep." He left for his room.

"Yeah, all right," Mel said. "Goodnight, Amos."

He lifted his hand and waved without turning around.

Chase got up and pulled Mel up out of her chair, and they headed for the dorm area. The lights had gone off in the hall, but a few remaining lights from the command center provided a glow.

Chase stopped at Mel's door, took her in his arms and kissed her forehead. Then her cheek. Then her lips. He didn't want to let go.

But he couldn't rush into wedding plans. Too many unknowns. He dropped his arms and she pulled away.

"I love you," he said.

"I love you, Chase."

"I've got to get used to living without the exoself. To find a new way to fit in here. And there's a lot for me to learn about being a Christian."

"Welcome to the club," she said. "I'll get you a paper Bible. I was close, I think, to getting one into your systems. But…"

"Never mind. The Lord will provide. Right?"

"Chase, all that talk of marriage wasn't my idea. They were just playing. We have to do *something* for entertainment down here." She took his hand and then let it go. "There is no pressure. Not from me."

He bent in for a quick kiss.

She smiled. "We've been talking about having real services at Blue Sky Field. You were so right when you said we're too caught up in just surviving. I think we've all forgotten what we stand for."

"What *do* you…we…stand for? Why are we hiding in a hole in the ground? It doesn't feel right to me, Mel."

She yawned and reached for the door knob. "I want you to tell me what you're thinking."

"Tomorrow," he said. He kissed her one more time. "Sleep well."

"See you at breakfast," she said. "Or lunch."

He lifted her hand to kiss it. "See you."

She went into her room and closed the door.

On his way to his own room Chase passed Switchblade.

"Who woke the dead?" Chase asked him.

"Hah. Go on to bed," Switchblade said. "Don't trip over nothing. You ain't used to getting around without your super powers. Get some rest—we got stuff to do."

"Like what?"

"We gotta find Sparky and put him back where he belongs." Switchblade staggered off as he yawned and scratched his head. "By the way, welcome to the family, brother."

A few days ago Chase couldn't stand the guy. Now they were brothers. With a mission, it seemed.

Even if they found the exoself, getting it back inside Chase would be impossible. Unless he could get in touch with Robert. Or rather, get *Mel* in touch with Robert. Chase didn't have a chance without her.

Thinking of her, he smiled. Leaving her down the hall was a little harder tonight. There was a new kind of hole in him now. One that could only be filled by giving the people what they wanted—a wedding. He stepped into his room, closed his eyes, and muttered a wish. No, a prayer.

"I hope it can happen. Someday."

38

Chase awoke a few hours later. He'd been able to sleep only after telling himself to do so. He shut down. But how? When the WR gave up on the world's first transhuman and stripped Chase of his abilities, Robert said the exoself wasn't really gone. It was still inside Chase, only dormant. Was it true this time? It seemed as if it had physically removed itself and taken refuge in Mel's laptop. There was a bigger question: Without the exoself, how was Chase able to develop new abilities? Like healing a broken leg.

And how could a computer program look out for itself? If it was nearby, could it jump back into Chase the same way it left? Without anyone to do the reprogramming?

"Um, God," he said. "I don't understand. Well, You must know that about me by now. I don't get how this thing operates—how it could be gone and then show up again. I don't care that it's gone. But it might be helpful if I got it back, I guess. I don't know how this Spirit thing works either, but I know You're with me. Mel and Switch say You won't leave me the way old Sparky did. Well, thanks for that. Amen."

It'd get easier—talking to God. But even now it felt like flying with no fear. Like freedom. Like the first breath of real life. The exoself would be an intrusion to what was going on inside Chase. "I'm not going to look for it."

Switchblade could go on a mission if he wanted to. He'd never find it on his own.

Chase got out of bed and grabbed his toothbrush and clean clothes, among other items, for a trip down the hall to the bathroom. He needed a shower. Nothing in his changing body prevented what happened after a couple of days neglecting personal hygiene.

The lights in the hall weren't on yet—it must be early. Chase managed to find the bathroom in the dark, flipped on the light, and cleaned up. Then he took a look in the mirror and decided, once again, to let the beard grow. It'd work well with the hair covering the tops of his ears. He studied his eyes. The darker blue tone that had come from the night vision enhancement was still there. He was stuck with that, he guessed.

He didn't look any different since his...What was it? Conversion? He was the same old Chase.

"What are you thinking?" he asked his reflection. "The old Chase has *been* gone."

The eerie shading of his formerly baby blue eyes sent a shiver up his spine. No processors sparked, but he could almost count them as if they did. "You're still wired." He examined his wounded shoulder. Not a mark remained. "And you've got some creepy gadgets in your blood."

Shaking his head, he turned from the mirror and pulled on tattered jeans. The white shirt was missing a button. Not exactly the designer suit he'd have slipped into a few months ago.

He smiled. "This is the life."

Walking into the now lighted hall, he met a couple of guys coming toward him.

"Figured you'd sleep all day," one of the men said with a smile.

Chase shrugged. "It's a fine morning. No sense wasting it."

The men went on toward the bathroom. Chase headed for the dining hall, where he found a few people up early enough to prepare breakfast. Mel wasn't one of them—no surprise. Chase hoped she'd be able to sleep until noon. But there'd be work to do long before then.

He went into the kitchen and offered to help, but four ladies shooed him away, so he walked to the command center.

Amos sat at a station, his head resting on his palms.

"Are you all right?" Chase asked.

He strained his eyes upward and let out a breath. "Feeling pretty bad."

Chase sat beside him and patted his knee. "Is it getting worse?"

Amos didn't answer. Instead he put a smile on his face and opened a program on the computer in front of him. "Looks like we might be getting some corned beef."

"I wish—"

"No more wishing. Now, you hope. And pray. It's all we have. It's enough."

Chase opened his eyes wide. "I can't believe you just said that. I figured it out already, I think. Last night. But then I forgot."

"It's the way of the believer, Chase. We learn something and then we learn it again. And again."

"I guess I'm feeling like I should be able to do what I came here to do," Chase said.

"Melody told me you saved her life last night. Without any super powers."

"She wouldn't have been in that predicament if it wasn't for me. Women are always falling off cliffs—or buildings—when I'm around. Just another near disaster. A day in the life of a transhuman."

"Women have fallen off buildings?"

"Well, only one. Back in NYC. I should have dropped her."

"Let me guess—your director. What was her name? Kerstin?"

Chase quivered. He didn't want to tell anyone else about the vexing hologram. "Yeah. The point is I can't help you the way I could before," he said. "I can't even tell you if the Feds are coming."

Something thudded above them and the lights flickered.

"The Feds are coming," Amos said with a laugh.

Chase laughed too. "More like the construction crew." But it wasn't funny. He squeezed his eyes shut for a moment and rubbed his hands together. "They could find us down here, you know."

"Sooner or later they'll stumble into the room with the paintings and they might pull them out to haul off to a real museum. And they'll find the passage."

"What if we get rid of the paintings and board up the hole?" Chase asked.

Amos nodded. "Might work. We can use the passage in the alley to come and go."

"So you know about that. Switchblade thinks it's his own personal exit."

"I figured he was using it—he likes to explore."

Chase studied the computer screen. Information passed back and forth between various branches of the underground. The system worked. No exoself needed.

But spying on the WR and manipulating their

plans wouldn't happen again. Chase didn't know how it'd happened to begin with. Robert told him he was disconnected from the WR, but then he was right back in. Until the killswitch. He shook his head.

"God will provide," he said.

"Yes," Amos said. "Provide what?"

Chase smiled. "Whatever."

A few others entered, greeted Amos and Chase, and got to work. Mel lilted in, her hand extended. "Good morning," she said. She took Chase's hand in hers and gave it a business-like shake. Then she winked.

"Uh, yeah. Good morning, Miss Melody. Ready for another day of programming the underworld? Let me know if I can be of assistance."

"Cut it out, you two," Amos said. "I'll lay off the wedding stuff." He nudged Chase with his elbow. "Go ahead and give her a proper greeting. But be careful, young man. We do have rules."

Chase stood and put his arms around Mel and whispered in her ear. "Are you always so beautiful first thing in the morning?"

She giggled and gave him a quick kiss. "What's going on? You hardworking men are missing breakfast."

Chase pulled away and got her a chair. She sat beside Amos, and Chase took the chair on the other side of her.

"We were thinking about robbing an art museum," Chase told her. "You in?"

"What? Are you serious?"

What sounded like a wall collapsing above them shook the room. A computer fell from a desktop and crashed to the floor. Mel's gaze darted upward as she grabbed Chase's hand.

"Dear God, help us," she said. "They're going to find us."

"Don't be afraid," Chase told her. "But we need to be proactive. We're going to move the paintings and block up the hole."

"They'll hear you," Mel said.

"Not with all that noise they're making. Besides, that hall with all the doors is a long way from the main rooms where they're working. I doubt they'd think anything of it. Probably just think it's old pipes or something."

"How do you plan to get those paintings through a hole that's roughly four feet in diameter? *Ciel Bleu Domaine* is six feet wide. None of the rest of them will fit either."

"We'll have to take the wall out," Chase said. "Then we'll put it back. When we're done, no one will know the hole was ever there."

"Or we could cut up the paintings and slide them right through," Amos said.

What was he suggesting? Chase couldn't consider that. "I say we preserve them. They're part of the history of this town, and of the underground. Part of *our* history."

"I agree," Mel said. "I guess it might work, but you don't need to be doing this. There are plenty of other men here who can handle the job. You've been through enough."

"She's right," Amos said. "We'll get a crew together to move the paintings and get rid of that hole."

"I need to feel useful. I've recovered from my injuries. I'm not even tired. In fact…"

"What?" Mel gave him a firm stare.

Chase opened his mouth, inhaled, and pressed his lips shut.

"Right now, mister. No more secrets."

He nodded. "Last night, it seemed like the longer I stayed awake, the less I needed sleep. And then I sort of shut myself down. I had to make myself go to sleep. Can you explain that?"

Mel took his hand in hers and frowned.

Amos rubbed the back of his neck. "Maybe you were just hyped up from the party."

"I don't think so," Chase said. "Mel?"

"Nobody knows more than Robert Fiender how all this works. I really wish I could talk to him."

"No more wishing," Chase said. "We hope and we pray. And that is enough." He squeezed her hand and lifted it to his lips.

Mel smiled. "Now don't tell me that being a transhuman means you're growth as a new believer will be exponential."

"I have no idea, Miss Melody. But nothing surprises me anymore."

39

After breakfast, plans were made for the art heist. Switchblade, of course, would lead the small crew. They had tools but the work would be slow. Especially considering they had to try to keep the noise to a minimum.

Chase, Switchblade, Mel, and Amos gathered around a work station as Mel tried to get the computer system to jump into a WR program. She wanted to see the work orders for the crew continuing to make so much racket that most of the underground's residents were now hiding in their rooms. But there was no report to be found—not by the undetectable supercomputer.

Mel pulled up a holographic image of the town, something she'd accomplished using the cameras positioned at street level. She could temporarily program the cameras to show past images when needed, just like Chase had learned to do with the exoself. But she couldn't redirect a satellite. Life here had been safer before the killswitch had taken away Chase's power. Now they'd take a chance every time they went up.

The holograph showed four men going in and coming out of the museum. They carried wood planks and large pieces of plasterboard. Materials that would be useful in building a new wall to replace the one that was about to get knocked down.

"I need to be a part of this team," Chase implored. "I can't let them go without me. It was my idea. Besides…"

"What is it, son?" Amos asked.

"That painting sort of belongs to me, I think. More than anyone else. I want to be the one to move it."

"How do you figure, Charlie?" Switchblade rubbed his head and dropped his hands to his knees. "We was hiding behind it before you showed up."

"Mel, I told you about the dreams. They led me here. God brought me to Blue Sky Field by showing it to me."

"What do you mean he showed it to you?" Switchblade asked.

"I was searching for an actual field. You can ask Molly—I told her that's where I was going. But she sent me here. And I found what I was looking for in the painting."

"Amazing," Amos said.

"Don't mean you own the thing." Switchblade grabbed a duffle bag off the floor. "But I see why you want to be in on this. It's OK with me. Kinda used to you being my sidekick."

Chase exploded out of the chair and folded his arms. "I'm *your* sidekick?"

"Yeah, I thought it might go the other way. But now that you lost your super powers you can see how I would be the logical choice for being in charge over a has-been gameshow host. You ain't got no experience in covert operations."

"Covert—like knocking down a wall? I think I've had plenty of experience. The exoself didn't get here all by itself, you know."

Mel leapt to her feet. "If you two can't get along,

then you can both stay here."

Amos snickered. Chase smiled. Switchblade put his arm around Chase's shoulder and pulled him to the bolted door.

Mel huffed and then laughed. "Chase Sterling...Redding, you keep a VPad on you and answer me if I call you."

"Yes, ma'am. Don't tell my mother what I'm doing. She's even stricter than you."

Mel hurried to his side and wrapped her hands around his bicep. "I mean it. I can't just type a message to your brain anymore. You stay in touch."

Switchblade unlocked the door and pushed it open. "If he needs to talk to you, I'll let him use my VPad. If you need to talk to him, call me." Switchblade's tone rose higher and he wagged his head back and forth. "But don't be carrying on about how you miss him and you hope he's all right." He went through the door and recovered his deep voice. "The men got work to do and we don't need none of that."

Mel stomped into the tunnel. "I just want to be in touch, that's all."

Chase took her by the arm and spun her around. He kissed her hair, lifted her off her feet, and set her down on the other side of the doorway. "I'll let you know if we need anything. Go make room somewhere for the paintings."

She faced him. "OK, boss."

He raised his brow.

"Sorry. You were bossing me and it slipped out." She grabbed him around the neck and kissed him. "I'll tell the rest of your crew you're going up."

"Thanks. I'll see you in a little while."

Chase followed Switchblade into the dark passage and up the winding stairs. Footsteps echoed behind him. One of the five men chosen for the job swung a laserlight, and Chase appreciated the glow it offered. The others caught up as Switchblade pushed the painting out of the way and crawled through.

The first thing to do was secure the door. Switchblade nailed old plywood over it so that if the workers on the other side wanted in, the crew on this side would at least have a couple of minutes to retreat. But there'd be no hiding—not for long—with a gaping hole in the wall.

The men went to work removing the artwork from the walls. The pieces all slid free without a struggle, except for *Ciel Blue Domaine*. Switchblade used a screwdriver to remove the hinges that held the painting to the wall. Chase and two other men held it as it broke loose. They eased it to the floor.

"Now we've got to make a hole big enough to get them through," Chase said.

"Seriously?" one of the men asked. "Let's just chop them up and throw them in the hole we've already got."

"Leo's right," Switchblade said. "It'd save a lot of time. Those workers could come in any minute."

"No way we're destroying them," Chase said to the man named Leo. "Start cutting the wall."

"Look, I know you're the most important thing to happen to the underground, but we don't follow your orders, Mr. Sterling," Leo said.

"Charlie, we could make clean cuts and put the pieces back together when we get them in," Switchblade said.

Chase shook his head. "The way I got cut up and

put back together? This painting—"

"I know. God used it to lead you here." Switchblade picked up a laser saw and powered it. "We'll get it through in one piece." He aimed the silent beam at the plaster and made a clean cut.

Chase grabbed an old-fashioned handsaw and began cutting the beam behind the plaster. Leo grumbled as he joined the other men in breaking out sections of the wall in chunks large enough to put back. With some new plasterboard and a little paint, nobody would know the wall hid a passage that went down into the cavern.

As they worked Chase explained his dreams, and his recent induction into the family of believers, to Leo and the other men. They seemed to understand that Chase needed to keep the focal point of his visions intact.

"I got wind of it last night—about you getting saved," Leo said. "People were talking. Then Amos started in on all that wedding stuff. So, you and Melody getting married?"

"I haven't proposed to the lady," Chase said. "Someday. I hope."

"No point in waiting if you ask me. Might not be a someday."

Hours passed as boards were removed and laid aside to be put back in place later. Mel called Switchblade's VPad twice. Chase assured her they were doing fine. Sandwiches were shared during short breaks. The noise from just beyond the room continued until the day grew old and the crew left.

With the wall all but removed, the paintings were put through to the other side.

Switchblade pulled on his cap and dark glasses.

"I'm going up to see what I can find to repair this mess."

"I'm coming with you," Chase said.

"No, you're not. You and the guys get those paintings down the stairs. Which, by the way, won't be no easy feat." The big man shook his head. "Meet me back here in an hour and we'll rebuild the wall. You and me can get it all beautified from the inside. Then we'll come in through the alley."

"You sure you'll be OK?"

"Just bring me some supper."

"Will do."

Switchblade headed up and Chase and the others headed down. Each of the men carried one of the smaller paintings to the staircase and into the underground. Others, waiting at the unbolted door, took the artwork.

Chase went back up with Leo. The other men left to eat their well-deserved dinner. More than two men maneuvering the largest of the paintings down the winding stairs wouldn't work.

"Thanks for understanding my need to keep the art from being cut up," Chase said as he and Leo grabbed hold of the heavy wooden frame.

"Don't know that I understand. But we put the needs of others ahead of our own," Leo told him. "If we didn't, we'd be fighting all the time down here."

"That's foreign to me," Chase said. "To the old me, anyway. I used to brag on how I helped so many people, but truth is I spent most of my life seeing what I could get out of it for myself. Now I'm starting to understand what you mean. But don't you resent it sometimes?"

"Like right now? This thing weighs a ton." Leo

smiled as he strained and blew out a breath.

"I'm sorry I lost the upper body strength." Chase huffed. "Really sorry."

"You just keep your end up." The two sidestepped through the tunnel. "As far as resenting it when I don't get my own way, I figure after what's been done for me, I can't complain. I gave up my own agenda a long time ago. So did you, brother. Look at all you've given up for us. You didn't owe us anything. And yet, here you are."

Peace flowed into Chase at the words of a man who'd been doing this Christian thing long enough to know how it worked. "Thank you."

"For what?" Leo asked.

"Just thanks."

As Switchblade had warned, getting the big canvas down the spiraling stairs was not easy. Chase nearly dropped it a couple of times. But they got it through the door and into the compound. Setting it down, both men dropped to the floor and leaned against the wall.

Mel was there this time—Chase hadn't taken time to look for her when he brought down the smaller paintings. She sat beside him, a look of relief on her face. Which disappeared when he told her he was going back to help Switchblade repair the wall.

"We can't leave it that way, Mel. Switch is seeing what we can use that won't be missed. We've got to close up the wall."

"I'll go with you," Leo said. "You'll get it done quicker with another set of hands."

"I appreciate that," Chase said.

"Well, you at least have to eat before you go," Mel said.

"We're coming," Chase said. "I told Switch I'd bring him some."

She got up and pulled on Chase's arm. "I'll fix him a plate."

Chase pushed up off the floor and took her by the hand. Leo followed them to the dining hall. The people sitting at the long tables smiled when Chase entered. They seemed to wait in silence for something. Chase looked around the room. The paintings—the smaller ones—adorned the walls.

"How on earth did you get them hung so fast?" Chase asked Mel.

"We had the hooks up and ready before you brought them down. What do you think?"

He led her to the nearest table and took a seat. She sat beside him. "It's perfect," he said. "Now we can all enjoy them." A few people applauded and the rest joined in. Chase's mom brought him a plate of corned beef and cooked apples.

Chase shoveled in a forkful of the steamy fruit. Maybe he could get by on little sleep, but thankfully he hadn't lost his need for food.

"So, who's been up?" he asked. "Corned beef is new to the menu."

"I went," Mel said.

Chase dropped his fork. "What? I can't believe you went on a food run."

"Somebody's got to carry on with that sort of thing now that we don't have any contacts up top. Michael and Joseph went with me. And we did all right. I don't think we have anything to worry about as long as the Feds aren't in the area."

"But—"

"We all have to work together."

"You don't go up without me. Understood?"

"Yes, *sir*," she said. She bent near and kissed him. The giggling started before she backed away.

"Go fix that plate for Switchblade."

"Yes, sir," she said again, and she left him there. He watched her go then found his mother had taken the seat beside him.

"You love that girl." Mom smoothed down Chase's hair like she did when he was a kid in need of a comb.

"I do. I think I've loved her for a long time. Just took a while to convince myself."

"When you get back tonight, come to my room. Even if it's late," she said. "I have something for you."

40

Carrying a plate of corned beef and apples for Switchblade, Chase followed Leo, who had the laserlight. They entered the room where the paintings had hung. No need to climb through a hole in the wall—the wall was nearly gone.

No sign of Switchblade. He should have been back from his unlawful supply run. Chase set the plate on the floor. "Come on," he said. "We'd better go look for him."

Chase cracked the door—Switchblade had taken down the boards they'd nailed over it. The construction crew hadn't ventured this far.

Leo handed Chase the laserlight and followed him to the museum's front room with its view of the dark town.

"I can't believe this," Chase said. "Where did he go?"

Switchblade filled the open doorway. "I'm right here. Don't get yourself in a tizzy."

"What are you doing out there?" Chase demanded.

"Fresh air, brother. I need it."

"Did you get the stuff?"

"Enough for our little building project. It's piled in the hall. You walked right past it."

"Then get in here. Let's get busy."

Patching the old chunks of drywall with the tape

and plaster made easy work of rebuilding the wall. Blue paint didn't match the aged green of the rest of the room, but Leo thought it best to put a coat of the latex over the repair job. Enough remained to add some blue to an adjoining wall, which gave the appearance of an unfinished project. Hopefully, the workers wouldn't get to this part of the structure before the new paint smell diminished.

With the wall put back together, permanently cutting off access to Blue Sky Field, Chase and his cohorts headed out the front door of the museum and stuck close to the buildings as they slinked to the alley at the end of the street. No one was out—it was the middle of the night.

Chase had called Mel with Switchblade's VPad to tell her when to scramble the camera links. The refuse bin held a full load and it took all three men to push it aside. Once they'd crawled into the tunnel, moving the bin back into place was even harder. Switchblade and Leo leaned against the wall, puffs of frigid air escaping their lips. Chase got his second wind. There had to be a breaking point for this endless energy.

"Good work," Switchblade said when they got to the old stairs leading downward. He patted Chase on the back and gave a quick punch to Leo's arm. "I'll see you men tomorrow." He reached the compound and disappeared in the darkness.

"See you, Chase," Leo said.

"Yeah. Goodnight." Chase faced the hall leading to his mother's room. "Thanks for your help." He nodded as Leo went the opposite direction.

Before he got too far into the compound, Mel ran toward him with a laserlight in her hand. She threw her arms around him.

"I thought I could get to the tunnel before you got back," she said. "I don't know my way around this far out."

"You didn't have to come. You should be in bed asleep." But he was glad to see her. He kissed her and stroked her soft hair.

"Like I could sleep not knowing if you made it back. Did everything go as planned?"

"Does it ever?" He took her hand and started walking.

"Oh no. What happened?"

"Switch pulled a disappearing act—took a stroll in the moonlight. That's all. The repair on the wall looks good, as long as nobody looks too close. Come on, I'll walk you to your room. I told Mom I'd stop by when I got back. I'm sure she's waiting up for me."

"Okay, but first I want to show you something. Come to my work station with me."

He followed her lead and she flipped on the lights above the computers. Chase found the reason Mel had brought him here. High on a wall, overlooking the worldwide command center of the Underground Church, *Ceil Bleu Domaine* hung in its new location.

Chase gazed at the painting and squeezed Mel's hand. "I'm so glad we didn't tear it up. I'll never get tired of looking at it." He stood before it. "This is where it belongs—right here where we hold everything together."

"I'm glad you approve." She lifted up and kissed his cheek. "Now you can take me to my room."

They entered the hallway. "Are you tired, Chase? At all?"

"No. I feel as wide awake as when I got up this morning after three hours of sleep."

"I wish I could tell you what's going on in your body," she said.

"Don't look so worried. It'll be all right."

She nodded as they neared her door. He kissed her goodnight. Or good morning—what time was it anyway? Then he kissed her again. "I'll try to sleep in." He let her go.

"You do that and you'll miss breakfast."

"Let me guess—corned beef and cooked apples."

"That's right. You're gonna want some of that."

He walked backward as she spoke. "I'll see you there." He smiled, turned around, and headed a few doors down the hall to his mother's room. A quiet knock brought her to the door and she let him in.

"Oh, son, I'm glad you're back. I was getting worried." She sat on the end of her bed and pulled a small leather pouch from under the mattress.

"It took some time, but we got the wall rebuilt. Nobody will know what's behind it." He sat beside her. "What have you got there?"

"I wasn't able to hold on to much when I came underground. But I managed to keep a few things." She spread open the drawstring top of the bag and pulled out two rings. "Mine and your father's. Our wedding rings. I want you to have them."

Chase opened his hand and she dropped the golden circles into his palm. He flipped them over and over. Then he took his father's ring and placed it on his finger. A perfect fit.

"I'm sorry I don't have the engagement ring. The diamond made it worth a lot, and I sold it when I gave up my WR assignment. I needed the money."

"I'm sorry you had to do that, Mom. Tell me how you ended up here." He looked her in the eyes. "And tell me about my father. I saw the look on your face the other day when I told Amos that I thought Dad knew more about the Bible than he let on."

Her head bowed and tears filled her eyes. "Your father became a believer when you were about ten. I was so afraid of filling your mind with fairytales that I made him promise to keep it to himself. I thought he was crazy. It was a source of contention for a while. I told him I'd leave if he didn't let it go. Well, he loved me." She smiled. "And I loved him. And we agreed not to talk about it."

"He tried to tell me about it a couple of times," Chase said. "Now I know why he stopped short."

She nodded. "It was my fault."

He put his arm around her shoulder. "I didn't say that. Dad was just like the rest of the Christians I've met. He learned to be quiet."

"When he died, I didn't give it another thought. Never considered the possibility that what he believed was true. Didn't picture him in Heaven or anything. He was just gone."

"What happened to change your mind?"

She pulled her husband's ring from Chase's finger and rolled it between her thumb and forefinger. "About a year ago I met a man—Marty—when I took a trip to Orlando. He was a believer and he reminded me so much of your dad. Only he didn't keep quiet. He said it was time to unlearn bad habits. Of course, he got arrested. When they let him go, his Christian friends told him to go underground. He was being watched because...well, he was too vocal. We stayed in contact. But he got arrested again. And again. And then he led me to the Lord. He made sense. Everything your father had tried to tell me made sense then. I couldn't deny it any longer."

"What happened to Marty?"

"The last time he got arrested, I was with him. We'd gone to New York to a rally and the Feds raided it. They took me in too. I didn't admit to anything—especially not to being a Christian. The police let me go—they didn't even file a report on me. But it was Marty's fourth offense. I don't know where they sent him. I never saw him again."

Chase rubbed her shoulder.

"I couldn't admit I'd become a believer, Chase. I couldn't say it. After that, I wanted to atone for my cowardice. And I wanted to hide. So I sold everything, took up with a church house in New York, and asked how I could get into the underground. My plan was, and still is, to spend the rest of my life serving here. I feel like I have a purpose in this place. And I'm too afraid to try to live the life of a believer out in the open."

"Don't be afraid, Mom."

"It's easy to say, son. But so hard to live. I *am* afraid. I can't help it."

"I understand." He took the ring back and jangled it against the smaller one in his hand. "So, you met Mel at the church house in New York?"

"Can you imagine my surprise when I came face to face with the woman who had been your assistant? Who'd programmed you? When she joined the underground, I went with her. I'd only wanted a place to hide, but then I knew God had a reason for bringing me here."

"To give me these rings? It's a nice souvenir. I'll keep them in a safe place." He stuck the rings in his pocket. "Thanks."

She crossed her arms and gave him a motherly stare, and he laughed.

"Charles Alexander Redding…"

"Oh, the full name. I must be in trouble."

"You know what those rings are for. You go ask that precious girl to marry you."

"That's a wonderful dream. But do you really think this is any way to start a marriage? Living with constant danger? Not knowing what tomorrow holds?"

"So you face it together. You're together anyway. It could only make things better."

Chase shook his head. "I guess I'm the one who's afraid." He reached into his pocket to grasp the rings. "It's not that I don't want to marry her."

She handed him the leather bag. "Think about it, son. I won't say anything to Melody about the rings."

"OK. Goodnight. I love you, Mom. I'm glad you told me your story." He kissed her on the cheek and left for his room.

He returned the rings to their pouch and stuffed it under his mattress. Then he stretched out on the bed and began the process of convincing his body to accept sleep. His body that teemed with nanobytes and silicon. Fake organs. Processors that might or might not ever activate again. How could he subject Mel to all that? Why would she want to marry a transhuman? If they got married, they might end up—

What would the next generation be like?

41

Morning brought no answers. Chase had slept little. Not that it mattered. Except that lying awake most of the night led to worry. How long would that construction project up top last? What would happen when it was done? People would be in the building every day.

"God help us."

Where was the exoself? Switchblade hadn't gotten a chance to look for the rogue techno brain. Not with yesterday's job of closing up the passage between one world and another. Today, maybe he'd start looking. But not Chase. He would spend the day trying to convince Amos to make a trip to Gagnon to see Dr. John.

"Might be pointless, but we have to try."

Kerstin. What was she doing now that she'd activated the killswitch and lost track of Chase? She might be in the area for real this time. Looking for him.

"Please, God, don't let her end up in Herouxville. Send her to Montreal. Or to the frozen tundra."

Mel. Chase smiled. But he worried just the same.

"Protect her."

After a breakfast of hash and apples, Chase followed Amos to the command center. The noise picked up from above, but the people seemed less concerned now that the hole in the wall was gone. Just to slow down the workers who would come into that room sooner or later, Switchblade had jammed the lock. Maybe they wouldn't care enough about what was on the other side to force the door open.

Mel worked at her station, concentrating on the needs of some other branch of the underground. Chase slowed to kiss her on the top of her head. She reached behind her and clutched his hand for a moment before he kept walking.

He sat beside Amos. "I want to take you to Gagnon to see the doctor."

Amos didn't even look up. "I talked to Dr. John. There is nothing he can do for me."

"He could take some blood samples. Maybe tell us how long—"

"How long I've got to live? What good would that do?"

Chase took a breath and sat silent. It wouldn't matter at all. The man didn't want to know.

"What I need to be doing is preparing my replacement," Amos said. "I'm going to ask Melody to take over for me."

Chase flew out of the chair. He didn't know what to say. But he didn't like the idea.

"Sit down. I know you want to protect her. To take care of her. But I've prayed about it and I think it's the right decision." Amos pulled on Chase's arm until he returned to his seat. "It'll be all right, son. You'll be there with her."

"I'm afraid she'll get hurt."

"She won't be in any more danger than she is now. I'm going to talk with her tomorrow. Don't say anything."

"I had a plan to get you to the doctor tomorrow. We could arrange for a transport to pick us up in time to get to Gagnon before sunup. Did you know they don't even try to hide there? They just walk around town like they own the place."

"It's a different scenario. They don't have a drone plant nearby. And they do have a fair population of ousted folks. They blend in."

"Yeah. Must be nice."

Amos laughed. "I don't think *nice* is the word for it. Even if they do get to see the sun every day."

Chase smirked. "You're right. It's hard, no matter what." He leaned back and studied the computer screen in front of Amos.

"Seems like it's been a little harder lately." Amos typed as he spoke.

"Since I got here?"

Amos gave him a firm look. "Since Kirel pulled one over on us."

"Oh. OK, we'll blame it on Kirel, who happened to show up right after me." Chase lifted his eyes to the painting that now graced this sterile and serious room. He could almost feel the warmth, the radiance of the sun. The breeze against his skin. He could almost hear the voice.

Then something fainter than a whisper spoke in his soul and repeated what the voice had told him in a dream.

It's a place of persecution.

Chase shuddered. How much more could the people of Blue Sky Field take? He dropped his gaze to find Mel. She seemed pleased with the outcome of whatever she'd been working on and she looked up and smiled.

He scanned the room and found Switchblade staring at a computer screen then moving to the next station and staring at another screen. Was he looking for Sparky? Seemed ridiculous to think the exoself could jump from one computer to another.

Chase laughed under his breath. Then he wandered to the nearest station and looked for a message on the screen. A sign. It wasn't so unbelievable.

Mom came in and took her seat at a table in the center of the room. Leo worked nearby. The young girl, Finley, whose parents had been murdered by the WR, sat in the corner with an old laptop in her grip and a look of confusion on her face.

Amos leaned over the desk where he worked. He let out a soft groan. Blood poured from his nose and he dropped to the floor.

42

Prayers followed shrieks as everyone in the room rushed to Amos. Chase parted the crowd, dropped to his knees, and took off his shirt. He wadded it into a ball and pressed it against Amos's nose. Switchblade knelt beside Chase.

"I'll carry him to his room," Switchblade said. "You got any idea what happened? What's wrong with him?"

"He's sick," Chase whispered. "Leukemia."

"You knew about it? Why would he tell you and not the rest of us?"

"Let's get him to his room." Chase shouted to the people behind him, "Everybody back up."

Mel put her hand on Chase's shoulder. Then she backed away with the rest of the onlookers. Chase glanced at her as she crossed her arms and shook her head.

Switchblade picked Amos up off the floor. The bleeding had slowed but Amos didn't open his eyes. Chase dropped the bloody shirt and followed Switchblade to the leader's private quarters near the front of the hallway. Mel hurried to Chase's side.

When they were all inside the room, Mel addressed the concerned crowd gathering in the hall. "Go and tell everyone to pray." Then she closed the door. Her anxious eyes met Chase. "There will be no hiding it now. The people have to be told how sick he is."

"You knew about this?" Switchblade asked.

She nodded. "Chase didn't want to tell him without some support. He told Molly and me before he told Amos."

Switchblade lowered Amos to the bed, and she pulled a blanket over the ailing leader.

"I get it." Switchblade eyed Chase. "This is one of your transhuman tricks. Right? You know when somebody's sick?"

"Not anymore," Chase said.

Mel opened the door of a small closet and pulled out a red shirt. She draped it over Chase's shoulders, and he pulled it on and buttoned it.

"Sparky took that gift when he left, huh?" Switchblade grabbed a hand towel from a table and dunked it into a pitcher of water. He wrung it out and began wiping Amos's face.

"Yeah, it's gone. It was useless anyway. I could tell you if you were sick but I couldn't do anything about it."

Amos drew in a deep breath and opened his eyes. "What happened?"

Mel sat on the bed next to him. "You passed out. And you had a bad nosebleed. How are you feeling?"

"I could use some rest." Amos glanced up at Chase. "Melody, why don't you take care of things for the rest of the day?"

"Sure, I can do that. Amos, maybe we ought to try to get you to see the doctor at Storm on the River."

"That's exactly what I told him earlier," Chase said. "But he wouldn't agree to it."

"Well..." She put her hand on Amos's arm. "I think it would be a good idea. I can do your job for a while."

"That's exactly what I told him earlier." Amos grinned. "But he wouldn't agree to it."

"Wait, you told who what?" Mel asked.

"I told Chase I wanted you to take over as leader of Blue Sky Field," Amos said.

"Permanently? Amos, are you serious?" Her wide-eyed expression found Chase. "But you don't think it's a good idea?"

"I know you'd do a great job. It's just…" What was he supposed to tell her? She'd not only do a great job, she was the only person for the job. "I'm worried about you taking on so much. But I know you can handle it."

"All right then." She pushed her hair back and sat a little straighter. "I accept." She faced Amos. "You get some rest. I'll go…take care of things." She looked back and forth between Chase and Switchblade. "I'll need both of you out there. Switchblade, find somebody to sit with Amos."

"I don't need a babysitter," Amos said. "I just need a nap."

"I'm in charge now, Amos," she said. "Go on, Switch. Ask Kim."

Mel sure didn't have any trouble moving right into a role that only a moment ago had seemed a shocking concept. Maybe God had not only directed Amos, but had given Mel a clue as well. Her small stature didn't fit the look of determination she now showed. Chase wasn't surprised. She could do this. Even if he'd prefer someone else take the job.

"That's a good idea," he said. "Mom'll take good care of you, Amos."

"I'm on it," Switchblade said as he left the room.

"Amos, we'll be right outside the door," Mel said.

She took Chase by the hand. "Yell if you need anything before Kim gets here."

"I don't think I can yell. But I'll be fine. Go on."

Mel led Chase out of the room and closed the door. The crowd was gone—probably in the meeting room praying. Chase searched Mel's eyes, and she threw her arms around him and dropped her head to his chest.

He held her tight. "You OK, boss?"

She barely shook, and he didn't know for sure if she was laughing or crying. Turned out to be a little of both.

"Don't you dare start calling me boss," she said.

He rubbed her back and kissed her forehead.

"Why did you tell Amos you didn't want me in charge?"

"That's not at all what I said, Melody. I just don't want you to end up in any more danger than necessary."

"Well, that's ridiculous."

"Yeah, Amos pointed that out. And he was right."

"This scares me to death," she said.

He pulled back and studied her expression. "What are you scared of?"

"Making bad decisions. Letting people down. Proving that I'm too young and inexperienced for the job. Which I am."

"Amos said he prayed and he believes you're the one who should take over. Don't be afraid."

"I need you, Chase. You have to promise to stay right beside me. No more up top excursions."

He pursed his lips and drew a breath.

"Oh, no, you are not taking Amos to Gagnon."

"He needs to go. I don't know exactly why, but I

believe the doctor can help him. Even if it's only to keep him from dying a painful death underground."

"I agree, Chase. But let Switchblade take him."

"Until a couple of days ago I was a great system of defense. But now, Switchblade is the best security guard this place has."

Mel dropped her gaze, her eyes blinking. "I'll think about it later. Right now we need to have a meeting."

Chase nodded. "I imagine most people are in the meeting room. Let's join them."

Mom walked up with Switchblade, who'd been too late to fill her in on Amos's condition. Molly had joined the praying people and told them the truth about their leader. And about the mini Wilberton inside the transhuman.

"Molly said she didn't know if it still functioned, and I told the others it was gone," Mom said. "It *is* gone, isn't it, son?"

"Like the rest of the gadgets. The only thing I can do now, it seems, is heal myself." Chase realized as soon as he said it that the statement was contrary to the Spirit residing in him. He gazed upward. The God of Underground Church, of the universe, could give him information on a level far deeper than the exoself had ever done.

"Well, I can't heal myself. But there's something in my blood that…" Startled by what had just come to mind, he sucked in a breath.

"What is it?" Mel asked.

Chase wasn't sure if he should allow the direction his thoughts were taking. This time, the Spirit didn't seem to offer any insight. Surely God would have something to say about drawing the blood of a transhuman and shooting it into a man who was about to die. Chase shook off the idea. It'd never work.

"Nothing." He looked at his mother. "If everybody's waiting in line for a diagnosis, I can't do it anymore."

"There's no line." She rolled her eyes. "I hope you realize you don't have to perform for us, Chase. We all love you. Even if you're just a regular man."

They loved him? For no reason? Somewhere in the back of Chase's mind, a gameshow host still tried to please the masses. But that man was fading away as surely as the exoself was gone for good.

"Thank you, Mom. I'll try to remember that."

43

Chase, Switchblade, and Mel interrupted prayers in the meeting room. Dozens of faces looked up at Chase. People rose from their knees and inched closer. He wasn't so sure his mother was right about them not wanting anything from him.

Molly reached for his hand as she approached. "How's Amos? Is he worse, Chase?"

"From what we all witnessed this morning, I think he must be. But, you know I can't tell for sure. Not the way I could before."

"I know. I've just come to depend on you, young man. You're still my hero." She lifted up on her toes and kissed his cheek. "Now come and pray with us."

"We'll get back to praying in a little while." He took her by the arm and led her back into the crowd. "Melody has something to tell all of you."

Molly lifted her eyebrows and then nodded. She stepped back and Chase took Mel by the hand and led her to the platform. The one where only a few days ago he'd explained his reason for coming here. Everything had changed. Everything.

Mel stepped to the center of the make-shift stage. Chase took a seat in the front row. Switchblade shifted on his feet against the wall.

"Well." She scanned the crowd as they settled into chairs.

Chase leaned forward and prayed she'd find her

voice.

One of the young girls called out from the back, "Are you going to tell us about the wedding?"

Laughs filled the room. Mel's eyes grew big.

Chase went to her side. "No one has made any wedding plans," he said. "This is not the time. Melody has something important to share with you about Amos. And about herself." He moved to the side and nodded to her.

"Amos is too sick to continue as leader of Blue Sky Field," she said. "It's an awesome responsibility—more than the operation of the other branches of the underground. We run the whole organization from here. Well, you all know that."

She lifted her chin and took a step forward. "For the most part, I designed the programs that keep us going. I know how it all works. Even better than Amos does. But that's not the only reason for his decision. He says he prayed on it, and I'm the one he wants to replace him. I know I'm young and lacking in experience. I'm willing to try if you all are willing to take a chance on me." She crossed her arms then dropped them to her sides.

One person clapped. Then another. In a few seconds, everyone in the room was on their feet, applauding their new leader. Chase joined them. She had the people's support. There'd be no turning back.

She smiled. The fire in her dark eyes that Chase had noticed when he first arrived blazed brighter than ever. How beautiful she was.

Her expression grew somber. "We need to ready ourselves for Amos's parting." She glanced at Finley. "Some have lost family recently. But this will be a loss for all of us."

Chase shifted in his seat. Was she ready to let the man go without a fight? The trip to Gagnon had to happen before Amos got any worse. Chase wouldn't contradict the new leader. Not in front of people. But later, they'd have to talk about it.

Not much else was said as to how things would change, if at all. Mel encouraged the residents of Blue Sky Field to go back to whatever they'd been doing—especially the praying. She promised to keep them informed about Amos, but he didn't need any visitors. Not now.

People left for their work stations, kitchen duty, or cleaning detail. A few approached Mel with a personal word of gratitude for stepping up. They'd keep her in their prayers. They'd do whatever she needed to help make the transition smooth.

Mel seemed exhausted when the last of the crowd left. Chase pulled her to a chair and made her sit.

He put his arm around her shoulder. "You did great."

"I think I need to spend the afternoon in the command center," she said.

"Like you would have done anyway?"

She tilted her head as her lips curved upward. "Yeah. But I need to let the other branches know I'm taking on a new role." She took Chase's hand in hers. "Can you check on Amos for me?"

"I can do anything you need me to do." He lifted her hand and kissed it. "Come on, I'll walk you to your station."

They went into the active hub of the underground. Nothing seemed different. Except Amos was missing. Chase left Mel there. She'd make her announcement to the believers around the world. He'd be only a few yards away in Amos's quarters.

He found his mom sitting in a chair beside the bed, deep in conversation with Amos, who seemed to be feeling better.

"Chase," he said. "We were just talking about you. Your mother tells me you were a peculiar child."

Mom's hands flew to her mouth and then dropped to her lap. "Now, Amos, that's not what I said."

"Oh, what was it? Special?"

"I said I knew he had a destiny."

"Yes." Amos wheezed out a laugh. "Your mother says you were destined for…What was it?"

Chase sat on the edge of the bed. "You feeling all right, Amos?"

"I'm fine. Your mother says you were destined to help people."

The dream of a note in a bottle floated through his mind. Chase could almost hear the waves lapping the shore. He could see his young father pulling the bottle out of the gulf. But it was his mother who'd extracted the note. More than a dream, it had happened. A long time ago.

"You remember the note, Mom?"

"Of course. Whatever happened to it?"

"I cleaned out my desk when I was ten. Never saw it again." He had to ask her about the numbers. But they couldn't have been on that old note. "It said—"

"You will become a helper to those in need." Mom nodded. "And you have."

"Mom, was there anything else on that note? Numbers?"

"No, I don't think so. Just that one line. Why?"

Chase wasn't surprised. The numbers weren't there until the dream. God added them for the transhuman.

"Never mind." Chase studied Amos. "I still want to take you to Gagnon."

"Your new leader, I'm sure, would not allow it."

"What's in Gagnon?" Mom's expression lightened. "Oh, the doctor." She directed her attention to Amos. "I think you should go." Her eyes darted to Chase. "We could get him there. Right, son?"

"We?"

"Well, sure. Take your mom on one of your adventures. I could stay with Amos until he's feeling better, and you could come back here to help Melody run things."

"Kim, I'm not going to get better," Amos said. "Only worse."

"All the more reason for you to see a doctor," she said.

"Mom, you told me you were never leaving the underground. You don't want to be up top. Remember?"

"And you told me not to be afraid." She smiled. "So let's do it. I need to exercise my faith."

Chase shook his head. "When I said that, it wasn't an invitation to tag along on one of these missions. *I'm* too afraid of what might happen."

"There is no mission," Amos said. "No one is going to Gagnon." He yawned and his face drained of color. "I think I need to rest some more."

Chase got off the bed. "I'll be in the command center. Mom, do you need anything?"

"You can have someone bring us some lunch in a while."

"I'll bring it myself. See you at noon."

Amos closed his eyes. Chase eased out the door

and pulled it shut. He started for the bustling room only a hundred feet away, but he heard a soft groan from the other end of the hall. He swung around and found Finley sitting on the floor with a laptop. Her long brown hair hung to one side. Her narrow shoulders fell forward. She pounded her fist against the keypad.

Chase dropped to the floor beside her. "Finley, how are you doing? I know it's been tough. Coming underground is a big adjustment."

"I'm all right, Mr. Sterling. I just wish my parents could have become believers before they were killed."

"It's hard to understand why it worked out this way. But you have a family here who loves you." He reached for her hand and held it between both of his.

She looked up at him. "Yeah. I guess so."

"Where'd you get that old laptop?"

"Miss Melody gave it to me. She's got a few reconditioned laptops and tablets in a storeroom. I like to write, and when I told her I'd miss my computer, she gave me this one. I lost all the stuff I wrote at home. I stored it with a cyber-server, but Miss Melody said it was too risky to try to get it back."

"Well, she would know." Chase glanced down the hall. He needed to get back to the command center. But he'd spend another minute or two with this poor girl who'd lost everything. "What are you working on? You write stories? Or poetry?"

"Right now, I'm not writing much of anything. This computer's got some kind of problem."

"We'll get Mel—Miss Melody—to check it out. I need to go see her now. I'll let her know you're having trouble with it." He started to get up.

"Yeah, it's all these numbers. They just keep

scrolling across the screen no matter what I do."

Chase's arms tensed, but his legs turned to jelly and he dropped back down. "Let me take a look."

It couldn't be.

He took the laptop from Finley, crisscrossed his legs, and set the old computer in front of him.

The numbers lit up the screen. It was the code. All of it. In order, beginning with Mel's original clue.

"Nineteen, two," he said.

"Mr. Sterling, you're white as a ghost. What's wrong?"

"Day to day pours out speech. And night to night reveals knowledge."

"I think that's from the Psalms," Finley said. "Are you saying that's Psalm nineteen, two?"

Chase kept his eyes on the screen. The numbers began their scroll.

20-2
22-26
23-6
31-8
32-7
32-7
32-7

The last number repeated. Over and over.

"See what I mean?" Finely asked. "They just keep showing up like that." She took the laptop from Chase and slammed it shut. "It's junk, that's all."

"It's not junk," he told her. His eyes moved from her irritated expression to the laptop as she slid it off her outstretched legs and onto the cold floor. "It's me in there."

44

Chase picked up the old device. He pulled open the screen, but the laptop had powered down.

"It's probably dead," Finley said. "Doesn't hold a charge very long. But Mr. Sterling, what do you mean it's you in there? You mean the missing exoman?"

"Exoself."

"Yeah, sorry. I don't get all that stuff. I mean, I know you lost it while you were gone to Gagnon. And I heard Switchblade shot up Miss Melody's laptop. And—"

"Finley. Please. I need to take this. I'll see if Mel can get you another one. All right?"

She lifted her hand, palm up, and shook her head. "Yeah, take it. I hope you find your exoself guy. But, Mr. Sterling, I've got stuff in there I don't want anybody reading."

Chase hugged the laptop to his chest. "I'll make sure nobody reads your stuff and I'll get Mel to load it into another computer. Thank you, Finley." He took a few steps. Then he reeled back. "Listen, maybe we should keep this quiet. Can you do that?"

"Hey, I'm not saying a word." She tossed her hair behind her back. "God be with you, Mr. Sterling."

"Call me Chase. Could you please go get the charger and put it in my room for me?"

She smiled. "OK. Chase. I'll get it."

He headed for the command center. Mel would

know what to do. Maybe. He stopped walking. Did he want this? The past couple of days he'd been glad it was gone. Ever since he'd gotten the H.S. in him, as Switchblade had put it.

But Switchblade had also told him that his days with the exoself weren't over. The people of the underground needed Chase to get back what he'd brought to them—the transhuman.

He stole into the computer center where Mel and several others worked. Switchblade sat nearby at the monitors showing the feed from the cameras in town.

Chase went to him first and grabbed him by the arm.

"Hey, Charlie, what's got into you? I'm busy here."

"I need to see you. In private. Now."

"All right, all right. I'm coming." Switchblade left the station. "Where we going?"

"My room. I'll get Mel."

"This about Amos?"

"Just go to my room. We'll be right behind you."

The big man huffed and headed toward the hallway.

Chase hurried to Mel's station and dropped his hand on her shoulder. "We need to talk. Right now."

She turned to face him. "Amos?"

"No, there's no change. It's about something else. It's important."

"Chase, can't it wait. I'm kind of busy."

He held the laptop in front of him and tapped it. "I found something."

"That looks like the old laptop I gave Finley. What are you doing with it?" Then her eyes grew wide. "I'm coming." She told the others working with her, "I'll be back in a few minutes. I have to check…I have to…"

"Mel, come on."

She rose from her chair. "I'll be back."

Chase headed out of the room with Mel right behind him.

"Chase, you're telling me the exoself is in that old thing?"

"Did it belong to you, Mel?"

"Yeah. I brought ten devices down with me. Figured we'd have them for personal use as long as we could keep them running."

"But is it registered to you?"

"Sure. They all are."

Chase entered his room and dropped the laptop on the bed. "You were right, Switch. I found it."

"Sparky?" His eyes darted to the bed and back. "So, he found himself another laptop."

Mel sat on the bed and opened the device. Chase found the charger on the table. "It's dead. I told Finley to leave the charger in here." He handed Mel one end and then plugged the cord into the only electrical outlet in the room.

The screen sparked and blue swirls formed a small rectangle. Mel typed in a passcode. Several icons popped up—perhaps titles of whatever Finley had been writing. No sign of the exoself.

"Open a file," Chase said.

Mel clicked on one at random—third from the left. "The Reasons I Hate the Underground," she read from the top of the page. "Teens. They let it all out, don't they?"

Chase took the laptop and moved to the table with it. The cord barely reached. "Sorry, I told Finley I wouldn't let anybody read her stuff."

"Chase, how did you figure this out?" Mel asked. "What makes you think the exoself is in there."

Chase scrolled down. The computer flashed to black. And then the numbers started their roll. "Here's why." He held it up for Mel and Switchblade to see.

Mel stared at the screen. "Praise Jesus."

Switchblade shook his head. "I don't get it."

"It's code, Switch," Mel said. "The code I planted in the exoself to hook it up with the underground."

"Well, how 'bout that," he said. "Charlie, get it back inside you. We know there ain't nobody tracking it now. We turned that off, or whatever. Right, Melody?"

"You disabled the tracker that found us on the highway when you destroyed my laptop. But they've got to be looking for us. For Chase."

Chase sat the laptop on the table and looked at Mel. "You're unsure about this, aren't you? When I first got hold of this, I had second thoughts. I considered putting it away and not telling you. I don't know if I really want the exoself back inside me."

Switchblade walked as far as he could in the little room, his hands on his hips. He spun around. "Are you kidding me? We got to get this back in you, man. Unless you think that old laptop can do everything you could do with the exoself. Seems to me it can't do nothing but show us some numbers."

"It may not matter what we want or don't want," Mel said. "I don't know how to get the program restored in Chase's processors."

"And I sure don't know how," Chase said. "But the exoself was able to use your computer to destroy a drone. So, there's got to be more to it than simply putting the code out. Let's type in the safe travel code.

Seems that one does more than the others."

Mel knelt and took his hand in both of hers. "Are you sure? You said you had second thoughts. Nobody is going to make you do something you don't want to do. Not anymore."

"Oh, come on," Switchblade said. "You gotta do it, Charlie."

Mel let go of Chase's hand. She shot Switchblade a glance. "We could use a couple more chairs in here. Would you go get us some?"

"You want me out of here so you can baby the robot?" Switchblade pursed his lips and his nostrils flared.

Mel crossed her arms. "I want us all to be able to sit around the table and work this out. Now go get us some chairs."

"You're the boss." Switchblade opened the door and stepped out. "You all best leave the door cracked. Don't want nobody saying our leader don't got to live by the rules." He disappeared down the hall.

"He's right," Chase said. "I have to do this. Or at least I have to try."

"I meant what I said, Chase. If you don't want to go down that path, don't. It's your call." She took his hand and pulled him out of the chair and to the end of the bed. They sat side by side. "What do you think God wants you to do? Did you ask Him?"

Chase lifted his eyes upward. "Well, God? Do You care one way or the other if I'm more transhuman or less transhuman? This new connection I feel—is it going to end if I let Sparky back in?" He closed his eyes and took a breath.

"That's amazing," Mel said.

He opened his eyes and met her gaze. "What do

you mean?"

"The way you just talked to God. Nobody does that, Chase. Nobody just starts up a conversation with God like He's sitting right there."

"Oh. I just don't know any better. I told you I've got a lot to learn about being a Christian."

"Well, don't learn too much. Wouldn't want you to unlearn how to pray. You got an answer?"

"Yeah. Nothing will separate me from God. Nothing. You and Switchblade told me that. Tell me something from the Bible, Mel. Tell me I'm right about this."

"From the book of Romans. For I am convinced that neither death nor life, neither angels nor demons, neither the present nor the future, nor any powers, neither height nor depth, nor anything else in all creation, will be able to separate us from the love of God that is in Christ Jesus our Lord."

"Does transhumanism fall within the boundaries of *all creation*?"

"Back when we were at Synvue, I once told you nobody makes something from nothing. Nobody but God. The Helgen Institute didn't do anything God didn't allow."

"What was meant for evil, God used for good."

Mel smiled and brushed her hand against the side of his face. "That's right."

Switchblade pushed the door open and dropped two chairs to the floor. "There. Now what are we doing about this, Charlie? You in? Or are you a transchicken?"

45

Chase grabbed a chair and pulled it to the table for Mel, and he sat beside her. "Get yourself a chair and sit down, you big jerk," he said to Switchblade as he let a chuckle slide out. "We've got to figure out how to get Sparky back where he belongs."

Switchblade nearly smiled—a rare sight from what Chase had witnessed the past few days. "That's what *I'm* talking about. What do you do now, Melody? You need anything? Wires or pliers or something?"

"Pliers?" Chase asked. "What do you think she'd do with pliers?"

"I don't know—*you're* the robot."

"Well, I don't have any parts that require anything from a tool box, Switchblade."

"You boys keep it down," Mel said. "I can't think."

"Sorry," Chase said. "Type in thirty-one, eight and see what happens."

"Yeah, sorry," Switchblade said. "What's thirty-one, eight?"

"Safe travel," Chase told him. "Mel? Anything?"

"I don't think so," she said.

"Let me try." Chase reached for the computer and pulled it across the table. "When I was traveling, I asked the exoself to give me some instructions, and it did." He put his hands on the keys and began typing, Mel and Switchblade behind him.

CHASE   STERLING   REQUESTING

REINSTALLATION INSTRUCTIONS
   Nothing.
   RESTORE CYBER CONNECTION
   "This is a waste of time," Switchblade said.
   HEY, OLD FRIEND. I NEED SOME
INSTRUCTIONS. GIVE ME SOMETHING.
   The code on the screen mushroomed from a short list of numbers to a full page display of binary code. Chase touched the screen as the code scrolled down. His eyes drank it in. Even his fingertips seemed to take in the information he couldn't interpret. The processors in his back and arms surged.

   "I need to lie down." He rose from the chair and stumbled to the bed.

   "Chase, is this thing hurting you?" Mel knelt on the floor next to him as he dropped to his back. "I'm turning it off."

   "No," he said. "Robert was able to reactivate the exoself in an orderly fashion. Now it's just all rushing in at once. But don't try to stop it. It's coming back."

   "Don't want the thing to take you down or nothing," Switchblade said. "I didn't mean to push so hard for you to do this."

   The rush that Chase knew as the signature of the exoself seemed to slow. "Give it to me. I need to look at the code. I don't know what I'm looking at, but I think my eyes do."

   "Chase, are you sure?" Mel asked.

   He reached for her hand. "I'm fine." Sweat beaded on his upper lip. Other than that, and the lethargy that had overtaken him, his physical condition hadn't altered. He could count the beats of his heart. He knew his blood pressure and temperature. They were forever constant.

"Quickly, Mel. Give me the laptop."

Before she could stand, Switchblade handed her the computer. She placed it on Chase's stomach, the screen facing him. He lifted his head a little, and Mel folded the pillow underneath him so he could look at the scrolling code. The inner clock worked again. For three minutes, thirty-four seconds, he didn't blink. And it all came back.

Every branch of the Underground Church lined up in a sea of information organized by the four S's. The secret communication of the WR opened to his manipulation. Intel of arrests, of stake-outs, growing detention center population, and the increasing number of people dropping off the grid of WR support programs filled his mind. He checked the reports from the underground against the files of the WR. No base of operations had been flushed out. At least not since those of a few days ago. Chase hadn't missed too much, and the exoself filled him in on what had gone down during their separation.

He exhaled a groan.

"Chase, that's enough," Mel said. "I'm turning this thing off."

"Yeah, go ahead," he told her. "It's done. The exoself is back where it belongs."

Before he'd finished the sentence, the computer screen went black. Then a spark shot out and a whiff of smoke rose into the air.

Switchblade grabbed the laptop and dropped it on the table. He waved his hand over it as if that would stop the smoke. Then he slammed the lid shut. "I think it was too much for the old thing."

Chase sat up and rubbed his eyes. "I told Finley we'd get her stuff moved to another computer."

Mel raked her fingers through his hair. "Too late for that. She'll understand. All that matters is you're OK. You are, aren't you?"

"Yeah. Don't think I'm quite ready to bend a metal pole, and I don't know if I can see in the dark. Other than that, seems everything is in good working order."

"Hallelujah," Switchblade said.

Then a flash of code appeared from the corner of Chase's eye. It danced and curved until it began to take the form of a human.

Chase wouldn't allow this. That phantom would not haunt him again. He jumped off the bed, grabbed a chair, and threw it at the corner of the room.

Mel let out a quick scream. "Chase, what is it?"

Switchblade took Chase by the arms and tried to sit him down on the bed, but Chase sent him flying into the wall. The upper body strength was back.

"I will not accept this!" he yelled at the code replicating in the corner. "Get out of here!"

Then he dropped to the bed and breathed out a heavy sigh. He swiped his hands over the top of his head.

"Oh, God, thank you," he said. "Robert."

46

"I can see you, Robert." Chase stared at the apparition materializing in the corner. "Can you hear me?" The white coat worn by the doctor when Chase last saw him was as real as Kerstin's red dress the night she'd first materialized.

"I hear you, son, but I can't see you. It's how the program works." Robert didn't look directly at Chase but his lips moved when he spoke.

"I know—I've had this experience before. Though I didn't welcome the last person who intruded on the exoself. But now—"

"Yes, yes. Kerstin. Awful woman. I demanded she be sent back to the Synvue Estate. But the government took her somewhere else, I think. They were hard on her when she lost track of you."

"Then you know about that. Robert, I'm so glad to see you. Well, to see what the exoself has presented of you. I've got so many questions. That aside, it's just so good to talk with you."

Mel sat beside him and clutched his hand. "Chase, baby, is Robert Fiender really here? Right now?"

Chase pried his eyes off Robert and looked at Mel. "Same program as when Kerstin showed up. It's all right. He's on our side."

"Are you sure? We don't know what kind of tricks those people can pull. Maybe it's not really him at all."

"Chase, is someone there with you?" Robert asked.

"If so, then a change has occurred in the program. The exoself should not have allowed contact unless you were alone. Little visions and hints of a presence, perhaps, but not audio."

"Yeah, about the exoself—it's done some things you might call unbelievable. Not to mention what my body can do on its own. If you know about Kerstin, then you know about the Feds losing my trail so quickly. I mean, I was right there under their noses. Did the exoself throw them off?"

"I suppose it did. The Feds were baffled when the trail went cold. They picked up three men, assumed one of them was you, and brought them in. Didn't take long, of course, to realize their mistake, but they only scanned the area for your cyber imprint. None was found and they didn't even bother with a physical search. Then a drone caught your trail, only to crash before it could send back reliable data."

"The exoself was hiding in an old laptop when it blew up that drone."

The doctor's bushy eyebrows drew together and he wiped his mustache. Chase smiled at this. He'd missed the old man. His friend.

"I had a feeling it had come out of your systems when your imprint disappeared. But to hide in an antiquated device? I feared it may have jumped out of you completely this time, rather than remaining dormant after the killswitch was triggered. Its homing mechanism should have sent it here. But it was best that it stayed clear of me—I guess it knew better. I'm under constant scrutiny." The doctor paused. He blinked his thick eyelids. "Chase, I had nothing to do with implanting the device in Kerstin that allowed her to access the exoself."

"I know, Robert. I never thought you did. But I think the homing mechanism did what it was supposed to do. Only it sought out a closer familiar hiding place. The laptop—actually two laptops—were registered to Melody Reese. Do you remember that name?"

The doctor grumbled and his lips puffed outward. "Yes, yes, of course I remember. Your undercover programmer. The best friend you were so determined to locate."

"That's right. I guess the exoself knew her, so to speak, since she helped in the programming. It took up residence in her computer. A perfect hiding place."

"Amazing. And now it's back inside you where it belongs? And you're safely back underground? Somewhere in Quebec, I assume." Robert cleared his throat. "Before you answer, and because this whole situation appears so volatile and fluid, disregard my last question, Chase. The Feds have not given up."

"Thank you for wanting to protect us."

"Us?"

"Yes." Chase put his arm around Mel.

"Enough said. But how on earth did you get the exoself back into your processors?"

"I just asked. I typed in a message and the code started scrolling. I think my eyes did the work."

"Oh my. Your eyes are programmed to accept data, but you don't need to do that on your own, Chase. You're an amateur. When I instructed your processors to allow reentry of the exoself, I did it in an orderly fashion to avoid too much strain on your...human. Are you all right?"

"It was a little overwhelming but I feel good now."

"And all functions are operational? The vision and

hearing enhancers? The strength sensors?"

"Haven't tried out the vision and hearing, but the upper body strength is back for sure."

From across the room, Switchblade muttered, "You got that right."

Chase glanced his way. "Sorry, buddy." He turned his focus back to the phantom figure of his doctor and designer. "Robert, I suffered a broken leg when the truck I was in flipped—that's when the Feds lost the trail. It took two days for the break to heal. Two days, Robert. What can you tell me about that?"

The man cleared his throat. "Your blood contains—"

"Nanobytes?"

"More like nano*bots*. But yes, they are in your bloodstream. When I last examined you, they were non-functional. I expected nothing more from them than the validation that such mighty little warriors could indeed be added to a human being's blood and not cause death. Are you saying that your broken bone has healed completely, Chase?"

"Like it never happened. Are *you* saying adding this crap to my blood could have killed me?"

"It was a possibility. I didn't know you then, son. I didn't care about you as much as I cared about the experiment. Any number of things could have gone wrong. That you survived your transformation at all was a miracle. I must admit part of me longs to study how the techno-evolutionary process is changing you. Your body's ability to heal itself is just another miracle. If I could believe in miracles. As it is, I'm glad those who do believe have taken you in. You know I'm sorry for all this, Chase. I wish it had never happened."

"I don't wish that, Robert. I'm with the ones who

have become my people. I have to protect them. Are there any more surprises coming?"

"I can't answer that with certainty." The doctor's appearance seemed to change. A darkness fell on him. "The exoself may take over your own thought process as it strives to preserve itself. Or it may have developed such a dependence on you that it will do nothing to harm you, but only to help you. Either way, it will—it has already—taken on a personality and it's living inside you, Chase. Whether or not you can trust it…"

"Someone else has taken up residence inside me, and I don't believe He will allow harm to come to me. Or allow me to become a danger to anyone."

The doctor shook his head. Was his motion real, or was the exoself adding appropriate gestures to the conversation? "You have become one of the hiders," he said. "Am I correct? A believer?"

"Yes, Robert. The exoself may attempt to become more, or to make me less. But God is bigger than it or me and He's got this."

"Your secret is safe with me, son."

"My location is a secret, Robert. The work of the underground is a secret. But what I said about me and God is no secret. Tell the world if you want. Tell them Chase Sterling is a true believer. A follower of Jesus, whose blood is more powerful than mine."

Mel clutched his arm. Did she expect him to keep it quiet? One thought tripped over another. The blood. Actively regenerating healing bytes…or bots.

Amos could live.

"I can't say I agree with your decision, son. I fear you've been driven to the limits of reason by the torment I helped bring on you. Again, you know my sorrow over the matter."

"No regrets. There's no turning back. But tell me something, as my doctor and my friend. If my blood was injected into another human—not a transhuman—just a regular man, what would happen?"

Mel lifted her hand to his face, pulled his gaze to her. "Oh, Chase, you can't be serious."

"Didn't Christ give his blood for me? Why shouldn't I follow His example?"

"It's not the same at all, Chase." Her eyes filled with such fear, and Chase wrapped his arms around her. He couldn't bear to think she might come to fear him.

"Trust me," he told her.

She sniffed back tears and nodded. "Always."

Chase let her go and stared at the corner of the room. But the computer image his brain had interpreted as the likeness of Robert Fiender had faded to a line of code and a flash of white.

"No. Don't go. You didn't answer my question." He shuffled to the empty corner. "Robert?"

47

Mel put her hands on Chase's shoulders. "Is he gone?"

Chase drew her close, then gaped at Switchblade, who sat on the floor, his back to the wall, his hands resting on his knees.

"Is he, man? He didn't tell you nothing about the blood? Because I think you got something there, Charlie."

"Oh, Switch, you can't be serious," Mel said. "You can't just go pumping nanobytes into a sick man. Besides that, we don't know what would happen to Chase if we started pumping them *out*."

"Actually, it's nano*bots*. Is that even weirder?" Chase asked. "Because it sounds weirder."

Mel didn't answer—her attention remained on Switchblade. "I can't imagine any doctor would agree to it, much less one with no training in cyber-genetics. Certainly not Dr. John, and I know that's what you're thinking."

Switchblade got up and limped to the door. "Charlie, can you get that ghost back here for some more Q & A?"

"I don't think so. But he'll show up again. Somebody must have interrupted. He can't very well sit around talking to Chase Sterling with other people around."

Mel shook her head. "Chase, this is crazy—you

talking to him. Talking to Kerstin the way you did. They're going to find us."

"We know what happened the last time they closed in. The exoself took care of it."

"You really want to go through that again?" she asked. "Tell the exoself to stop bringing people here from your old life." She crossed her arms.

"Robert will be careful. I need to talk to him again."

"About a blood transfusion? *That* is even crazier. As leader of Blue Sky Field, I forbid it."

"Mel. Seriously? You're going to stop me from doing something to save Amos's life?"

"I've got to get back to the command center." She opened the door. "If Fiender shows up again, I want to know about it immediately." She left without waiting for a response.

"Yes *ma'am*," Chase said. He pointed at the door and lowered his brow at Switchblade. "That woman…"

"Yeah, you got your hands full, Charlie. But she's just looking out for you. At least you got Sparky back. You really saw that doctor of yours? I only heard one side of a conversation, and I didn't see nothing but you staring at the corner."

"He seemed as real as you, Switchblade. I mean, after he coded in and before he coded out."

"I think I got the gist of it—the talk you had with the man. You went right out and told him you're a believer. Took guts, Charlie. More guts than I ever had."

"Nobody ever taught *me* to be quiet, Switch. And nobody ever will."

"You got some power in you, brother. All that

stuff you said about Christ giving His blood for you—you understand it. But you ain't had no teaching."

Chase sat on the end of the bed. The exoself ran through every branch of the underground. That world, at the moment, appeared safe. Well fed. Equipped. Transportation requests flowed through his mind. A branch in the EU had accepted thirty-two believers seeking shelter after a raid of church houses. No one was lost in the crackdown.

Everything Mel could see at her work station amassed in Chase's head without any prompting. The Underground Church moved on in its quest to remain an entity apart from the obstructive forces of world government. Hidden, protected. In part by the programs brought to them by a transhuman. But surely it was God watching out for them.

Was the rest of the population to be left godless?

Chase shifted from Mel's programs and the code uniting the underground, and locked into the workings of the WR. He'd been kicked out of this trail of information when Robert first removed the federal ownership of the exoself and placed it solely in Chase's possession. But the exoself took a one-way street back to the Western Republic. That street was still open. Nothing had changed since Sparky took shelter in Mel's old computers. Chase roamed the government programs at will.

The nearest detention center—the one with the awful machine designed to harvest gray matter—had a few new prisoners. Dissenters. Kirel was one of them. He might talk—tell the Feds all about Blue Sky Field. His file showed nothing but a medical report stating trauma to the brain resulting in short-term memory loss. A temporary condition being treated with techno-medical procedures. Kirel wouldn't be out of his mind forever.

Chase shuddered as he attached a report demanding treatment cease immediately due to insufficient data supporting a positive outcome of the procedure. Then he prayed Kirel would never remember he'd been beneath an old museum in Herouxville.

He looked up to find Switchblade sitting beside him.

"Man, you been off on a trip or what? You got an update from Sparky?"

"Yes. Most of it's good. Some of it's troubling. I'll monitor the situation."

"Tell me if I can be of assistance. You serious about helping Amos, in spite of what our fearless leader says? Because I'm ready for a trip out of this cave."

"Switchblade, if I get Mel to change her mind I want you to stay here. I'll feel a lot better knowing you're watching over Blue Sky Field."

The big man huffed and shook his head. "I'd feel a lot better doing what Amos assigned me to do—watching your back."

"I can handle a run to Gagnon. But before we plan anything I need to talk to Robert again. No point in putting Amos through that if the maker of the nanobots says it's a waste of time."

"This stuff just keeps getting weirder, Charlie."

"Yeah. And useful. I hope."

48

The command center buzzed with excitement. Eyes stared at Chase. The people knew their transhuman was back in full service. He could hear every whisper across the room. Sure didn't take long for news to travel in this place.

Chase pulled up a chair and sat next to Mel at her work station. She lifted her gaze from the computer screen. No smile. Not even a welcoming gleam in her deep brown eyes.

"Mel, I can't help it if people back at the Helgen can visit me through the exoself."

She focused on work in front of her. "We shouldn't have allowed the exoself back in. I didn't know you were going to get another visitation right off the bat. We would have been fine without—"

"I'm a transhuman, Melody. Can you live with that?"

She dropped her hands from the keypad and swiveled in her chair. Her expression softened. "I love you."

That ever-present giggle of teenage girls rippled through the space between Chase and Mel. He smiled.

"Can we go someplace a little more private?" He took her hand and rubbed her fingers. "I'll leave the door open."

She smiled at last and rose from her seat. She said nothing, but tightened her grip on his hand and led him down the hallway to her room.

He followed her in. As he said he would, he left the door cracked. But it made no difference to him—he took her in his arms and kissed her. "Can you?"

She seemed dazed, and said nothing before her lips met his again. Then she fixed her eyes on his. "Can I what?"

"Live with the fact that I am a transhuman."

"Oh, that. Can you live with the fact that I'm not going to let you take Amos to Gagnon?"

He dropped his hands from her waist. "What if Robert says it will work? That it won't harm either Amos or me?"

"That's a big *if*."

"Well?"

"You get me conclusive information about what might happen, and I will consider the *two* of us taking Amos to see Dr. John."

"You'd leave your post? You're the boss now."

"Well, that doesn't seem to matter to *you*. You're going to do as you please. And I'm going to follow you wherever you go." She cupped his face in her hands. "I just have a bad feeling, Chase. Like if you leave we might not ever see each other again."

He took her hand and held it to his lips. "Mel, you've got to believe me. I will do whatever it takes to make sure that never happens. I can't live without you."

"Then don't go."

A young man pushed the door open. "Sorry to interrupt," he said. "Amos seems to be getting worse. Mr. Sterling, your mother wants to see you."

Chase pivoted toward the door and heaved a breath. "I'm coming." He faced Mel. "Let's go see him.

He might not approve any more than you do, but I want to tell him."

"All right, but—"

"I know. Robert's got to show up again and give his approval."

"I hope that crazy old doctor—"

"Mel, be nice. And don't be afraid, sweetheart. Don't be afraid."

49

Amos was worse, all right. Chase didn't need to touch him to find that out. Mom leaned over him with a damp cloth. His ghostly white face was all that showed in the bed covered with multiple blankets. Breathing seemed harder than two hours ago. Open eyes gave the hint of a man wavering between hope and all-out terror. The pain must have grown worse.

Chase knelt by the bed and looked up at Mel. "Did we bring back anything in those medical supplies to help ease his discomfort?"

"Codeine. I'll go get it." She left the room.

Mom dropped the little towel into a bowl of water beside the bed. "Chase, I heard you got the exoself back."

"It's all there."

"I don't know how I feel about that."

Chase shook his head. "I'm not sure either. But it's me, Mom. It's who I am." He got up off his knees and sat on the bed opposite his mother. "Amos, can you hear me?"

The man grunted and looked at Chase. "Yes, son. I'm feeling a little better now." He winced and his eyes shut tight.

"We're going to give you something for the pain. But it'll have to be in pill form. Can you keep it down?"

"Kinda doubt it. But we'll give it a try."

"Good," Chase said. "Mel went to get it from the supplies we brought back from Gagnon. Amos, we need to talk to you about taking you there."

"I told you before there is nothing the doctor can do for me."

"You may be wrong about that, Amos. Remember how my leg healed? And Mel said I might have some techno blood flowing inside me?"

"I remember."

"She was right. And I think my blood might be what you need."

Mom's eyes grew wide. "What on earth? You can't be serious."

"Mom, I talked to my doctor—the one who designed me."

"He called you?"

"No, Mom, he didn't call me. It's complicated."

"And what did he say about this foolish idea of yours?"

"Well, I didn't get an answer. But I'm hoping to know for sure if it'll work. And if it will, or even if there's a possibility, then that trip to Gagnon might just save Amos's life."

Amos lifted his arm out from under the covers. He reached for Chase but his hand fell to the bed. "Son, why would you take a chance like that for a dying man? I've made my peace with this."

"Amos, what would it hurt to try? If God wants you to go, then you'll go." Chase took the man's hand in his. "But maybe He wants you to stay a while longer."

Amos blinked and then stared at the ceiling. "You don't know if it will work?"

"I'm hoping to find out soon. Will you do it?"

"I've always loved a good scientific experiment."

Mel slipped into the room with a small pouch. "I've got it." She sat beside Amos and took out a pill.

Chase lifted Amos's head, who opened his mouth just enough for Mel to drop the pill on his tongue. Then she reached for a water glass and held it to his lips.

Mom crossed her arms. "Melody, do you know what he's planning?"

"Oh, yeah. Crazy idea. Might kill both of them. But hey, I'm just the leader of the worldwide command center of the Underground Church. And the transhuman's girlfriend. My opinion doesn't count for much."

"Mel, take it easy," Chase said. "I thought we'd reached an understanding."

"You talk to that crazy doctor again?"

"Not yet."

"Then you still have some convincing to do."

Chase tightened his jaw, his eyes on Amos. "I'll let you know what happens. Hang in there." He headed for the door. "Mom, do you need a break?"

"I got one earlier. Can I just call you...you know, in your head if I need to?"

Chase nearly laughed. "Only if you have a coded VPad on you. Right now, Mel's the only one who's got one. You can't summon me with your brain. Unless you got chipped since the last time we talked."

She smiled and brushed the graying hair from her eyes. "I'll just send for you."

Chase nodded and left the room.

Mel was close behind him. "I'm going back to my station," she said. "You gonna go try to conjure up your doctor?"

"I can't do that. At least, not yet. Maybe the exoself will refine the program and allow it. For now, I'll just have to wait."

"Amos could die before Fiender shows up again."

"Then it wasn't meant to be. I'm going back to my room."

Mel grabbed his hand. "We've got to do this together. No matter what happens."

"You've got no argument from me. I'll check in with you in an hour or so."

"It'll be supper time in an hour."

"I'll see you there." Chase squeezed her hand, then let her go. He went to his room, shut the door, and sat in one of the chairs Switchblade had brought in earlier. And waited.

No amount of hoping or praying would bring the phantom of the man back. Maybe Mel was right. Maybe this wasn't God's plan for Amos. Or for Chase. "She's right—it's a stupid idea."

He leaned forward with his elbows on his knees and rested his head in his hands. Then a flash rushed through his mind. The line of code. A white coat materialized beside the table where the lifeless old laptop still remained. "Robert."

"Yes, yes. I'm here, son. I had to exit the program earlier. That asinine man who chipped Kerstin blew into my office."

"Young Dr. Jack. Does he suspect anything?"

"Nothing. And I've altered the exoself to disallow contact from any processors other than mine."

"Robert, do you have a chip in your brain like the one Kerstin got?"

"Had it for years. It's a bit antiquated and I don't know how long I can maintain contact with the exoself.

Getting an updated implant right now would only bring more questions than I care to answer. But rest assured, no one else can come in. If Kerstin tries it again, the exoself will not only disallow entry, it will wipe out her processor."

"That's a relief. I almost got caught. The underground would have been compromised. I can't allow that, Robert. Are you positive what you're doing now is safe?"

"Yes, of course. You know how I feel about you, son."

Chase wanted to put his arm around the old man's shoulder. "I know. Robert, did you hear my last question before you had to cut out?"

"About your blood? Yes. I'm guessing someone is ill."

"The leader here—the former leader—is dying. Leukemia. He had to step down and now he's in bad shape."

"The technology is so new, Chase. You're the only man in the world with nanobots in his bloodstream."

"Just give me your professional opinion. Would it make any difference at all in his condition? Would it matter if we didn't have the same blood type?"

The doctor's image varied a bit but rectified in a flash. "Blood type, for you, no longer matters. It's the same as with your organs, which are made to be universally acceptable by any human being. Once we added the technology to your blood, it lost some aspects of its humanness. It regenerates with no specific type. A transfusion would not harm your leader. As to whether or not it would help him, I can only tell you that it would take over in his body the same way it has in yours. It would latch on to the organic blood cells and eradicate malfunctions. At least, in theory, Chase."

"Then it's a cure for all kinds of disease. That's incredible."

"In *theory*, son."

"But you think it would work. Don't you?"

"The data indicates that it should produce major, positive changes when applied to most conditions. Now that I know of its function in you, I'm hopeful that it will become a viable treatment. But son, the nanobots don't regenerate. Your human blood still does, of course. However, this is not something you could do repeatedly. Once, maybe twice, but no more. Now that your organs and your blood are functioning together, doing this repeatedly might have dire consequences."

"The recipient wouldn't benefit," Chase said.

"No, son. The donor wouldn't survive."

Chase drew closer to the image. "Robert, can you send the data to me? I mean, only if it can be done in an untraceable program. I don't have access to the Helgen."

"Do you remember when you contacted an old computer of mine to let me know you were safe? Does the exoself still have the code, or was it wiped clean after the first contact?"

Chase ran a scan of the coded trails of the exoself and found the connection. "I have it."

"I'll move the data to that location. Give me until tomorrow morning. Chase, this will be my last visit, at least for a while. They're bringing in a new subject and I'm being forced back into the laboratory. Security will be too tight for me to try this again."

"A new subject? They're going to build another

one, aren't they? Another transhuman."

"Yes, son. But he will be inept. I'll see to that."

Chase grinned. "Thank you, Robert. For everything. I miss you."

"And I miss you, son. Maybe one day…"

"Maybe."

The image faded away. Chase reached for the door, but stepped back and sat in the chair. Then he dropped from the chair to his knees. "God, thanks for this. It'll work. But it won't be me that saves Amos—I know that. I can't save anyone. Only Jesus can."

He stood up and swung the door open. A smile on his face, resolve in his step, he headed for the dining hall.

Meals waited on the counter for the evening's servers to pick up and deliver to the tables. Mel sat on the far side of the room. An empty chair waited beside her. Chase made his way to sit next to her.

"I talked to Robert," he told her.

"And?"

"Good news. He thinks it'll work."

"I need—"

"He's sending me the data. I'll have it by morning. But Mel, we can take him at his word."

"I know you trust him. But to me, he's just the man who turned you into…" Her eyes showed the sorrow for what she almost said. "I need to see the data."

"It's coming. But I don't think that's the only thing you're worried about. I have to ask you, one more time, if you can deal with what I am. I'm not the same man you once knew."

Her lips curved upward and tears puddled in her eyes. "I know that. I didn't love that man the way I love you."

Her words took his breath away. Even lab-grown lungs had to respond to the unexpected confession of this lovely young woman.

She wiped her eyes. "I'm just so scared of you going off. You can tell yourself it'll all work out, but the truth is that you being up top in the real world is dangerous. And you made a promise that we would never be apart again."

He studied her face for a moment. "We need to talk, Mel. You've got to see the data before you let me go. Well, there's something I've got to do too."

"What is it?"

"Not here. Meet me in my room after I tell Amos the good news."

"But Chase, he needs to understand—"

"I know—the data. Half an hour. OK?"

"Yeah, but aren't you hungry?"

He grabbed a slice of bread from her plate. "This will do." He left her there. Looking back, he met her eyes and held the sight of her. Then he headed out as he stuffed the bread into his mouth.

She had her stipulations. Well, so did he.

50

Amos seemed hardly able to comprehend what Chase had to tell him. Would he even survive the trip to Gagnon? Mom still sat at his bedside. She'd eaten her supper in the room and tried to feed Amos a bit of cooked apples. He didn't take much.

Even through the pain and mental haze, Amos accepted Chase's word that what they were about to do offered hope and promise.

"We'll leave tomorrow night—around midnight," Chase told him.

"The three of us," Mom said. "Right?"

"Come on, Mom. You can't be serious about that. You're as bad as Mel."

"Well, you can't stay with him—you'll need to get right back here. He needs to have someone with him, Chase. Someone he knows. We've become close friends. And I want to go."

Amos had closed his eyes. What would *he* think about dragging her along? Chase huffed. "You'll need to get permission from the boss."

His mother smiled. "How are we getting there, son?"

"Assuming it's *we*, I'm working on it. I met a funny guy called Shorty who owns a hearse. That's how I got to Gagnon when I was injured."

"Kind of morbid—putting a sick man in a hearse."

"It may be our best option. He'll be more

comfortable than if we try to move him in a livestock truck."

"All right. Whatever you say. So you'll make the connection from the command center tonight?"

Chase smiled. "No need for that. I just made it. Waiting for a response."

She shook her head. "Wonder of wonders."

"I need to talk to Mel. You OK? You need anything?"

"A couple of the young men have been helping me. If you see Michael or Joseph, ask if one of them can come in about an hour from now. I'll go to my room and get a few hours' sleep."

"OK." He bent to kiss her cheek. "I can't believe you talked me into taking you. You're stubborn. You know that?"

"Where do you think you got it from?"

Chase left for his room. But he slowed his pace. "God, is this the dumbest thing I've ever done? I planned on waiting a while."

He found his door open and Mel resting in a chair, her eyes closed. He left the door cracked and knelt in front of her just to watch her.

After a minute, she opened her eyes and smiled. "Hi." She blinked and sat up. "How'd it go?"

"Between the pain and the codeine, I'm not sure he understood everything I told him. But he knows what we're planning."

She wiped her eyes. Worry swept over her face, but she didn't argue about the plan. "What did you want to talk about?"

Chase didn't answer. He only looked at her.

"You're scaring me."

He reached to take her hand. "I don't want to scare

you, Mel. I want you to trust me. I need you to know I never want to be apart from you. And I think there's a way I can show you." He paused.

"I'm listening."

He kissed her hand before he rested his head on her knee and closed his eyes.

She ran her fingers through his hair. "Chase?"

He lifted his head and looked into her dark eyes. "Marry me. Tomorrow. Before I leave. Then you'll know I'm coming home. There's no way I'd let anything stop me from getting back to my beautiful wife."

She breathed in. He couldn't read her expression. Shock? Doubt? Then she tilted her head and smiled.

"Tomorrow," she said. "Yes."

He wrapped his arms around her. "It'll be a great day. The best day ever. I love you, Melody."

51

By morning all the residents of Blue Sky Field had one goal—to orchestrate a wedding. What could possibly have them working so hard? They had no means for preparing a grand event. This would be a simple ceremony officiated by one of the ordained ministers. Nevertheless, platters filled with finger sandwiches and fruit seemed to come out of nowhere.

Some of the ladies joined together to craft a white coverlet into a gown. Chase had nothing suitable to wear. He never planned on a wedding devoid of a designer suit, a proper venue, and the best caterers.

"What am I thinking?" he prayed out loud. "I never planned on a wedding at all. Chase Sterling would *not* approve of any of this. Good thing he's no longer with us."

Then he had a wretched thought. He had to talk to the bride.

He found her in her room, struggling to rearrange the furniture.

"What are you doing?" he asked from the doorway.

She stood straight and brushed back her hair. "Oh, nothing."

He hurried into the room and nudged the door closed behind him.

"Leave the door cracked," she said.

"Mel, we're getting married in an hour."

She folded her arms. "Well, we're not married *yet*."

He pulled the door open. "I had an awful thought. Is this even legal—getting married in the underground?"

"You want to apply to the WR for a permit and wait six months?"

"I just want it to be official."

"We have a document. We sign it. Witnesses sign it. The pastor signs it. We say our vows before God. It's official. And it is binding. And we don't have a process in place to dissolve what's binding. So, you in?"

He lifted her off the floor and swung her in circles.

"I'm in," he said. "Nothing like an impromptu wedding to make a transhuman come unglued."

She put her hands on his chest. "Whatever happens, we're in it together. You and me. And the Lord is with us." She pulled away. "Now get out."

"What?"

"Do I look like I'm ready to get married? Go get Amos a chair. He says he's feeling better and he doesn't want to miss this."

"I'm going." He pulled on the door. "I don't think anybody's making me a suit and tie out of an old bedspread."

She let out a laugh. "But you are going to shave. Right?"

"Yeah, of course." He smiled. "Don't you want me to help you with whatever it is you're doing? I'm super strong, you know."

She pointed at the door. "Out."

He left her for a trip to the bathroom, where he showered and shaved, though he hadn't planned on shaving. Back in his room, he pulled on a clean shirt and black jeans. The best he could do. Before he had a chance to follow instructions concerning Amos, a rush of information entered the exoself. The data. Chase didn't understand much of it. He sent it to Mel's work station.

In Amos's room, he asked his mom to go and tell Mel to take a look at the files.

"But she'll be getting ready," Mom said. "Can't it wait until after the ceremony?"

"I've postponed the transport—Shorty's not coming until two in the morning. That gives me twelve hours with my bride. We're not going to spend our honeymoon—"

"Enough said." Mom bounced on her toes. "Have I told you how happy I am?"

"A couple of times. Now go give Mel the message. If you want to go on a road trip, she's got to see that data."

"All right, son."

She left the room and Chase devoted a few moments to Amos, who did seem a little better. The man laughed about the twelve-hour honeymoon. Chase got him up and dressed, helped him to the meeting room, and propped him in chair.

Others arrived. Switchblade—the best man— joined Chase in a circle of guys offering advice and joking about Chase's change of heart regarding the timing of the nuptials. Mom took a seat beside Amos. Chase spoke with the pastor—an older man who'd been elected to officiate by the two younger ministers.

When he'd gotten a minute's worth of pre-marital counseling, he joined his mom and Amos. Fifteen minutes until the wedding.

"Mom, did Mel get a chance to look over the data

from Robert?"

"I think she's still looking. She'd better hurry it up."

"Maybe I should go check on her." Chase rose from the chair.

"You can't do that, Chase. I'll go." Mom headed away from the oddly festive meeting room. White paper flowers bloomed everywhere. A table against the back wall held an elegant display that included a little white cake.

From the platform, Switchblade called to Chase. "Charlie, get on up here. It's almost time."

Mom returned and took her seat. Every resident of Blue Sky Field waited. A boy pulled out a little flute and began to play a tune. Chase had never heard it. But even without lyrics, the exoself supplied the name of the old song: "Great is Thy Faithfulness."

Young Finley entered the room. Her only mark of being the maid of honor was a bouquet of paper flowers. She stepped lightly up the aisle formed by careful placement of old white resin chairs and took her place on the other side of the pastor.

Melody stepped into the room with no one to give her away. Her make-do dress hung loose off her shoulders. A strand of pearls graced her neck. She smiled, seeming to glide toward Chase.

A power tool blared above them, but no one seemed to care. Mel took Chase's hand as they stood before the gray-headed pastor with reading glasses perched on his nose.

He welcomed them to the sacred altar. "Friends, today we come to encourage these who've chosen to commit their lives to one another and to bless their union."

The matter of reciting common vows happened too quickly. Chase wanted to slow the man down.

But the preacher rambled on. "Do you promise to love, honor, and cherish her until you are parted by death?"

Chase had more to say. And so he answered with the unexpected. "Not exactly." He grasped both Mel's hands and faced her.

She laughed. "Then tell me what it is you're promising."

He wanted to reach into her soul. "You are a blessing I don't deserve. I regret the time I knew you and cared about you, but didn't know you were my gift from God. He changed me and now I know. I'm so glad you're mine. Until we are parted by death? No. I love you forever."

She breathed in and squeezed his hands. "Forever."

The pastor asked if they had rings to give each other.

Mel shook her head. "Maybe someday."

Chase slipped the pouch from his pocket and opened it. He held up Mel's hand and dropped his parents' rings into her palm.

"Chase, where did you get these?"

"From my mother. She likes you."

A ripple of soft laughter rose behind them as Chase placed the ring on Mel's finger. A tear fell down her cheek as she lifted his hand and slipped the band onto his finger.

He bent close enough to feel her breath on his face, but Switchblade smacked his arm. "The man didn't say you could kiss her yet."

The whole assembly laughed and the pastor lifted

his hands. "By all means, you may kiss your bride."

Chase pulled his wife close and softly kissed her lips. Then her sweet smile filled him. Together, they faced the cheering residents of Blue Sky Field.

The hugging from wedding guests went on longer than the ceremony. But soon everyone had a plate of treats concocted, no doubt, from hash and old bread. Chase cut the little cake and fed a slice to Mel. She returned the gesture. Not nearly sweet enough, the cake tasted more like a big biscuit with waxy cream on top. No loss that there wasn't enough for everyone.

Chase led Mel to a corner and kissed her. "Hello, Mrs. Redding."

She ran her hand up his arm. "Do you know how many women wanted to marry you a year ago? I kept a file of all the proposals from your fans."

"Thanks for not marrying me off to one of them."

"I'm no dummy."

He lifted the string of pearls from her neck and then dropped it back in place.

"One of the older ladies loaned them to me."

"Mel, did you look over the data from Robert?"

She lowered her gaze. "Yeah. I think it might work." Her eyes met his. "But I'm speaking as someone trained in A.I., not as a doctor. Something could go wrong. Not to mention it could harm you to give up too much blood."

"Robert said a pint or two won't matter. After that I'll never do it again. I promise."

She tilted her head and huffed before fixing her gaze on Amos. "He needs to rest up for later."

"So we have your approval?"

"You have my *consent*."

"I'll get Switchblade to help him to his room. Do

you think all these people will notice if you and I disappear?"

"If they do, there's going to be a lot of giggling from Finley and company."

Chase laughed as he motioned for Switchblade and asked him to take care of Amos. Then he put his arm around his bride and walked her to her room. The door was wide open. More paper flowers adorned the table beside a double bed.

"This is why you were moving furniture? Where'd you get the bed?"

"I'm the boss around here. I get what I want." She kissed his lips. "This is *our* room now."

He walked to the bed and glanced back at her as he rubbed his moist palms against his jeans. He thought he felt the rapid beat of a heart that never altered its rhythm.

Mel gave him a smile. "Now all the rules have changed." She reached behind her.

And then she pushed the door shut.

52

The command center was normally deserted after midnight. Not tonight. Chase sat with Mel at her station. Nearby, Switchblade monitored the world up top. Others milled around checking on security and travel conditions. Mom sat with Amos near the hallway leading to another hall that held the only exit left from Blue Sky Field. It'd be a chore getting Amos up the stairs and out the hole behind the dumpster. Shorty would meet them at the end of the alley.

Chase watched his wife as her fingers moved over the keypad before her. But then she stopped typing. A tear fell on her cheek.

Chase leaned forward and grasped her hands. "No, sweetheart, don't cry."

"I just wish we had more time. I want to go with you. It's our wedding night and you're going off with your mother. That's not right."

"I'd prefer to leave her here, but Amos likes the idea of having her there while he recovers."

"*If* he recovers." She pulled her hand away and wiped her face.

Switchblade pulled a chair close and dropped beside Chase. "If anybody ought to be going with you on this outing, it's me. Leave the women folk behind, Charlie."

"I told you I'll feel better knowing you're here, Switch."

"How you getting back? You'll be on your own. I don't like that."

Mel rested her hand on Switchblade's arm. "I don't like it either."

"Look, I've still got a flight pack," Chase said. "I'll travel at night and I'll be back in twenty hours."

Switchblade shook his head and breathed out one of those obnoxious snorts.

Chase narrowed his eyes. "Could we have a little time alone?" He jerked his head to one side, hoping the man would get the hint.

"I'm going." He left them, mumbling about "another asinine idea."

Chase grabbed hold of Mel's hands, pulled them to his lips, and filled them with kisses. "Twenty hours. I'll be back and we'll pick up where we left off." He couldn't help but smile.

She frowned but then a quivering smile overtook her. "Can't we just put this off for a couple of days?"

"Our transport will be here soon and Amos is getting sicker."

"You can tell from the touch?"

"Yes."

Her eyes lighted on the computer screen. "I've been working on something since you got that God-forsaken exoself back in you."

"Mel, that's harsh."

"I'm sorry. It's who you are—I know. And I love you. And all your inner workings. Well, this is kind of a wedding present for you and Sparky. I've been reworking the entry point of the code I put in you."

"Nineteenth processor, second factor."

"Yes. I think I've got a Bible ready for you. Concordance and study guides too."

"What's a concordance?" He shifted from Mel's code to general intel. "Never mind, I've got a dictionary." He found the meaning but not the Biblical application. What did it serve the government to extract Christianity from the cyber world?

"It'll help you understand the Bible better," Mel said. She pushed a few keys and then looked up at Chase. "Well? You got it?"

Chase sparked the processor. He shook his head. "Only the few Psalms that led me to your code."

Her shoulders sank and she stared at the screen. "I'll keep trying."

He put his arm around her and rubbed her back. "I know you'll get it."

She reached to the other side of her station and grabbed a VPad. "You take this with you so you can answer me when I ask the exoself if you're still alive."

"I've got a little present for you too." He sat back in the chair and closed his eyes. "Type a message to me."

Her fingers clicked against the keypad.

Chase opened his eyes wide and then jerked his head from one side of the command center to the other. "Uh, Mel, you didn't need to get so personal. Delete that." He smiled. "But first, watch the screen."

She kept her eyes there and then brought her hands to her cheeks. "You can answer me. How?"

"Just another development in my…in me."

She reached for his hand as she stared at the screen. "It's wonderful."

"Yeah, but don't talk to me like *that* anymore. Not until I get home." He bent near to kiss her.

Mom joined them, and Mel's eyes showed a hint of panic as she reached forward and punched the delete key.

"Hi," she said. "Mom."

Mom put her hands on Mel's shoulders and kissed the top of her head. "I know you must feel bad about me going off with your groom. Doesn't seem right."

Mel cocked her head and raised her brows at Chase. Then she said to Mom, "I know Amos wants you to go. And I need to stay here and do my job. It might be a while before the two of you can return. You all right with that?"

"Whatever happens, we're all under the watchful eye of the Lord. We'll be back together soon enough."

Mel nodded. "It's almost time. Isn't it?"

"Yes. Some of the men are helping with Amos. Chase, you can meet us in the upper hall whenever you're ready." She left them.

Chase fell into his wife's dark eyes. He'd never be ready. "Don't come up with me. Let me say goodbye here under *Ciel Bleu Domaine*. There's nobody left in the room but us."

She rose from the chair. "But—"

He stood and weaved his fingers into her hair. He put his lips to hers and lingered there. Pulling back, he wiped another tear from her sweet face. "Stay right here. I'll see you tomorrow."

"Twenty hours," she said.

"That's all. And then I'll be home."

53

Chase rode in the front of the hearse with Shorty. Mom sat beside Amos, who was stretched out in the back. Maybe the verses above his head would be a comfort. Chase perused the programs of the underground in hope of finding Mel's implanted Bible.

The ride to Gagnon, if a covert operation could be called carefree, was just that. No sign of federal deputies. No drones. They passed only two vehicles.

Chase hoped Mel had gone to sleep, but he sent her a message anyway.

We're almost there. No problems. I love you.

Her reply was instant—she wasn't sleeping. *This bed is too big without you. I love you forever.*

She must be on one of her old laptops. Good to know that'd work with this new capability. "Just don't jump ship, Sparky."

"Excuse me?" Shorty held the wheel with one finger. He maneuvered through the dark at full speed.

"Sorry. I was talking to my wife."

"You can do that in your head?"

"Yep."

"Did you marry that pretty girl with the dark curls?"

"I sure did."

"Congratulations. Happened awful fast. You been hitched, what…two days?"

"Fourteen hours. And thank you."

The transport pulled into Gagnon and stopped in front of the old schoolhouse. Dr. John met them outside. He'd read the data. Residents helped Mom get Amos inside. Chase and the doctor remained under the starlit sky.

"From what I understand, Chase, this procedure will deplete you of your own ability to heal. Is Amos aware of that? And your mother?"

"It's nothing to be concerned about," Chase told him. "No sense in worrying them."

"We'll let Amos rest until dawn. The whole procedure shouldn't take more than an hour. We'll be making medical history and no one will know."

"So you think it will work."

"I believe there's a good chance," Dr. John said.

The two went inside, and the doctor went to his quarters to get some sleep. Chase found his mom sitting in a chair in the hallway that led to the clinic.

"Is Amos settled in?" he asked her.

"He's sleeping."

"You should do the same. Dr. John says there are a couple of sofas in a meeting room back the other way."

"Will you stay with me?" She followed Chase down the hall.

"Sure. I don't need much sleep, but I'll sit with you."

They found the room with mismatched old sofas. Mom stretched out on one. Chase sat on the other. Not a sound resonated in the place called Storm on the River.

"I don't know if I should leave Amos alone," Mom said.

"I'll go check on him in a while. It'll give me something to do besides think about…"

"About the honeymoon you should be on right now?"

"Yeah. I can't stand being away from her."

"You made quite a sacrifice for Amos. You just met him a few days ago. And yet, you're willing to give up so much for him. Why?"

"The overwhelming urge in my gut, I guess. I had to do it."

"Sounds like God directed you." She smiled.

"I'm going to turn the light off, Mom. Get some sleep."

"OK, son."

Chase reached for a small lamp and twisted the switch. He stared at the window, its filmy curtain not holding out the light of the stars.

"Chase?"

"Yes, Mom?"

"If anything happens after you leave us here, and you have to move on—you and Melody—don't look back. Follow God's lead, son. I'm so glad to have spent these last days with you. But if you can't come back for me, I'll understand. We'll see each other again."

He powered his night vision to see her face. "What on earth are you talking about?"

"Oh, I don't know. Something in my gut, maybe."

"Well, stop talking like that. I don't know about all these feelings that come from the gut. Maybe we ate some bad meat. Now go to sleep."

She didn't say another word. Chase powered down the night vision and ran through WR programs. All quiet in Quebec. Some rumblings in the EU. Nothing new about that.

But then a communication in progress crept into his mind. A dispatch to federal agents throughout the

Northwest Territory called for anyone not assigned to essential activities to report to the detention center north of Herouxville with all available transport vehicles.

What were they planning? Were they ready to activate that awful machine, Bloodless?

Had Mel intercepted the information yet? Should he notify her? No, he'd wait for more intel. During the pre-dawn hours he went to sit by Amos's side. An hour before sunrise, Amos opened his eyes and reached for Chase's hand.

"Soon, Amos. You'll be feeling better soon."

"Perhaps. This is the most ridiculous thing I've ever done. And I've pulled some crazy stunts these last few years in the underground."

"It's meant to be," Chase told him. "You're needed here."

"Here? You mean here in Gagnon?"

Chase remembered his mother's unsettling words. "I don't know about that, but it's a nice place. I wouldn't mind staying here."

Amos shrugged. "I don't know if I want to be living anywhere—not on this planet. Why am I willing to put off Heaven? That's where I belong."

"But you know this is supposed to happen. Don't you, Amos?"

"It's hard to imagine why." He closed his eyes.

"Rest," Chase said. "It'll be time soon."

54

Amos seemed to fade in and out during the transfusion. Chase sank into a cot nearby, a pint of blood gone from him, days of little sleep catching up to him. He couldn't hold his eyes open.

Mel, I'm done with my part. Amos is receiving the blood. I'm fine. You might have picked up on some WR movement north of you. We need to find out what they're up to. But I'm so tired. I have to sleep.

Her answer all but quickened his replicated heart.

Rest well, my love. It's probably just some sort of drill. Tell me when you wake up.

He pulled up his heavy eyelids when he heard someone near. Dr. John hovered over him.

"Why did I crash?" Chase asked "I haven't felt tired since the last time I was here."

"I guess giving up some of the stuff in your blood was enough for your human body to feel the effects of sleep deprivation. In the future, if you can find a way to sleep on a normal schedule, you should do it."

"I can shut down when I want to. Just haven't had time the past couple of days." He smiled. "This little trip interrupted my honeymoon, you know."

"I heard. But while you're here and your bride isn't, get some sleep."

Chase didn't need to be told. He drifted into dreams of Blue Sky Field. Of Melody. Of the Spirit lifting him and letting him fall. Over and over. No voice. No message. Just a flight into the brilliant blue sky and a drop close enough to the ground to view the green hills that seemed fluid.

Like they were moving.

He sat straight, his eyes wide open. "Something's wrong." The exoself informed him he'd been asleep for four hours and twelve minutes. Intel coursing through him reported WR activity. A transmission from Mel had been deposited into his brain…forty-seven minutes ago.

Panic overtook him.

The town is being evacuated. Cameras show it's turning into a ghost town. Like the one we talked about, Chase. Remember? I sent Switchblade up to see what's going on. Please tell us what you can find out. I need your help.

He jumped off the cot.

Mel, I'm so sorry, I just got your message. I was in a deep sleep. Please tell me you're all right. I'm running reports now.

He forced his way into every agency in the area— local police and rescue units, federal reports and operations. It didn't take long to find out a test of new chemical weapon-equipped drones had gone wrong over Herouxville. It took less than twenty seconds to discover that report was a ruse. The Feds only wanted to empty the town.

Whatever you hear, there is no danger from chemicals.

The exoself caught a WR directive. A raid on the Underground Church might involve actions not supported by local residents. Panic might occur if bloodshed became necessary. Federal status in the eyes of the citizens would suffer if they witnessed the extraction.

Mel, you've got to get out. Everyone should join the

evacuation. I know it's a major risk, but they're coming for you. They're going to find you.

No response. "Mel, answer me," he said. "Right now. Please." Nothing.

He sparked her code and searched for communication between branches. In an instant he arranged transportation disguised as a federal evacuation vehicle and sent word to Mel. They'd have to find a way to hide until the big truck on its way to Montreal changed course and headed north. It would take hours.

"Mel, why won't you talk to me?" He went into the system again to look for a hiding place outside of town. They'd have to be invisible until that truck arrived.

But the code from the Psalms had ceased its flow into the exoself. It appeared as a stagnant line in Chase's mind. Everything after the starting point—19-2—had shut down. Only 32-7 remained. A code from the Psalms Chase knew before the four *S*'s, apart from Mel's programming.

Now it raged inside the exoself.

Dr. John stepped into the room. "Good, you're awake. We seem to be experiencing some problems with our computers."

"I have to go." Chase grabbed his shoes.

"You can't go. I need to check you over. Don't you even want to know how Amos is doing?"

Chase reached for the black jacket he'd thrown over a chair. "How is he?"

"His white blood cell count is down. Way down. But it'll be a few days before we know if this worked."

"Tell him I'm praying. And tell my mother I love her. I don't have time for goodbyes. They'll understand." He eyes darted around the room. "I left a flight pack here somewhere."

"It's in my office. Chase, what's going on? Why are we cut off from the new programs you brought to the underground? It's like there was a killswitch and somebody just pulled it."

"For your own good. Blue Sky Field has been found. Mel must have cut communication to protect you." He called out to her in his mind. But he knew she wouldn't answer. "To protect *me*. I'm sorry."

"How—"

"A dissenter got in and then he got caught. I thought I took care of it but he must have talked." Chase started out the door, but he stopped and clutched the door frame with both hands. Then he drove his fist through the wall. "I should have done more. This shouldn't have happened."

"I'll get your flight pack," the doctor said. "You sure you're up to this?"

"I have no choice."

55

Chase strapped on the flight pack as he headed out the front door of Storm on the River. Dr. John told him his mother and Amos were in a meeting with the branch's leader, Haley. They were waiting for him. They must be wondering about the system failure. The doctor would have to fill them in.

The pack powered and Chase lifted off the ground. "God, protect Storm on the River," he prayed. "Watch out of for Mom. Please. I didn't even tell her goodbye." She'd understand.

During the flight, he continued trying to make contact. He should've brought that VPad Mel offered him. But if everything he'd delivered to the supercomputer had been shut down, any device could be tracked.

The flight took nearly two hours. Drone activity increased as Chase got close to town, so he landed in a field to walk into the evacuation zone. The sun still shone bright in the western sky. No hiding in darkness. He re-angled a satellite and shut down street cameras while he was half a mile out.

A drone swooped down in front of him. He didn't have to spark the code—the exoself blew the thing to pieces. Another approached. It fell in a fiery heap to the ground. Two more flew close. Both crashed. Not a good way to get into town unnoticed. But so be it. He tore off the fight pack and threw it onto a burning drone. He wouldn't need it anymore. Everyone would be all right and he'd never leave Blue Sky Field again.

Before he could even think it through, the exoself took out local communications. Then it destroyed the cyber systems of every WR office within a hundred miles. But not before planting reports of multiple sightings of Chase Sterling in Montreal. "I don't care about protecting myself," he yelled. "Get back my connection to the underground."

Nothing.

He watched several federal vehicles race away. The smoking drones didn't even slow them down. Were they on their way to hunt him down in Montreal?

He ran into the town. No one remained. Not even local police. Vehicles brought in to haul off misled residents were gone. He entered through the front of the museum. The construction project hadn't changed. Maybe the underground bunker had gone undiscovered and the Feds had left empty-handed. Running down the back hall, he prayed the new wall remained intact.

Every door in the long hall hung open. Plaster dust hung thick in the air. In every room—most of which Chase had never peered into—a destructive force had knocked out the back wall. Littering the hall nearest the room where Chase had first entered the underground was a trail of wires and keypads. A broken monitor. And a bag, ripped open and spilling apples onto the path.

Chase stepped over the debris. A hole torn through the new wall opened into the dark tunnel. Chase rushed in and ran down the spiraling stairs. The bolted door that hid the underground was ripped from its hinges. He didn't stop until he was in the command center.

Every computer was either gone or destroyed. Work stations were overturned, holograph display centers smashed. Above it all, *Ciel Bleu Domaine* hung at an angle, a red X painted from one side to the other.

Chase hurried to the closest dorm area and pushed open the door to Mel's room. The gown made from a coverlet lay across the double bed.

"Mel!"

He turned a circle in the hallway. No one remained. He ran to the dining hall.

In the far corner he saw them. Eleven bodies were laid out orderly, all facing upward, their arms at their sides. His eyes moved from one to the next. The pastor who officiated the wedding. An elderly woman with a strand of pearls around her neck—the necklace loaned to Mel.

Molly.

He ran to her and dropped to his knees. He touched her face. She'd been dead for hours. These were the oldest residents of Blue Sky Field. No sign of how they died. Tears fell as he looked over the group of seven women and four men.

He wrenched his head toward the ceiling "How could you?" He stood, his eyes scanning the paintings hung in the room. All destroyed.

"Why?" he screamed. "Where is my wife?"

He stumbled back to the command center and fell into the chair in front of Mel's overturned station. He wept aloud and refused the comfort of the Spirit pulling at him. But a word flooded through anyway.

Don't be afraid.

He dropped his head forward and shook as he

cried. Fear could have him. He saw no way out of it.

Hours passed. Darkness fell on the town up top. A skeleton of communication programs the exoself took out had been restored, and intel showed residents were being allowed to return. Forty-seven people were delivered to the detention center where the machine—Bloodless—waited. No identities listed.

He went deeper into the file. They were from a homeless camp. The one near Mist Covered Hill. Had believers there been caught? Chase didn't want to know. They'd taken his people somewhere else. His wife. He let his eyes fall shut.

Hands gripped his shoulders and he jumped from the chair and spun around.

"Switchblade," he said. He lifted the splintered work station and threw it across the room. Then he lunged at the man and sent him flying. The laserlight Switchblade carried rolled across the floor. Chase jumped him and held him in a strangle hold. "Where were you when this happened?" he screamed.

"Man, let me go," Switchblade said, his voice barely audible as Chase pressed his airway shut. "You're gonna kill me."

Chase rolled to the side and sat on the floor. He said nothing before dropping his head to his knees.

Switchblade coughed and gasped for breath. "Mel sent me up, Charlie. I was following orders. I heard what the Feds were telling people and I headed back. They spotted me. I tried to run but I got a laser band around me and they put me in a bus. They set up a camp outside of town. I had to wait it out, man. Just got released. Whatever *you* know is what I know. I can't believe this." Switchblade sucked in a breath and let out a whimper. "They destroyed it all. There's nobody left? You look around real good?"

"Eleven bodies in the dining hall. All elderly."

"Molly?"

"Yes."

"Lord, where are the rest of them? Maybe they got away before—"

"They wouldn't leave people behind."

"Why would the Feds kill the old folks and take everybody else?"

"I don't know."

"Melody said she could talk to you now. Right through Sparky. She didn't tell you nothing?"

"She said she needed my help. Then she cut me off. Seems she had a killswitch of her own."

"Only one reason she would do that." Switchblade leaned against the wall and rubbed his neck. "To keep the Feds off you."

"It's more than I could do for her. Before she shut the system down, I found a transport and sent it this way. But the situation was too volatile. I doubt the driver even tried to get into town."

"Say they got picked up. Where would they go?"

"They got picked up by the Feds," Chase shouted. "They're in a center. Or they're dead."

"Sparky would know if that was true."

"Official reports about killing prisoners are deeply coded. So far I've got nothing."

"Then we got some hope," Switchblade said.

Chase swiped his hands through his hair as information rushed in. "They don't want older brain tissue for their research. That's the reason for the bodies. It can only mean one thing for the rest of them. There is no hope."

"You think what you want, Charlie. I won't stop

praying."

Chase staggered toward the hall.

"Where are you going?"

"To my room. My old room—not the one I shared with my wife for ten hours." Chase kicked a chair out of his way. "Don't bother me, Switchblade."

"Man, we can't stay here. We need to get out of town tonight. While it's dark."

"Go ahead. Best of luck. Sorry I tried to kill you." Chase continued on his way as Switchblade yelled after him.

"You can't give up. You know Melody don't like that. Come on, man."

In his room, Chase fell on the bed. He didn't power the night vision. Didn't allow more input from the exoself. Didn't speak to God except to pray for dreamless sleep. He got what he wanted.

56

Long before dawn—the exoself said it was half past three—Chase woke in a start. He powered the night vision. Switchblade lay on the floor in front of the closed door. The man hadn't fled. Would he ever forget about his bodyguard assignment?

WR reports filled his head in a scrambled mess. They were chasing a man in Montreal who remained hidden in a place they'd already destroyed. How many would suffer because of the misinformation Chase planted? Without Mel's four S's, he could do nothing to help them.

But something rushed into the void left by the terminated code. Words welled up inside Chase and he let them pour off his tongue.

"In the beginning God created the heavens and the earth. Now the earth was formless and empty. Darkness was over the surface of the deep and the Spirit of God was hovering over the waters. And God said, 'Let there be light,' and there was light. God saw that the light—"

"Man, what are doing?" Switchblade sat up and rubbed is face. "You got a Bible in your head or something?"

Tears fell. "Yes."

Switchblade lit up his laserlight and crawled to the end of the bed. "I don't think it's compliments of the Helgen Institute." A smile crept onto his face.

"It's a wedding gift. Mel was working on it when I left for Gagnon."

"Then she's out there." Switchblade jumped to his feet.

"On one of her old laptops," Chase said. He tried to contact her, but he knew it wouldn't work. He couldn't send her messages anymore, or receive them from her. But she'd sent this one sign. He bent his head and wept.

"Thank you," he cried. "Thank you. Thank you."

"Pull yourself together, Charlie. We're getting out of here."

Chase could barely lift his head. "I don't know where to go. I have no idea where to look."

Switchblade grabbed him by the arms and lifted him from the bed. "You find anything you been through lately *easy*, Charlie?"

Chase shook his head.

"Then this ain't nothing new. We're going up. We're getting out. And we're praying over every step we take. You got it?"

Chase nodded.

Switchblade led the way through the command center, where Chase gazed one last time at the beautiful painting, now marked with an unbearable message from the WR. He couldn't move.

Switchblade joined him. "We torching the place before we go?"

"We either cremate our people or let them…" Chase took a breath. "You got a lighter?"

"There's one in the kitchen."

In the dining hall, they said a prayer over the gray-haired patrons of the underground. Switchblade went into the kitchen and came back with an old-fashioned lighter. He handed it to Chase.

They piled the torn and broken paintings in the center of the room, and Chase set them ablaze. Then he followed his friend through the bunker, up the stairs, down the tunnel, and out the hole in the alley wall. No use putting back the refuse bin.

They left Herouxville behind and took a southward direction. Switchblade prayed out loud. Chase searched the Bible in his mind for the verse Mel had recited.

"For I am convinced that neither death nor life, neither angels nor demons, neither the present nor the future, nor any powers, neither height nor depth, nor anything else in all creation, will be able to separate us from the love of God that is in Christ Jesus our Lord."

"That's right, Charlie."

But the separation from Mel would rip him apart. He'd bleed to death looking for her.

"Don't be afraid," he said as he wiped a tear.

"Man, I ain't afraid of nothing."

"Just talking to myself, Switch. But I know one thing you're afraid of. You don't want anybody to know your real name. So face your fears and spit it out."

The big man puffed a frozen white breath in the pre-dawn twilight. "OK. But you can't tell nobody."

"Deal."

"Leslie Honeywell."

Chase couldn't hold back the laugh. "That's kinda pretty."

Switchblade punched him in the arm. "Don't you ever...*ever*...call me that. Now concentrate. You think we should go back to Gagnon?"

Chase yearned for that gut feeling he knew must

be the Spirit's call. And it came. Mel's last message played in his mind.

...a ghost town like the one we talked about.

A town with no computers. With family.

"We're going to Detroit," Chase said.

"Oh, no way. Man, I had some trouble there."

"Come on, Leslie, we've got no choice. God says we're going to Detroit." The exoself found the nearest westward road. They'd move far past Montreal before heading south. Chase Sterling was still hiding there— so said the reports.

Switchblade gripped Chase's shoulder as the first hint of daylight greeted their path. "I'm right beside you," he said. "Robot."

Thank you

for purchasing this Harbourlight title. For other inspirational stories, please visit our on-line bookstore at www.pelicanbookgroup.com.

For questions or more information, contact us at customer@pelicanbookgroup.com.

Harbourlight Books
The Beacon in Christian Fiction™
an imprint of Pelican Ventures Book Group
www.pelicanbookgroup.com

Connect with Us
www.facebook.com/Pelicanbookgroup
www.twitter.com/pelicanbookgrp

To receive news and specials, subscribe to our bulletin
http://pelink.us/bulletin

May God's glory shine through
this inspirational work of fiction.

AMDG

Free Book Offer

We're looking for booklovers like you to partner with us! Join our team of influencers today and receive at least one free eBook per month. Maybe more!

For more information
Visit http://pelicanbookgroup.com/booklovers
or e-mail
booklovers@pelicanbookgroup.com

www.ingramcontent.com/pod-product-compliance
Lightning Source LLC
Chambersburg PA
CBHW020933260626
47169CB00006B/1708